A sacred place

A sacred place

A NOVEL BY

Bonnie Leon

BROADMAN
&HOLMAN
PUBLISHERS

NASHVILLE, TENNESSEE

0-8054-2152-1

Published by Broadman & Holman Publishers, Nashville, Tennessee

Cover photograph by Steve Terrill Photography, Portland, Oregon

Dewey Decimal Classification: 813
Subject Heading: HISTORICAL FICTION / ALASKA—FICTION
Library of Congress Card Catalog Number: 00-037864

Library of Congress Cataloging-in-Publication Data

Leon, Bonnie.
    A sacred place : a novel / Bonnie Leon.
        p.   cm.
    ISBN 0-8054-2152-1 (pb)
    1. Married women—Fiction. 2. Alaska—Fiction. I. Title.
PS3562.E533 S23 2000
813'.54—dc21

                                                    00-037864

1 2 3 4 5 04 03 02 01 00

Acknowledgment

Thanks, Mom, for delighting in God's creation.
You helped me to see.

Chapter 1

Leaving the door ajar, Mary Matroona fled the hut. She stepped into the cold and stumbled up a crude stairway cut into the earth. Biting wind clawed at her and frozen snow crunched beneath her boots as she ran for the shed. She yanked open its broken-down door and ducked inside. Quiet darkness enveloped her; it felt safe and comforting, momentarily hiding Mary from the world and its awful demands.

Gulping down air, she sat on a stack of driftwood. It gave beneath her, then steadied. No longer required to keep her emotions in check, the eighteen-year-old native covered her face with her hands and wept.

"How could they ask me to marry Sean Calhoun? They know I love Paul." She rubbed away the tears, then balled her hands into fists and stared at the ceiling. Closing her eyes, she gave a shuddering sigh, then wrapped her arms around herself.

She shivered. In her haste to escape, she'd forgotten her coat, and now the cold penetrated her outrage.

With no fire to warm the shed, the February cold anchored itself inside the small room. Ice layered the walls and frost blanketed the floor. Rubbing her arms, Mary glanced at the door. *I wish I'd brought my cape. I can't go back now. I can't face them. I hate them.*

Thoughts of Paul swirled through her mind, and the ache of loss settled in her chest. He was so vibrant and alive, always smiling. When they'd first met at the Chemawa School in Oregon, she hadn't liked him. He'd been too brash, too intimidating. But he'd persevered and won her over with his gregarious teasing.

Now he was gone. He'd gone to work on a revenue cutter. Before leaving Unalaska, he'd pledged his love to her and promised they would marry when he returned. In his usual enthusiastic way, he'd vowed to bring back enough money to set up a real home for them, insisting no wife of his would live in a primitive barabara.

"I love you, Paul. Please come home soon," Mary whispered. A sob escaped and tears spilled onto her cheeks. "Please, before I have to marry Sean." She rocked forward, bracing her elbows on her thighs. *We should have married before he left. Now we'll never have a life together.*

The shed door creaked open and cold air swept into the room. Mary's mother, Luba, stood in the doorway. "May I come in?"

Mary didn't look at the small woman. She didn't want to talk to anyone. All she wanted was to be left alone and allowed to choose her own husband, her own life. Finally, unwilling to hurt her mother further, she said softly, "Yes. Come in."

Luba lit a lantern hanging just inside the doorway and stepped into the room. Closing the door, she crossed to Mary and stood in front of her. "I thought you might need this," she said, holding out a heavy coat.

Not wanting to see the pain and disappointment in her mother's eyes, Mary was careful not to look directly at her as she took the fur-lined coat. She pushed her arms into the sleeves and huddled inside it. Silence settled over the room.

Luba finally asked, "May I sit?"

Mary nodded.

Luba sat beside her daughter and placed the lantern on the floor beside her. The flame flickered, casting eerie shadows across the walls. Somehow, the light only made the room feel darker. For a long while, no one spoke.

Staring at the hot flame of the lamp, Mary finally said, "Mama, I'm sorry for running out, but I couldn't listen to you and Daddy any more." She pressed her lips together, then continued, "I can't marry Sean. I . . . I'm going to marry Paul."

Luba took a slow, deep breath. "Mary, I know this is not easy for you. Your father and I understand how you feel about Paul, but he's gone, and Sean is here. . . ."

"But Paul is coming back. He asked me to marry him, and I said yes."

Luba carefully folded her hands in her lap, then looked at Mary. "Sometimes what a person wants isn't what is best for them." Taking Mary's hands in hers, she gently continued, "Try to understand. Your father and I want you to have a good life. We don't think Paul can give you that." She paused. "He's not right for you, Mary."

"How can you know that?" Mary looked straight at her mother, wincing inwardly at the anguish she saw in the woman's eyes. "What do you know about Paul? Why shouldn't I marry him?"

Luba didn't answer right away. When she did speak, she chose her words carefully. "He's not a Christian. And more than that, he has made it clear that he'll have nothing to do with the Christian faith."

"I don't care about that. I don't feel the same way you and Daddy do about church. Christianity is your faith, not mine."

"You feel that way now, but you won't always," Luba said, her voice breaking slightly. "I know the old ways of our people pull at you and that you've struggled to find the right path. But Christianity and many of our traditions can be joined. There are differences that can never be brought together, but that does not make the truth of Jesus Christ and his love a lie."

"I don't mean to hurt you, Mama, but I can't pretend I agree. I don't think I'll ever believe the way you and Daddy do." She pursed her lips. "My real father didn't agree with you either."

Pain touched Luba's eyes. She took her daughter's hand and squeezed it gently. "You have always been straightforward, and I respect you for being so. But, Mary, there are some things you don't understand. As you grow older, you'll see more clearly."

"I see clearly now. I know Paul and I are meant to be together. And it's wrong for you to keep us apart."

"And what if he is not what you think? People aren't always what they seem."

"I don't know why you're saying these things. You don't know Paul. I do. He's good and kind, and he makes me laugh. And he loves me."

Luba smiled sadly. "When I married your father, I thought love could overcome anything and that the difference in our beliefs didn't matter, but I was wrong. I married him although my parents didn't want me to, and I knew God disapproved." Luba met her daughter's eyes. "Mary, I paid for my disobedience with years of grief. Your father didn't know God and couldn't understand my faith. He felt threatened by it. Loving someone who doesn't share your faith, who can't understand what it means to serve God is . . ." She searched for the right words and finally said, "It is a sorrow that eats away at your heart. I would never want you to go through that." She reached out, caressed her daughter's hair, and looked into her dark brown eyes. "In the end I watched as his fear and unbelief killed him. It's a horrible thing to watch someone you love destroy himself. I don't want that for you."

"It was alcohol that killed him, Mama," Mary said dryly, pulling away from her mother's touch.

"He drank to hide from fear and hopelessness. Without God he was like a branch floating upon the sea—forever cut off from the tree—forever lost. And no amount of drinking could help him find his way back. Each drink drew him further and further from the one who could help him."

"What does that have to do with my marrying Sean?"

Luba met her daughter's eyes. "Sean is a good man, and he goes to church regularly. He loves you."

"He barely knows me. We only met a few months ago and only see each other when I take lunch to Daddy."

"He knows you well enough." Luba smiled. "He told your father he fell in love with you the first moment he saw you."

Mary pursed her lips and said nothing.

"Sean comes from a good home. His parents immigrated from Ireland, but they're American citizens now. And although Sean was raised a Catholic, he grew up fearing God and attending church. And . . ." A gust of wind swirled across the rooftop and Luba looked at the ceiling, then continued hesitantly. "And although I know you do not want to speak about race, it does make a difference." She glanced at her hands. "Sean is white and . . ."

"I don't care if he's white. I don't love him."

"Mary, please listen to me. Sean is a good man, but more than that, he's not native and can give you so much more than you've had. Too many doors are still closed to us. Natives were not even considered citizens until 1915, only two years ago." She gently placed her hand on Mary's shoulder. "Marrying a white man will make life better for you."

"I don't see what's wrong with living as we always have. I like my life. I'm happy as I am. I wish we'd stayed at the village. Can't you see that Sean and I are from two different worlds? He can't understand mine, and I don't want to understand his."

"You two are not so different as you might think." Luba straightened her spine and set her jaw. "Marrying Sean is the right thing for you to do."

Mary stood and turned her back to her mother.

"Our answer to Sean is still yes," Luba said. "You will marry him. It is the best we can do for you."

Mary turned and stared at her mother. "I won't marry him," she said before whirling around and walking out of the shed.

————————————————

Sean hoisted a gunnysack of cornmeal onto his thigh, tossed it onto the loading platform, then turned and grabbed another. After placing the grain on top of the stack, he took off his hat and wiped his brow with the back of his hand. In spite of the cold, he was hot and sweating. Stripping off his outer coat, he sat and leaned against a bag of cornmeal and took a container of water from his pack. He swilled down two mouthfuls before replacing the cap and turning to gaze at the tiny town of Unalaska. A few small businesses hugged the shoreline, and a street running parallel to the bay divided the businesses from several shabby-looking homes. Snow-covered hills rose above the hamlet. Soon the white would melt away and be replaced with lush grasses as deep as a man's shoulder and hillsides splashed with brightly colored flowers. Sean liked Unalaska and planned to stay.

His thoughts turned to Mary. He remembered their first meeting. When she'd turned and smiled at him, her warm brown eyes set against amber skin and her bright smile had captivated him. All he could think about was spending more time with the lovely native girl. He had to know her.

She came to the waterfront almost daily to bring her step-father, Michael, his lunch. Michael, a teacher on leave from the local school, had been repairing an old boat, trying to get it into shape for the summer fishing season. He worked at the docks nearly every day.

Sean often invented reasons to visit Michael at the lunch hour, hoping for an opportunity to spend time with Mary. She was always gracious and friendly and laughed easily at his clever remarks. And on more than one occasion, the two enjoyed a sparring match of words. Sean soon found himself in love with the open, friendly young woman.

Although he and Mary didn't know each other well, Sean knew she was the one he wanted to spend his life with. Hoping she felt the same, he'd gone to Michael and asked for her hand. Michael readily agreed to the union but insisted on speaking to Mary first.

She will make a fine wife and mother, Sean thought.

"Hello there," came a familiar voice, pulling the young Irishman from his musings.

Michael leaped from his boat to the dock and strode down the pier toward Sean. "Looks like you're working hard," he teased.

"Takin' a break."

"I can see that," Michael said with a grin.

"Noticed ye were out this mornin'. Did ye do some fishin'?"

"Yes. And I did well too. I pulled in two fat cod."

"So, it's fish for supper?"

"There's nothing as good as Luba's fish stew."

"I've made a batch or two in me day," Sean said. "I'm not a bad cook. After me mother passed on, I did a lot of the cookin'. Got pretty good at it too." He paused and looked up the dock toward town. *There's no reason to put it off,* he reasoned. *I have to know.* He looked at Michael. "So, did ye speak to Mary?"

Michael edged his hat back a bit. "Yes . . ."

"And?"

"You need to remember she's young." Michael kicked a pebble into the water.

"Yes, but how does she feel about marryin' me?"

"Well, you know about Paul."

Sean's heart thudded. "Yes."

"She insists she loves him."

"I'd hoped she'd gotten over him. He's still out to sea?"

"Yes, and I wish he'd stay there, but he's expected back this summer."

Immediately deflated, Sean said, "So, I guess that's it then?" He pulled at his work gloves.

"No. That's not it." Michael grinned and rested his hand on the young man's shoulder. "I still think you two should get married. You're a fine person. She'll come around to the idea. We just need to give her some time."

Sean nodded dully. In the past weeks Mary had seemed to like him well enough, and he'd hoped she had feelings for him. He forced a smile. "Well, I better get back to work." He hefted a bag onto his shoulder.

"I've got work to do myself," Michael said. With a warm smile and a pat on the back, he returned to his boat.

Sean couldn't pry Mary from his thoughts the rest of the morning. If she loved Paul, there was no way she'd marry him. He remembered the young native man. He was handsome and bold. And although Sean thought him superficial, he could see how the man's charm could attract someone like Mary. *I'm nothin' like him. I'm sure when Mary looks at me, she just sees dull and ordinary.* He looked at the docks and watched the boats bob placidly in the waves, then scanned the hamlet of Unalaska. He'd always been quiet and peaceable with little flash, very much like this place. His mind wandered to his own two-room cabin. *I haven't much to offer, and workin' at the local store here isn't goin' to help much,* he thought dismally.

He secured a rope around the stack of grain sacks, then leaned against a piling and watched the squawking gulls swoop beneath the pier picking at the leavings of gutted fish. Wind cut across the top of the quiet bay, sifting over the waves and raising a fine spray. Sean pulled his hat down tighter over his dark brown hair and lifted the collar on his coat.

Footsteps approached from the harbor side of the dock. They hesitated. Sean turned. Mary stood only a few feet away. She glanced at him, then at her father's boat and back again. "I've got to take Daddy his lunch," she said without her usual enthusiastic smile, then hurried past him.

As Sean watched her walk away, his throat tightened. Had he ruined everything? They'd been friends, and he'd hoped for more, but now he could see clearly that she felt nothing for him. If only he'd given it more time. *Maybe Michael is right and she'll come around,* he hoped. *I know I can make her happy.*

Sean returned to his work but kept watch, waiting for Mary to come by again. The moment she stepped off her father's boat and started up the pier, he waved and called, "Mary!"

She managed a small smile and a nod. Her skin had lost its radiance, and a haunted look had replaced the customary warmth in her eyes.

He could see her discomfort, but his need to speak with her overrode his good sense. His stomach quaking, Sean took long strides to close the distance between them. "Hello," he said quietly. The wind caught at her hair, and he fought the desire to reach out and touch it.

"Hello." Mary glanced at him, then turned her eyes toward town.

"So, ye and yer father had a bit of lunch?"

Mary nodded. "I have to go. Mama needs me." She quickly moved past him.

Sean searched for something he could say to keep her there, but he only nodded and watched her walk away.

Chapter 2

$\mathcal{M}$ary stood at the top of the stairwell that led to her family's subterranean hut. Wind swept over the snow-covered grass roof, lifting a dusting of white and carrying it into the air where it settled on frozen bushes alongside the house.

Thoughts of Sean and the promised marriage whirled through her mind. She liked Sean. He'd always been kind and friendly. His thoughtful, quiet demeanor was engaging and his good looks enticing, but she'd never thought of him as anything more than a friend. The tall man with dark hair and hazel eyes would make a fine husband—for someone else.

Wind whistled down the stairwell, and Mary pulled her coat tighter, then shoved her gloved hands into her pockets. Her eyes roamed over snowy fields and across the bay. One day Paul would return. What would happen if he found her married to another man? She could feel his hurt and anger. Her eyes teared. "What can I do?" she asked, a gust of arctic air carrying away her words.

The door at the bottom of the stairway opened, and Luba looked up at Mary. "Dinner is ready," she called. "Are you going to join us?"

Mary nodded, and with a heavy sigh and a final look at the bay, trudged down the steps. She wasn't hungry, and the last thing she wanted was to join her family. Her brothers would undoubtedly prattle on about the upcoming wedding, her father would act too cheerful, and her mother would serve quietly, unable to erase the worry lines from her brow.

Mary stood in the doorway a moment before entering. Although lanterns glowed, the living chamber remained dim. It was always so in the barabara. Without windows there never seemed to be enough light. *It would be nice to live in a wood-framed house with windows,* Mary thought, remembering Sean had such a house. Quickly, she reminded herself of the pettiness of such desires. Her eyes scanned the dining area. Her father and brothers occupied three of the wooden chairs around the kitchen table.

"Come in and close the door. You're letting in the cold," Michael said.

Mary stepped inside but hung back, feeling uncomfortable and angry.

Michael looked at Luba. "It smells good. I'm hungry."

Luba set a pot of steaming fish chowder in the center of the table. "Mary, could you get the pitcher of water, please?" she asked, retrieving a platter of fried bread from the stove and setting it beside the soup.

Mary did as she was told, then sat beside her brother Erik.

"Can we eat now?" Alex, the youngest boy asked as he reached for the bread.

"Wait for prayers," Michael said.

Luba ladled out soup and handed a bowl of it to her husband. "This is made with the fish you caught this morning."

Michael stirred the steaming stew. "I'm glad the fish were cooperative," he said with a smile.

Eleven-year-old Alex propped his elbows on the table and watched as his mother spooned out his portion and set it in front of him. He breathed in the fishy aroma rising from his bowl. "Mmm, smells good." He dipped his spoon into the chowder.

Michael eyed the youngster. "I said, wait for prayers."

Frowning, the boy released his spoon, allowing it to slip into the bowl, and folding his arms over his chest, leaned back in his chair.

After everyone was served, Luba sat down. Heads were bowed, and Michael offered a brief prayer of thanks.

Immediately slurping up a mouthful, Alex announced, "Very good."

Nodding in agreement, fourteen-year-old Erik tore off a large chunk of bread, dunked it in his soup, and shoved it into his mouth.

Pensively Mary swirled her spoon through her broth but didn't eat.

"Mary, you need to eat," Luba said kindly.

Giving her mother a weak smile, Mary took a bite.

"There's pudding for dessert," Michael offered cheerfully.

Erik grinned. "What kind?"

"Tapioca. It's one of Cora's recipes," Luba said.

Alex took a bite of bread, and mouth full, said, "I remember Cora, Grandma's friend. She's nice. When can we see her again?"

"I think we'll invite her to the wedding. Would you like that, Mary?"

Mary stared at her mother. Her spoon clattered as it dropped into her bowl. "Would I like that?" She scooted her chair back from the table and stood. "I'm sorry. I'm not hungry." She hurried from the room.

Once safely closed off in her bedchamber, Mary dropped onto her bed and allowed the tears to come. For a long while, she cried, then sat in the dark, buried in wretchedness. There seemed no way to escape her destiny. Clearly her parents had made their decision, and there would be no changing it. The thought of fleeing flitted through her mind, but she knew it would be impossible. She had no money, and even if she did, there was nowhere for her to go. Paul was out to sea. He couldn't help her. And her grandmother would side with her parents. No one could help.

Finally, Mary pushed herself up from the bed and lit the lamp. She paced the room, then her eyes fell upon the bookcase and her scant collection of books. Hoping for a distraction, she took *Little Women* from the shelf. It was one of her favorites.

Sitting on the bed, she turned to the last page she had read. Her eyes read the words, but they didn't penetrate the clamor of her thoughts. Instead of losing herself in the story, thoughts of Sean and the upcoming marriage tumbled through her mind. Finally, she slammed the book closed. "I can't marry him! I can't! I won't!" She stood, dropping the book onto the bed. "I will make them understand." Straightening her skirt and blouse, she glanced in the mirror, smoothed her hair, then marched into the front room.

Erik stood in front of the dish pan, his hands immersed in soapy water, while Alex rinsed and dried. Her father sat in an overstuffed chair reading a newspaper, and her mother sat across from him darning socks. Luba glanced up from her sewing. "Hello, Mary. Are you feeling better?"

"Yes."

Michael peeked over the top of the paper at his daughter, then looked at Luba. "According to the article here, the war in Europe is expanding."

"What does that mean to us? Do you think the United States will go to war?" Luba asked.

"I don't know, but the reporter says President Wilson has cut off diplomatic relations with the Germans. That doesn't sound good."

"Mama, Daddy, can I talk to you?" Mary asked.

Luba set her mending in her lap, and Michael closed up the paper. He looked at Erik and Alex. "Boys, it's time you got yourselves to bed."

"But, Daddy," Erik protested.

"I'll finish the dishes," Luba offered.

"Just because she doesn't want to get married doesn't mean I have to leave," Erik complained. "I'm old enough to stay."

Michael leveled a stern look at his oldest son. "To bed."

Wearing a pout, Erik wiped his hands dry on his pants and shuffled toward his room. Alex followed. Both boys glowered at Mary as they walked past her.

Mary ignored them. Taking a deep breath, she walked into the front room and stood before her father.

Leaving her sewing in her chair, Luba crossed the room, sat on the floor beside Michael, and leaned against his chair.

Setting his newspaper aside, Michael looked at Mary and waited patiently.

Nothing was said for a long moment. Finally, Mary began, "I know you love me and think you're doing what is best, but I need you to understand how I feel."

"We want to understand," Luba said. "And we're trying."

"I think Sean is a fine person, and I believe he will make a good husband, but I don't love him. How can I marry someone I don't love?"

"Love is something you must choose to do," Luba explained. "Sometimes in marriage love isn't present in the beginning, but comes with time."

Mary's frustration swelled. *I knew they wouldn't understand. Why am I even trying?* Remembering what was at stake, she tried to relax and said calmly, "I don't agree with you. A person can't create love." Placing her hand on her chest, she continued, "It has to be here, in the heart. And with me it's not."

Michael smiled indulgently. "Mary . . ."

"You aren't hearing me. Please listen. I can't marry a man I don't love."

"Not even if it's what is best?" Luba asked gently.

"Best for whom?"

"Best for you," Michael said. "I think God wants this marriage."

"God? Why would God want me to marry a man I don't love and barely know?" Her arms at her side, hands rolled into fists, Mary took several paces back and forth in front of her parents.

Michael leaned forward, resting his forearms on his legs. "I thought you and Sean were friends."

"We are. But being friends isn't enough, and we haven't known each other very long." Fighting angry tears, Mary closed her eyes, unclenched her fists, and forced herself to breathe slowly. When she opened her eyes, she looked directly at her father. "I love Paul. I want to marry him. And he wants to marry me."

Michael leaned back and folded his arms over his chest. He clenched his jaw and stared straight ahead, looking through his daughter.

Luba stood and crossed over to Mary, placing a hand on her daughter's shoulder. "Mary, sometimes our feelings for someone are so strong we don't think clearly. And it's possible that the person we believe we love isn't who we think he is."

"But I know Paul. We spent months together at school. I love him."

In an uncharacteristic outburst of anger, Michael exploded, "Paul! I've heard enough about him!" He bolted out of his chair and marched to the barrel stove. Opening it, he shoved in a piece of wood, then turned and faced Mary. "He's not right for you. He's nothing more than a . . ."

"Michael, I thought we were not going to do this," Luba cautioned.

He looked at his wife. "I know." His shoulders slumped. "But we have to. She needs to know." Slowly he closed the stove door and looked at his daughter.

The grief in her father's eyes frightened Mary. Something was very wrong.

"We didn't want to hurt you." Michael glanced at the floor. "Didn't you wonder why Paul left in such a hurry?"

"No. I just thought he found out about the job and had to leave." A sick feeling twisted in Mary's stomach. "What are you saying, Daddy?"

"If Paul had stayed in Unalaska, he wouldn't have lived another day. He had to go."

Mary's queasiness tightened into a knot. "What do you mean?"

"We never wanted you to know. . . . We hoped you would get over him." Michael took Mary's hand. "Paul had a . . . he had a relationship with a married woman. Her husband was going to kill him."

Mary felt as if someone had slugged her in the stomach. Stepping back, she yanked her hand out of her father's. "No. That's not true. He wouldn't."

"It is true. We know the people involved very well," Michael said, his voice heavy. "He betrayed you, Mary."

Barely able to breathe, Mary took another step back. "I . . . I don't believe you," she said as she wrapped her arms about her waist.

"Have I ever lied to you, Mary?"

She shook her head slowly. The awful truth crashed over her in a cruel wave and threatened to crush her. A wail welled up inside, but she forced it back, and as tears threatened, she blinked them back. How could she have been so wrong?

"I'm sorry. I'm so sorry," Michael said, pulling his daughter into his arms.

Mary stood stiffly in his embrace.

After a few moments, Michael held her away from him. "Now do you understand why we want you to marry Sean? He's a good man and he'll love you."

Bereft and empty, Mary straightened. What difference did it make? She might as well marry Sean. Without looking at her parents, she said quietly, "All right. I'll marry him." She crossed to the door and took her coat from its hook. "I'm going for a walk."

"It's awfully cold," Luba said, unable to keep the worry out of her voice.

"It will feel good." Mary opened the door and stepped outside.

———————————

As she walked through town, the words, "He betrayed you," played through Mary's mind. Unaware of the world around her, she placed one foot in front of the other. She didn't see the wooden cottages that lined the streets or the old man who nodded at her as he passed by. Her mind was a palette of memories and confused emotions—love, regret, betrayal, and anguish.

Her thoughts wandered back to her time at the Chemawa School in Oregon. They had been good years. It was there she'd discovered so much about the world and had met Paul.

At first Mary hadn't been interested in the handsome native. He was two years older than her and considered a rogue. She'd been warned about him but was taken in by his charm. His eyes always seemed to be laughing, and when they fell upon her, they would warm with admiration. The young man of contrasts intrigued her, and she fell in love. When Paul asked if she would be his wife, she had readily said yes. She trusted him.

Mary took in a tremulous breath as she gazed at the bright winter moon, its beauty only causing the pain to burrow deeper into her heart. *Why Paul? Why? I loved you. I thought you loved me.* Tears burned, but she quickly blinked them away, unwilling to yield to the grief.

For a long while she stared at the place where the cloudless sky met the glistening white hills. The cold bit into her lungs and penetrated her clothing. Finally, with her hands tucked into her pockets, she started for home. She glanced at the bay. The yellow moon cast its light over the quiet waters. Drawn to its tranquility, she turned toward the beach.

Pebbles and black sand ground beneath her feet. Its coarseness felt good—real. A blast of wind snatched at her coat, and Mary drew the hood tighter about her head and pulled the coat close. As she gazed out over the bay, she watched small waves break against the shore. The unfailing steadiness of the sea was a sharp contrast to the turmoil within. Her world had been shattered, but the waves ceaselessly continued their rhythmic commission. What was it that pulled them toward shore?

Maybe there is a God who created and watches over all the universe, Mary thought. She glanced back at the town. With only a few lights winking out of the darkness, it looked sleepy and lonely.

The quiet of the night reminded her of the village where she'd been born. There, each day passed into the next with little change, its quiet and expected constancy bringing calm. She'd only been eight when they moved to town. Although she visited the village and her friends periodically, it wasn't the same, and she wished her family had never left.

As Mary turned away from the water, a form separated itself from the shadows beneath the pier. Her skin prickled with fear. She watched as the figure approached. "Who's there?"

"It's just me," came Sean's reply. "Is that you, Mary?"

"Yes, it's me." Mary wanted to run. She didn't want to speak to anyone, especially not Sean. But there was no way she could leave and ignore him without being exceedingly rude, so Mary waited. When he stood in front of her, she said, "I thought I was the only one foolish enough to walk the beach late at night in the middle of winter."

"I couldn't sleep, and sometimes the ocean soothes me." He stared at the water.

"I know how you feel." The wind caught Mary's hair, and she tucked the loose strands inside her hood.

An uncomfortable silence fixed itself between them.

"I've been workin' down at the docks, but I haven't seen ye there lately," Sean finally said. "So, how have ye been?"

"Fine. I am fine."

"Good."

The two silently watched the waves.

Sean turned his gaze on Mary. "Mind if I ask what ye're thinkin' about?"

Mary looked at the handsome man. He cocked his head slightly to the right as he often did. *A peculiar habit,* she decided. The wind whipped his dark hair across his face, and although she couldn't see him clearly, she knew his hazel eyes radiated warmth. He was certainly a man who would be easy to love, but she could never love anyone again. She returned to staring at the harbor. "I was thinking about us," she said quietly.

Sean cleared his throat. "Me too."

"Mama said the wedding should be in April."

"That sounds good. April is a good time for a weddin'."

Again, silence wedged itself between them.

"Do ye mind?" Sean took a deep breath. "Marryin' me, I mean."

Mary did mind, but what else could she do? Paul had deceived her, and her parents insisted she marry Sean. She sighed, her desolation growing. "No. I don't mind."

From somewhere down the bay, a man hollered and a dog yelped.

Glancing toward the noise, Mary said, "I better get home. Mama will worry." She turned and headed up the beach.

"I'll walk with ye," Sean said, striding along beside her. "I'll write me father in Seattle and tell him about the weddin'. He's been feelin' poorly though, so he probably won't be here."

"I'm sorry he's not well," Mary said without emotion. "What about your mother?" she asked, hurrying her steps and longing for the dark solitude of her room.

"She died years ago. Got scarlet fever when we were movin' out west from New York. I was only ten."

"My father died when I was a little girl." Abruptly, Mary turned down a narrow lane. "Michael's my stepfather." Neither of them spoke again until she stopped at the top of her stairway. "This is where I live," she said, taking the first step.

"Mary . . ."

Mary stopped and looked at Sean. He took her hand. She wanted to pull away but forced herself to be still.

"I'll do me best to make ye happy. Ye don't have to love me. Not just yet, anyway."

Mary nodded, took her hand back, and hurried inside.

Chapter 3

*H*er stomach quaking, hands clutched tightly, and eyes focused on the path in front of her, Mary walked down the hill toward the Church of the Holy Ascension. Luba matched her daughter's steps.

Mary's eyes settled on the impressive building. The cathedral stood on a narrow strip of land sandwiched between Illiuliuk Bay and Lake Unalaska. It basked in spring warmth, the bright sunshine illuminating its broad, white walls. Mary wondered how many weddings the grand sanctuary had witnessed throughout the years. She stopped and stared at the building.

"It is beautiful," Luba said reverently. "It feels like an old friend to me. I've spent many wonderful hours safe within its walls." She looked at Mary. "We need to keep walking, or we'll be late. Your father, brothers, and grandmother are waiting for us."

"I'm glad Nana is here," Mary said. With a steadying breath, she continued on, but her eyes remained on the house of worship. She'd attended this church since moving to Unalaska and only now realized that she'd never really looked at it. Even from a distance it looked impressive, its roof higher than all the other structures in town. Her eyes wandered to the bell tower that was crowned with a traditional Russian onion dome. Another dome adorned the roof sheltering the sanctuary. Mary wondered what the onion domes symbolized and decided she'd have to ask the father one day, but not today.

Beyond the church, the water of the bay looked dark and somber. Seagulls carried on warm air currents floated above the harbor. Momentarily, they perched on the church roof, then lifted their wings and allowed the breeze to carry them into the air and back over the cove.

As she watched the gulls, Mary wished she could fly—to be free to soar above the earth and seek whatever course she wished, or none at all. But that could never be. Her future had been determined. She would become Mrs. Sean Calhoun and take on the responsibilities of spouse and, eventually, motherhood.

The wind caught her skirt, billowing it away from her. She captured it beneath her hands, allowing her eyes to roam across the bay to the mountains rising up from the waters. Wisps of clouds clung to their peaks. Her gaze settled on the hills and the tough Aleutian grasses just sprouting. It was still too early for many flowers, and the green tufts reminded Mary of frayed knots on a worn quilt. She longed for the brilliant splash of color that came with the spring bloom and tried to imagine herself racing across the fields, then stopping to pick a bouquet and resting beneath the warm sun.

If only she could find peace. Today her life would change, and there was nothing she could do about it.

Luba caught hold of her daughter's hand. "It's a beautiful day. Perfect for a wedding." She looked at the church and smiled softly. "I remember the first time I visited the church. You were just a baby. I was troubled and came seeking God. Foolishly, I thought I might find him in a building." She chuckled. "I was young and had forgotten I didn't have to go into a sanctuary to speak to God. He's everywhere. It impressed me then, and it still does. This is a lovely church." She stopped and allowed her eyes to roam over the hillsides and the sea. Taking a deep breath and opening her arms wide, she continued, "But even such a holy house looks plain against the beauty of God's creation."

"Were you and my father married here?"

Luba bent and plucked a fresh strand of grass. "No, but Michael and I were, after I returned from Juneau. Your father and I were married on Kodiak. The church was much like this one. He arranged everything." Her expression turned tender.

"I don't remember him," Mary said sadly.

"You were still a baby when he died." A shadow darkened her eyes, and she let the blade of grass drop. "He was stubborn and hardheaded, and we disagreed about many things, especially religion, but he could be softhearted at times. And, oh, how he loved you. He took you everywhere and doted on you—sometimes too much," she added with a grin.

"Norutuk used to tell me stories about him." Mary considered the old medicine man she'd known while living in the village. "I think he missed him as much as anyone." She looked south, in the direction of the distant village. "I wish my father were here today. I feel as if he would help me be strong." Tears blurred her vision and she managed to say in a whisper, "Mama, I'm scared."

Placing a hand on Mary's arm, Luba said gently, "All brides are, but there is strength and peace in the one above."

"There is no peace for me," Mary said, her voice trembling. She rested her hand on her abdomen. "I'm afraid my stomach won't stay put."

"Nerves are normal." Luba patted her daughter's arm. "I know this isn't what you want, but all will be well. You will see."

The two women continued on. With each step the church grew larger, and Mary's heart grew heavier. A steamer moving out into the bay caught her attention. She wondered what it would be like to sail away—to leave this place and never return. Ships left the harbor every day, traveling to exotic places, including some she'd never heard of. She could take one, maybe even find Paul. As the young man's face fixed itself in her mind, she was reminded of his betrayal. No, she couldn't go to him. Clenching her jaw, she stepped up to the church gate.

———

Michael greeted the guests at the front entrance. He wore a smile and gave each new arrival a hearty handshake.

Mary lifted her long, cotton skirt and carefully stepped through the damp grass leading to the porch. A small blue flower pressed against the wall of the church, tentatively reaching for the sun. "Oh, a forget-me-not," Mary said as she bent and touched the fragile blossom. Tempted to pick it, she quickly straightened, its continued existence somehow important.

Erik and Alex raced around the corner of the building and up the steps, colliding with their father.

"Slow down, boys. This is not a free-for-all," Michael scolded.

"Sorry, Daddy," the two said almost in unison and quietly walked into the front foyer.

The last few guests were still arriving, and doing her best to hide her inner turmoil, Mary greeted them graciously. When she reached the small porch, Mary stopped and stared at the double doors of the church. Only one side was open. She knew it was silly, but the interior looked dark and menacing. She wanted to run.

"Mary," Michael said. "You look beautiful!" He smiled broadly.

"Thank you." She glanced down at her full white skirt. "It's Mama. She's the one who made the dress." Slowly, she climbed the steps and stood beside her parents.

Michael placed his arm about Luba's shoulders and planted a kiss on her cheek. "You're a good seamstress."

"It's not the dress but the one who's wearing it," Luba said. She studied her daughter and her eyes glistened. "You are beautiful. Not just on the outside, but inside too. I'm very proud of you, Mary." She gave her daughter a hug and a kiss, then stepped back.

Mary forced a smile. She didn't feel beautiful, but old and frayed.

Adjusting the tight-fitting collar that hugged her throat, Mary gave herself one more inspection and smoothed the fitted waist and flattened a tiny pucker in the delicate lace stitched into the bodice. It was a lovely gown. But what difference did it make? Paul had betrayed her and nothing mattered any more.

Michael held out his hand. "Are you ready?"

No! Mary wanted to shout. Her stomach knotted, and she felt cold and anxious, but she took her father's hand and quietly said, "Yes."

"Everything will be fine," Luba reassured her as she reached up and gently tucked a strand of Mary's hair into place. She gazed at her daughter, then blinking back tears, said, "You're all grown up. How did the years go by so quickly?" With a sad smile she continued, "You'll always be my little girl. Remember, Mary, you're never alone. We'll be here for you, and God is always with you."

Mary nodded.

"I better go in," Luba said, dabbing at her eyes. She walked to the sanctuary entrance, took Erik's arm, and allowed him to escort her into the church.

Mary thought her brother looked very grown-up in his borrowed suit and couldn't repress a smile.

"It is good to see you're feeling better," her grandmother said from an unlit corner.

"Oh, Nana. I didn't see you there."

"I've been waiting to speak to you." The tiny woman stood and crossed to her granddaughter. She glanced at Michael. "Could you leave us a moment, please?"

Michael gave Anna a small bow and stepped inside the sanctuary.

"I'm so glad you're here," Mary said. "You live so far away, and it's hard not seeing you. Will you ever move to Unalaska?"

"One day, but for now I still have things to do in Juneau," the native woman said with a smile. She took Mary's hands. "I remember the day your grandfather and I were married. It was the best day of my life." She raised an eyebrow. "But I do not think you feel the same."

Mary struggled to control her emotions, but tears came as her grandmother pulled her into a tight embrace. "Nana, I don't love Sean. This is something he and my parents want, not me."

"I know. Your mother told me." Gently Anna loosened her hold, stepped back, and looked into Mary's eyes. "This is very hard for your mother and father. They love you and hate to see you hurting, but they want what is best for their only daughter."

"But Nana, how can this be best?" Mary turned and looked out a small side window. The outside world seemed far away.

"I cannot answer that, but I do know your mother and Michael are good parents and they have much wisdom. You can trust them."

Mary gritted her teeth in frustration. Even her grand-mother didn't understand. No one did.

The sanctuary door opened, and Alex peered out. "Grandma, everyone is ready."

Anna glanced at her grandson. "Just a moment." She looked at Mary and took her hands in her own. "Trust God to work out the things you do not understand. He is here, you know, and he loves you." She kissed Mary gently on the cheek, turned back to Alex, took his arm, and disappeared into the sanctuary.

Her hands balled into fists and arms rigid at her sides, Mary stood alone. She wished she could believe her grandmother, but how? Clearly, if God did exist, he wasn't interested in her or her struggles.

The door creaked open again, and Michael stepped into the foyer. "It's time," he said soberly, knowing full well this was something his daughter dreaded. He tried to smile but only managed a crooked grin.

Mary solemnly took her stepfather's arm and stood beside him at the entrance to the church. She closed her eyes, fighting the rising panic she felt.

Tightening his grip on his daughter's arm, Michael moved forward. He whispered, "Try to smile. This isn't a funeral."

Then why does it feel like one? Mary wondered as she walked into the church. The familiar heavy fragrance of incense hung in the air. Candles washed the sanctuary in soft light. Along the walls icons of saints radiated in the glow.

As Mary made her way down the aisle, her legs felt like lifeless stumps, and she feared she might fall. Friends smiled brightly. Her aunt Olga reached out and patted her arm as she passed, and her mother's friend, Polly, snuffled into a handkerchief.

Unable to smile, Mary only nodded politely.

Her mother and grandmother stood at the front of the church, their eyes trained on Mary. Nana's eyes sparkled with tears. She looked happy. Didn't she understand how sad this day was? She'd always been wise. Could it be her grandmother was right and this was a good thing? An unexplained calm settled over Mary as she stepped up to the altar.

Sean stood to the priest's left, his back straight and stiff. He gazed at her with open admiration, and as he looked into Mary's eyes, she felt he could see into to her soul. Unable to return his affection and knowing he would see that, she quickly looked away. Once more she fought the urge to run. Instead, she took another step forward. Michael placed her hand in Sean's, and this man she barely knew held onto her with strong assurance.

Afraid to meet his eyes, she swallowed hard and turned her attention to the altar. She focused on the huge Bible and candles resting on the elegantly draped table. They blurred into a mix of light and dark, and the room tipped oddly. For a moment, Mary feared she might faint. She breathed deeply and forced her eyes to focus. The flickering candles became clear and their light burned brightly.

As the priest motioned for the couple to move toward him, Michael stepped back and joined Luba.

Mary risked a glance at Sean, then studied him a moment. His hazel eyes were clear and intense. She sensed a mixture of joy and anguish in the man. When he met her gaze, she quickly looked back at the priest.

As the priest blessed the couple, family and friends, and visitors, Mary's mind wandered to the surrounding hillsides, and she didn't hear. As he read Scriptures, she thought of the sea and didn't hear. During the ceremony of crowning, she crawled further into her mind and didn't hear. Even as she took a lighted candle and obediently walked beside Sean around a small table, she didn't hear. And while hiding within a cocoon of indifference, she drank from the common cup.

The priest prayed, and Paul's face intruded into Mary's thoughts. Paul—if only it were he who stood beside her. If only she had promised to spend her life with the man she loved. Tears burned, but she willed them away.

Sean slid a plain gold ring on her finger. It felt cold and unfamiliar. His face replaced the image of Paul's, his eyes warm and kind.

Prayers, then Scriptures followed. The melodious chant of the priest filled the room. And then after a final blessing, the priest turned to Sean and said, "You may kiss your bride."

Obediently, Mary lifted her face to her husband.

Blushing slightly, Sean placed his hands on her shoulders and tenderly pressed his lips to hers.

Although the kiss lasted only a moment, Mary recognized his devotion. Guilt welled up at her inability to return his love, but she quickly rejected the emotion. He knew she didn't love him, and still he'd decided to marry her.

As the couple turned and faced the congregation, the priest placed his hands on their shoulders, and with a paternal smile said, "I am proud and pleased to present to you, Mr. and Mrs. Sean Calhoun."

The words, *Mrs. Sean Calhoun* echoed through Mary's mind. *That is who I am now,* she thought and tried to calm her thumping heart and shaking hands.

Sean looked at his wife and held out his arm.

Mary linked hers with his, and the couple made their way down the center aisle through the throng of well-wishers.

Mary felt alone. Then she saw her grandmother in the crowd. The tiny woman's face crinkled into a smile, and she held out her arms. Mary walked into her embrace and felt a peace she couldn't explain. She wished she could remain folded within the cocoon of love forever. At that moment, Mary almost believed everything would be all right.

Finally, Anna stepped back, keeping hold of her grand-daughter's hands. "He is a fine young man. You love him."

"But how can I?" Mary whispered.

"You are his wife now."

Mary heard the words and felt stunned at the realization. For a moment she didn't reply, then quietly said, "I will try."

"You must do more than try, Mary. He loves you and needs you."

"Yes, Nana," Mary said, hoping to appease her grand-mother, but she had no idea how she would actually fulfill the old woman's request.

Anna stood her granddaughter at arms length and looked into her eyes. "Love will come," she said with assurance. "Enjoy your new life."

"Let's go to the school for the reception," Sean said as he joined them.

Mary moved away from her grandmother, plastered a smile on her face, and with an effort at gaiety, said, "All right, I'm ready." She offered her arm to him.

As they walked down the street, she stared at the young man. He looked almost boyish, his dark hair curling onto his forehead and his mouth turned up in a smile. Although tall and lanky, his long strides were graceful. He was certainly hand-some and seemed kind, but who was he really? Would she ever be able to love him?

"Am I that funny lookin'?" Sean asked.

Mary could feel the blood rush to her face and quickly looked away. "No. You're not funny looking at all."

"Good. The way ye were starin' at me, I was wonderin' if I'd grown another head or something."

Careful to keep her eyes on the road in front of her, Mary did the best she could to match her husband's steps. *I'm sorry, Sean, but I will never love you,* she thought.

Chapter 4

Sean opened the door of the Methodist School. "After ye," he said with a smile and ushered Mary in ahead of him.

Mary gazed about the room. It had been transformed. In place of desks, school papers, books, and chalk were brightly colored ribbons that stretched from one corner of the room to the other and delicate bell cutouts laced together with garland hung beneath doorway arches. The hardwood floor glistened. Sunshine slanted through the windows, and the room looked as if it had been freshly painted a soft gold. On the far wall, a long table covered with an elegant white lace cloth displayed a large, two-tiered cake. China plates, silverware, and napkins had been arranged on one end of the table, and a large crystal punch bowl surrounded by transparent glasses rested on the opposite end.

Captivated by the charming transformation of the school-house, Mary relaxed. She crossed to the table and studied the cake. It had been frosted with white icing and trimmed with butter cream roses. She turned to her mother. "Who made this? It's beautiful."

"Susie. You know how she loves to bake. As soon as she heard about your wedding, she offered to make this for us."

"I didn't know," Mary said, realizing she'd been so unhappy about the wedding that she'd remained detached while others took care of the preparations. She felt a flush of regret over her self-absorption. "I need to thank her." Mary scanned the room searching for the longtime family friend. When she found the plump, native woman, she waved and joined her. Taking Susie's hands in hers, she said, "Thank you for the cake. It's beautiful."

A smile lit Susie's round face. "I wanted to do something. I'm glad you like it."

Mary squeezed her hands. "I do." She surveyed the guests. Everyone chatted gaily. *This is a nice party. I just wish it wasn't my wedding reception.*

"My brother-in-law brought his recording machine," Susie said, pointing to a cabinet in the corner. "Tonight we can listen to songs from the outside."

Surprised and fascinated, Mary looked at the phonograph. "I've never seen one." The two women cut through the crowd, Mary politely greeting guests, then moving on until she stood in front of the remarkable device.

A phonograph was a possession reserved only for the prosperous. Mary had never known a native who owned one. She touched the rich mahogany cabinet that housed the workings of the rare machine. It felt smooth, almost like satin. She allowed her hand to travel over the cool metal of the fluted horn.

"That's where the sound comes from," Susie explained.

"How does it get there?"

Susie shrugged. "I don't know. You just put a record on, wind it up, and music comes out."

"Can we play a song?"

"I'll ask Jonathan." Susie searched the room. When she spotted her brother-in-law, she called out, "Jonathan."

A young, rotund, white man smiled and waved, then shouldered his way through the guests until he stood in front of Susie and Mary. He nodded at Mary, then asked Susie, "What can I do for you?"

"Could you put a record on the phonograph?"

He turned cheery eyes on Mary. "So, you'd like to hear a record?"

Mary nodded. "Yes. I've never heard one before."

"Anything for the bride."

As he took a round disk out of its paper cover, Mary wondered if Susie's sister, Sophie, was happy. Just like she and Sean, Sophie's marriage to Jonathan had been arranged by her parents. The couple had been married only a short time. *I should talk to her,* Mary thought.

"I think you'll like this one," Jonathan said and placed a record on the turntable. He cranked the handle and set a long skinny attachment that looked like an arm on the black disk. At first there was a crackling sound, then sweet-sounding music filled the air.

Mary smiled brightly. "It's wonderful," she said, then closed her eyes, allowing the soothing symphony to enfold her.

Quiet settled over the room.

Susie beamed, obviously proud. "I'm the one who suggested he bring it. I thought it would be a special treat."

Mary looked at Jonathan. "Thank you for sharing this with us. It makes beautiful music."

"I'm glad I brought it," the young man said and tipped his hat.

When the song ended, Mary hoped Jonathan would play another record. Before she could ask, Luba said, "I think everyone is waiting for you and Sean to cut the cake."

"Oh," Mary said soberly, feeling the numbness that had protected her from reality return. She'd much rather remain distracted by music and friends.

Luba circled her arm around her daughter's waist and escorted her to the table.

Mary glanced around the room and found Sean staring at her. His eyes glowed with admiration and affection. For a moment she held his gaze, then wishing he wouldn't look at her that way, she turned her attention back to her mother.

Luba motioned for Sean to join them and called over the din, "It's time to cut the cake."

The guests jostled one another as they crowded around the table, and Sean took his place at Mary's side. She picked up a knife and set it on the cake. Sean placed his hand over hers, and together they sawed through the top tier. Remaining reserved, Mary took a small piece and held it up for her husband to taste.

Taking a bite, Sean smiled. "Very good."

As Sean fed Mary her piece, panic enveloped her. *This man is my husband! I barely know him, and he's supposed to be my mate for the rest of my life!* She forced down the confection.

Cheers and clapping erupted from the bystanders.

Michael raised his glass. "A toast, to the bride and groom."

The guests lifted their glasses in salute.

Michael turned and faced his daughter and son-in-law. "May the Lord bless you with a long and happy life. And may he grant you the blessing of true love."

Although he smiled, Mary could detect sadness behind her stepfather's eyes. *He knows this is wrong, that I won't be happy,* she thought.

"And may you be blessed with many children," someone added.

Mary felt heat rush to her face and was grateful when Michael swallowed the last of his drink. Careful not to look at Sean, she quickly emptied her glass.

"You two should begin the dancing," Luba said. "I will serve the cake."

Mary set her glass on the table and stared at her mother. *How can she expect me to dance? Doesn't she understand at all?*

"It is proper for the bride and groom to share a dance," Luba pressed.

"Yes. You should," her mother's friend Polly added.

Mary cast a look of annoyance at Polly. She'd always liked her, but at the moment couldn't remember why.

Sean took Mary's hand. "Shall we dance, then?"

Mary didn't want to dance. She didn't want to be in this man's arms. She didn't want to be here at all. Nevertheless, without a word, she allowed Sean to escort her to the center of the room.

Music spilled from the phonograph, and as Sean took his wife in his arms, Mary complied, feeling stiff and clumsy. Mechanically, she followed him around the room. He was too close. She couldn't think. Panic set in, and she pulled away, stepping on his foot. "I . . . I'm sorry. I haven't done much of this."

Sean gave her a half grin. "I'm not so good meself, but maybe we can learn together."

Mary didn't know how to answer, so she stared at his shoulder and allowed him to waltz her around the room. Gradually the music settled over her, and Mary felt the stiffness leave her neck and back. She relaxed her hold on Sean's hand and actually began to enjoy the feel of her skirt as it swished away from her legs, the sounds of the orchestra, and the feel of her husband's arms. The song ended, and they moved apart, standing awkwardly and uncertain what to do next.

The onlookers applauded. Mary glanced around the room. She hadn't realized that she and Sean had been the only two dancing. Her face warmed, and she put her hands to her cheeks.

Jonathan set another record on the phonograph, and once more, music filled the room. Others moved onto the dance floor.

Sean looked at Mary. "Again?"

With a nod, Mary allowed him to sweep her back into his arms and around the room.

Laughter, music, and conversation filled the schoolhouse. Brightly colored skirts swirled above lightly moving feet. Women flirted and men swaggered. Youngsters played childish games; some danced, trying to imitate the adults, while others chased one another, darting between couples. It was a good party—so good that Mary nearly forgot the reason for the celebration.

Late in the evening, Luka Glotoff, a lifelong resident of Unalaska, suggested they share a traditional native song and dance with the nonnative groom. The guests agreed, clapping their approval.

Four tribal elders sat together at the far end of the room. Each held a drum that looked like a large tambourine attached to a wooden handle. As their hands fell upon the tightly stretched skin surfaces, a pulsating thrum reverberated throughout the schoolhouse.

An old man named Yeagor stepped into the middle of the room. Stomping his feet in time to the rhythm, he pranced across the floor. Soon another man joined him, and another.

As the beat pulsated, Mary struggled to keep her feet still. But the young bride couldn't ignore the call of the music and rocked back and forth.

Anna joined the dance. Her body moved to the drum's pulse and she no longer looked old, but vigorous and graceful.

For several minutes Mary watched, then unable to hold back any longer, she joined her grandmother. She forgot all but the music. Its cadence filled her and she swayed, then beat the floor with her feet. Others joined them, a mix of young and old, male and female. Free of inhibitions, they moved about the room aware only of the drums.

Abruptly, the music stopped, and the dancers slumped to the floor.

A man stood up and stepped to the center of the room. Everyone moved aside, sat in a wide circle, and waited expectantly. His expression serious, he studied the onlookers and finally walked across the floor, stopping directly in front of Sean. Leveling a solemn gaze on the young man, he said, "There is a story of a great seal hunter who took a wife . . ."

Some of the women giggled, and all the guests smiled as they looked from Sean to Mary.

Allowing her mind to wander, Mary retreated from the present. She'd heard this story many times. She didn't want to hear it now. She wasn't the wife of a great seal hunter, but the wife of a white man who knew nothing of native ways. Sean had never lived off the land. He didn't know how to hunt the whale or walrus, or how to handle an umiak or baidarka. Their worlds were divided by a chasm that could never be traversed.

Mary remembered her years in the village. They had been good years. She looked around the room and saw many who still lived there. Polly and Olga sat together, intent on the story. They had been a large part of Mary's early years. Polly, who had always been good-hearted and spirited, had made certain that Mary knew how to have fun. She taught her young friend many games and dances. More conservative, Aunt Olga had always been attentive and kind and made certain that Mary learned to weave and sew.

The music brought back memories of Norutuk, the village medicine man. Mary had loved and revered him. The old man had seemed to possess mystical powers, but he never shared his knowledge of the spirits with her. She'd asked many times, but he'd always refused, saying it was much too dangerous for one so young. Mary sighed. So much had been lost when he died. A pang of grief filled her. She missed the uncomplicated life she'd once known.

The drums thrummed again. The storyteller stood in front of Mary and held out his hand. Knowing what was to come, she reluctantly allowed him to pull her to her feet. The man motioned for Sean to stand, then led the couple to the center of the floor. They were expected to dance, and Mary felt a twinge of apprehension. She didn't want Sean to feel like a fool. He knew nothing about their ways and stood awkwardly, awaiting instructions. Mary stepped close to him, and looking into his eyes, she said, "Do as I do." She moved to the beat. "Let your spirit hear the music."

Sean blushed, then did his best to imitate Mary, stomping, turning, and swaying to the drums' pulse. He looked silly, nothing like a mighty hunter, but he kept trying. Mary admired his spirit and smiled at him, hoping to encourage him.

Giggles broke out among the spectators. Sean laughed but continued to move. Others soon joined the couple.

Gaining confidence, Sean threw himself into the dance. Grinning, he spun and swayed, moving more gracefully to the rhythm. With a sense of pride, Mary watched as this outsider found freedom in the music.

Finally, with a loud thump the drums fell silent, and again, the dancers dropped to the floor. Panting for breath, everyone laughed.

Sean stood and held his hand out to Mary. "That was fun."

Mary allowed her husband to help her up. He pulled her too close. Mary stepped back. "I'm thirsty. I think I'll get some punch."

"I'll get it." Sean left her and joined the line of people waiting to fill their cups.

"You look beautiful when you dance," Anna said, joining her granddaughter.

"Me? You're the one. You're wonderful." She bent and kissed the tiny woman.

Anna hugged Mary with one arm. "It felt good to dance again. I've missed it."

"I wish you would stay in Unalaska, Nana."

"Some day. But not now. Cora needs me."

"How is she?"

"Not good. She is getting old." A look of sorrow crossed Anna's face. "She will be gone soon, and I will miss her. She's been a good companion." She brushed a strand of hair off her face. "She was my first friend when your grandfather brought me to the white man's world." Her eyes teared. "I do not like good-byes. I never have." She smiled softly. "But at least it is only temporary. One day we will be reunited."

"How can you be sure of that?"

"God said we will live with him in eternity, and he does not lie, not ever."

Mary didn't want to hear about God and his promises. She'd grown up with a mix of the old wizardry left by her ancestors and the new Christian faith. It was Norutuk's magic that tantalized her. He had possessed power. Her parents' faith, though it seemed to provide peace for them, held little appeal for Mary. Wishing to change the subject, she asked, "When are you going home?"

"Soon. On the next boat, I think. I have been teaching some of the younger native women in Juneau the old ways. It feels good to share the skills I was taught by my mother and grandmother."

"I know some of our ways, but there is still much I need to learn. I wish you could teach me."

Anna looked incredulous. "There are many here who can guide you—your own mother."

Mary frowned. "It's not the same. And now that my life has changed, I will have less time for such things."

Anna studied Mary a moment, then kissed her on the cheek and pulled her into her arms. Stepping back, she held Mary's hands. "Change is never easy. Now you are a married woman, and you must think not only of yourself but of your husband also. It is a beautiful thing to share your life with another person."

Mary sighed and looked at Sean. He visited with a friend, unaware of her scrutiny. He was animated and seemed happy. She wished she could feel the same.

The evening passed quickly, and soon the guests began to leave. Mary knew that it was time to leave with Sean, but she didn't want to face being alone with her husband. She wasn't ready for that. So she stayed and helped clean.

"You shouldn't be doing this," Luba finally said. "It's time you and Sean went home."

"I don't want to leave all this work for you."

"Don't worry about me. I have a lot of help."

Mary swallowed hard and looked at Sean.

"Are ye ready to go?" he asked.

"I guess so," Mary said, searching for a way of putting off the inevitable. But there was nothing she could do except to take his arm and allow him to escort her home.

Sean stepped onto the porch. Instead of opening the door, he stood looking uncertain, then unexpectedly swept

Mary up into his arms. With a shy grin, he said, "It's our weddin' day. I'm supposed to carry me bride over the threshold."
He pushed the door open and stepped into the dark cabin. For
a few moments he stood just inside the door holding Mary close
to him, as if reluctant to let her go. Finally, he set his wife on
her feet.

Mary stood rooted where he'd set her. She didn't know
what to say. While Sean lit a lantern, she smoothed her dress
and hair, unable to keep her hands from shaking.

Lifting the lamp to shoulder level, he said, "Well, this is it."
His face looked anxious in the dim light as he surveyed the
room. "It's not very big, only two rooms. . . ."

Mary gazed at the modest quarters. Although neat and
clean, the tiny house clearly needed a woman's touch. The
night's blackness peered through naked windows, and empty
walls clamored for animation. There were no quilts or afghans
decorating the meager furnishings. A wooden table with two
chairs sat in front of a small window at the front of the house.
An overstuffed sofa rested against the far wall. The kitchen consisted of a wood cook stove, two cupboards, and a single sink
with a hand pump for water.

It will be nice not to have to carry water from outside, Mary
conceded.

"I plan to make some new furniture," Sean said. He set
the lantern on the table.

"This is a fine house." Mary searched for something more
to say. She crossed to the pump and rested her hand on it. "I've
never had indoor plumbing before."

Sean combed back his hair with his hand and cleared his
throat. "Would ye like some coffee? I can make some."

"No," Mary said, then wished she'd said yes. It would have given them something to do.

For several awkward moments the two searched for something to say.

"Well, I guess ye'll want to freshen up." He glanced toward the back of the cabin. "The bedroom is right here." He quickly crossed to a door and pushed it open. "It's not much, but there is a feather bed. I remember when I was a boy growin' up, me mother always said a feather bed was a must if a person expected a good night's sleep."

Mary's hand rested at her throat as she walked to the doorway. Her heart beat wildly as she stepped into the small room. A lumpy, double bed had been pushed against one wall where a bare window stared down upon it. On the opposite wall stood an aged bureau with a mirror. One of its drawers tipped at an angle. A pitcher and a glass sat on top of the chest. To the left of the dresser, a wooden rack huddled in the corner. Sean's lightweight coat hung limply from a peg, and a hat had been carelessly tossed over the top hook. Long johns drooped off the other side, balancing out the hodgepodge.

Sean snatched his underwear from the rack and stuffed them under his arm. "I . . . I'll have to keep some of me things in here. There's no where else to put them." He pulled open the bottom drawer of the dresser, stuffed the long johns inside, and shoved it closed. "Ye can have the two top drawers." He straightened and clasped his hands behind his back. "I . . . I'll be out here," he stuttered and backed out the door.

After he'd gone, Mary pushed against the door to make certain it was tightly closed, then removed her coat and hung it on the rack. Her small trunk, which had been brought over earlier, sat on the floor beside the chest of drawers. She knelt beside it, untied the straps, and carefully sorted through the clothing until she found her nightdress. Holding the plain, cotton gown out in front of her, she studied it. It was certainly nothing special for a wedding night, not that she wanted it to be. She glanced at the bed she and Sean would share; her stomach knotted and her heart hammered.

Mary then set the nightdress on the bed and poured herself a glass of water. She sipped slowly, but the water didn't seem to wet her mouth. She turned back to her trunk, carefully removed the rest of her clothing, and put it in the dresser.

With that done, she glanced around the room. There was nothing else she could do. It was time to dress for bed. Methodically, she unbuttoned the top row of hooks on her dress. Her eyes fell upon the blackness beyond the window, and her hands lay still. What was out there in the darkness? She'd always thought that living in a house with glass windows would be nice, but now she felt exposed and vulnerable. All she wanted was to return to the safety of her family's snug barabara. She shivered, and fighting tears, asked herself, *What am I going to do? I'm someone's wife. I don't know how to be a wife.*

A soft rap sounded at the door.

Instinctively, Mary closed the top of her dress. "I'm not ready."

"Just checkin'," came a muffled reply.

Mary finished unbuttoning her dress and carefully stepped out of the gown. For a moment, she held it against her face. It smelled of home. Tears brimmed over, and she buried her face in the soft cotton. Straightening, she said, "That's enough of that." Wiping at her eyes, she carefully folded the dress and placed it in her trunk.

Donning her night clothes, she walked to the mirror and brushed out her hair. A stranger with large, dark eyes stared back at her. Mary remembered a deer she'd once encountered. Ready to bolt, the animal stood with its sides heaving, staring at her from dusky, terrified eyes, eyes similar to the ones she now saw in the glass. She'd stood very still, hoping the animal wouldn't flee, but with a flick of its tail, it had darted into the bushes.

She wished she could run.

Mary set the hairbrush on the bureau top and walked slowly to the door. When she opened it, Sean looked up from a kitchen chair where he sat with his feet propped against the wall and a pipe between his teeth. Smoke rose lazily from the bowl. The scene looked oddly serene until Sean's booted feet thudded to the floor. He sat up and stared at Mary but said nothing.

"I didn't know you smoked," Mary said.

Taking the pipe from his mouth, Sean studied it. "It's not somethin' I do every day. Just now and again."

Mary liked the pleasant lilt of Sean's voice.

Setting the pipe on a rack, he stood, and taking long strides, he stopped just in front of Mary.

She pressed her back against the wall.

Sean moved past her and into the bedroom. "I just need to get some blankets, then ye can go on to bed."

Mary didn't understand why he needed blankets but was too embarrassed to ask.

A few moments later, he emerged from the bedroom with a quilt tucked under each arm and a pillow beneath his chin.

Without looking at Mary, he stepped into the front room, dropped the pillow on the floor, folded one quilt in half and spread it out, then laid the other over the first.

Confused, Mary watched silently.

Wearing a half smile, he glanced up at his bride. "I guess ye're wonderin' what I'm doin'." He straightened and joined Mary. Standing very close, he gently took her hands in his. Taking a breath, then letting it out slowly, he said, "I could claim me husbandly rights . . ."

Mary's stomach tightened. She could feel his breath against her cheek.

Sean searched her face. "Don't be frightened. I'm not goin' to hurt ye." He caressed her cheek. "I know ye don't love me . . . not yet anyway. And I won't force meself on ye. I'm willin' to wait until ye *want* to become Mrs. Sean Calhoun."

Mary's eyes flooded with tears. "Why did you marry me?"

"I love ye. And I was afraid if I waited ye would marry someone else." He turned her hands over and kissed the palms, then looked into her eyes.

Mary moved away a little. He didn't understand. *I can never love you. I love Paul. Paul, how could you do this to me?* She pulled her hands free. "Good night, Sean."

Chapter 5

Bang. Bang." The sound hammered itself into Sean's dream. He tried to ignore the noise and linger a little longer in sleep, but the racket continued and he forced one eye open, then the other. "Bang. Bang." Rolling onto his back, he tried to identify the sound. Turning blurry eyes on the door, he realized someone was pounding on his front door.

"Sean! Wake up!" a familiar voice called.

"I'm comin'. I'm comin'," Sean mumbled, throwing back his covers and pushing himself up on one elbow. Stiff and sore from sleeping on the hard floor, he raised onto one knee, then slowly pushed himself upright. Fumbling in the half-light, he located matches, lit the lantern, then grabbed his pants off the back of a chair. The pounding continued. "I'm comin'." He pulled on one pant leg, then the other, while hopping on one foot. He glanced out the window, but darkness hid his visitor.

"Why would someone be here at this hour?" he wondered aloud. "It's the middle of the night." With a sense of uneasiness, he opened the door.

"I thought you'd never answer," Marcus said as he pushed past his sleepy friend.

Incredulous, Sean stared at him. "What are ye doin' here?" The smell of tobacco smoke and alcohol hit him. "Have ye been tossin' down the drinks again?"

"I've got news!"

"It couldn't wait till mornin'?"

"Well, if you'd bother to look at the clock, it is morning."

Sean looked at the wall clock and brought it into focus. It read four-thirty. "Barely," he said sarcastically.

"I knew you'd want to know." Marcus slurred his words, clearly inebriated.

"Know what?" Sean closed the door.

"You won't believe it." Marcus' eyes slid to the pile of bedding on the floor. Momentarily sidetracked, a crooked smile touched his lips.

Sean steeled himself against what he knew was coming.

"Thrown out already, huh?"

"No."

"No?" Marcus chuckled.

Sean realized that before the day was out every man in town would know he'd spent his wedding night on the floor. He nearly groaned aloud, but instead he squared his jaw and asked, "Why are ye here?"

Marcus removed his hat and with his hand combed back his short-cropped black hair. He refocused on Sean. "Oh, yeah." He took a deep breath. "War. They've declared war."

"Who's declared war?"

"President Wilson. It came over the wireless."

His embarrassment forgotten, Sean's stomach knotted. "Ye sure?"

"I heard it myself."

Sean crossed to a threadbare wing chair and dropped onto it.

Marcus dragged a wooden chair across the room, planted it directly in front of Sean, and sat. Gripping his hat in his hands, he stared at his friend. His eyes looked eager, his expression animated. "First light, I'm signing up. There's a lot of us ready to fight. It's about time someone showed those lousy Huns a thing or two. They'll be sorry."

The room momentarily disappeared behind a haze, and Sean felt numb. "War?" He looked at Marcus. "War is madness." Slowly shaking his head, he said, "Why couldn't they find another way?"

Marcus leaned back and rested his right ankle on his knee. "What other way? The Germans won't give up, and the British don't have a chance without our help."

Sean said nothing for a long while. Finally, he said, "I need a cup of coffee." He stood. "Would ye like some?"

"No thanks. I've got to get moving. There'll be a lot of men wanting to sign up." He stood and walked to the door.

Sean realized what lay ahead for him and the other men of Unalaska, and anger surged through him. "Innocent people are going to die."

"Yeah, well, that's reality."

Sean followed his friend to the door. "Marcus, ye don't know what's ahead of ye."

"Yes I do. I'll see you later." With a quick salute, he turned and marched down the lane.

Sean watched the big man disappear into the morning gloom. Enjoying the coolness, he remained on the step for a long while. Dawn's light caressed the clouds with color, illuminating the dark hills. Beyond the bay, a heavy mist veiled the horizon. Sean sucked cold air into his lungs. This was the only reality he wanted.

"War," he whispered, shaking his head and remembering the ghastly stories his father had told him about the Irish Land Wars. The people rebelled and were nearly annihilated. Famine and the blood of Irish peasants became his father's reality. This war would be no different. Men would die, families would perish, and in the end, no one would win.

His spirit heavy, Sean turned and walked inside. Closing the door, he leaned against the wooden entrance and eyed the pile of bedding on the floor. An ache gnawed at his gut. *If only she loved me. Then anything would be bearable.*

He studied the bedroom door. Would she wait for him while he was away at war? And if he didn't return, would she forget him as the years passed?

Mary sat up and hung her legs over the side of the bed. Who was at their door so early in the day? The voices sounded troubled. She listened closely but couldn't distinguish who was speaking or what was being said. She considered joining Sean and his visitor, but without knowing who was with him, she decided it would be best to stay put.

Still sleepy, she lay back down and burrowed into her feather pillow. *I hope everything is all right.* Pushing against the cushion with her elbow, she turned onto her side. The bed gave beneath her weight. It was too soft. For years, a pallet on the floor had been her bed. She'd only recently changed to a firm spring bed. Sighing, she thought, *How will I ever get used to this?*

Mary tried to sleep, but she had too many questions about who had visited and why, so she finally gave up and climbed out of bed. Taking her cape from the cloak rack, she threw it over her shoulders, then stepped to the door and listened. Hearing nothing, she cautiously opened the door. A wedge of lantern light brightened the room. Sean stood looking out the window, arms folded over his chest. He didn't notice her, but as she stepped through the doorway, the floorboards creaked and he turned.

"Good mornin' to ye. Ye're up early."

"I couldn't sleep. And I thought I heard someone earlier. Is everything all right?"

"Marcus was here."

Mary waited for an explanation.

With a breath that sounded more like a sigh, Sean stepped around the table and sat down. He leaned forward, rested his elbows on his thighs, and momentarily covered his face with his hands. "He had news that couldn't wait."

Something in Sean's voice set Mary on edge. "What kind of news?"

"Seems . . ." Sean sat back, took another deep breath, then slowly let it out. "It seems the United States has joined the war in Europe."

A pulse of adrenaline surged through Mary's body. "War? How does he know that?"

"Heard it over the wireless."

Mary grabbed the back of a chair. "But why? Why would we go to war? The Germans have done nothing to us."

"No, but they're threatening our allies in Europe. If we don't help, who will? Someone has to step in."

"What will happen now?"

"Troops will be sent overseas. And the army needs men. Marcus plans on signin' up first thing this mornin'." He looked into Mary's eyes. "I'm goin' too." He picked up his pipe. "War is despicable." Taking a pouch out of his front pocket, he sprinkled tobacco into the bowl and packed it down. "When I was growin' up, me father often told me about what it was like. He didn't want me thinkin' it was somethin' it wasn't." He lit his pipe and took two puffs, allowing smoke to escape the sides of his mouth. "All the same, I'll be signin' up."

For months the paper had been filled with frightening news from overseas. Reports of terror and death had been recounted again and again. Still, it had seemed far away, part of someone else's life. Now it was real.

Mary studied her husband. Gripping his pipe between his teeth, he stared out the window. As he took a drag, the tobacco glowed red and a plume of smoke lifted into the air. He glanced at his wife, then returned to watching the early morning shadows dissolve.

Though Mary didn't know Sean well, she knew he was a peaceable man and it would be wrong for him to be thrust into a war. There must be another way. "Do you have to sign up?" she asked.

Sean puffed on his pipe and watched the smoke slowly

billow into the air and drift toward the ceiling. "I've no choice. I'll be goin'."

Mary knew he meant what he said and didn't argue. "Do you know when you'll be leaving?"

"I expect soon. They'll be needin' as many men on the lines as they can get."

Mary remembered Paul. He would have to fight too. She dropped into a chair. "Dear God."

"What is it?" Sean asked.

"It's just that . . ." Mary searched for a reason for her words. She didn't want him to know she'd been thinking about Paul. That would be too unkind. "I was just thinking about all the men from here who will have to go," she finally explained.

Hurt flickered across Sean's face. "Yeah, everyone, even Paul." He let his pipe rest on the table. "It's cold," he said as he pushed himself up and crossed to the wood box. Picking up a chunk of driftwood, he opened the firebox, shoved in the tinder, and replaced the stove lid.

"I . . . I'm sorry Sean. But I can't help but think about him. I'm trying, but . . ." There was nothing more she could say.

Sean shoved his hands in his pockets and stared out.

"I . . . I do care about you," Mary said feebly.

Sean kept staring.

"I'll make coffee." She searched a cupboard and found the coffee, then spooned it into a pot. Unaccustomed to indoor plumbing, she gingerly pushed down on the pump's handle. When nothing happened, she repeated the process, and finally water spurted from the spigot. She filled the pot, careful not to churn the grounds, then set it on the stove top.

Sean continued to look out the window.

Now what? Mary glanced at the clock. It was still early.
Muted light washed the interior of the cabin. *I better get dressed,*
she decided and quietly retreated to her room.

Mary pulled a white cotton blouse over her head, but-
toned it, then stepped into her dark blue skirt and cinched
it at the waist. After pulling on socks and shoes, she crossed
to the mirror, brushed her hair, and pulled it into a single
braid. The water in the pitcher was cold, but she poured a
little into a washbowl and splashed her face with it. She
patted her cheeks dry, then studied her reflection in the
mirror. The panicked look of the previous evening had
been replaced by worry. Straightening, she said, "Stop that.
Being afraid won't help. There is nothing you can do about
a war."

She turned away from the mirror and looked over the
room. Except for the bed, it was tidy. Quickly she pulled the
covers up, plumped the pillows, smoothed the quilt with her
hand and returned to the front room.

The aroma of coffee greeted her.

Sean stood at the stove, cup in hand. "Would ye like
some?"

Mary nodded. She sat at the table while he grabbed a cup
from the cupboard and filled it. Her hands folded on the table
in front of her, she glanced at the heap of bedding still piled in
the center of the room. She looked away and caught Sean staring at her. Guilt pierced her conscience. She hadn't fulfilled her
wifely responsibilities. But hadn't Sean told her she was free of
them? *But only until I fall in love with him,* she thought, wondering what he'd say when he finally realized that would never
happen.

"Sorry. I meant to clean that up," Sean said. "Just didn't get to it yet." He handed her the coffee and sat at the table.

Looking at the bedding, Mary said, "I'll put it away." Prodded by her guilt, she continued, "It's not right for you to sleep on the floor. This is your house."

"It's my choice."

"But . . ."

"It's my choice," he repeated firmly.

"You're stubborn, aren't you?" Mary challenged.

"That I am, but I'll bet ye'd give me a run for me money," Sean said with a wink.

Mary couldn't keep from smiling.

He leaned back in his chair. "It's good to see ye smile."

Mary could feel her face heat up and turned her attention to her coffee. It looked awfully strong. She tasted it and wrinkled her nose in distaste.

"I like strong coffee," Sean said and took a drink. "This way, I know I've had a cup." He cradled the mug between his hands. "Marcus woke me so early, it already feels as if the day is half over." He gazed out the window. "Mornin' is my favorite time of day. It's peaceful before the rest of the world wakes up." He took another drink. "Looking out there, it's hard to believe a war is goin' on overseas."

"Most of my life I've stayed right here on Unalaska Island. The world has always been far away. But I like it, being detached from the outside. It feels safe here."

"Some places in the world aren't so bad. In fact, I kind of like explorin'."

"I could never leave here, not for a very long time anyway." Mary's eyes wandered over the hillsides and steep cliffs

that rose up from the bay, then settled on the hamlet of
Unalaska with its boxy houses and weathered bay-front businesses. "I'd miss this place too much."

The door closed behind Sean. He was on his way to sign
up. As Mary cleared away the breakfast dishes, she watched
him amble toward town, hands in pockets. His step was slow.
Clearly, he took no pleasure in what he was about to do.

She carried a pan of hot water from the stove and set it in
the sink, then added cold water. As she plunked the dishes into
the water, Paul's face intruded on her thoughts. Would he return
to Unalaska before enlisting? If he did, would he come to see
her?

Shame pressed down on Mary, and she forced his image
from her mind. *I'm married,* she reminded herself. *Sean is my
husband now.* Sadness settled over her. Why did life have to be
so complicated and painful—so unfair? Why couldn't Paul have
been honorable? Why did Sean marry her knowing she didn't
love him? "I shouldn't have married him. It was wrong."

She returned to the table and wiped it clean with a damp
cloth. She stopped and scanned the sky. A heavy band of
clouds had settled over the bay and clung to the mountains. She
sighed. A storm had moved ashore. There would be no sunshine today.

Wind moaned as it swept around the house, and bushes
scratched the windows. Mary shivered and rubbed her arms.
The traditional barabara did a much better job of holding off the
cold. Her family was one of the few remaining residents on
Unalaska who still lived in a hut, and Mary had always believed

that living in a wood house would be better. Her discontent had been foolish. She realized it now and longed for the quiet snugness of her family's barabara.

She shoved another piece of wood in the stove, picked up a blanket from the floor, wrapped it about her shoulders, and sat on the sofa. She still felt cold. Pulling the blanket tighter, she realized it wasn't the temperature that chilled her, but life, with its frightening possibilities.

Someone rapped quietly on the door.

With the blanket still around her shoulders, Mary crossed the room and opened it.

Luba stood on the step. She smiled. "Good morning."

"Mama, what are you doing here so early?" Mary hugged her mother. "Have you heard?"

"Yes. That's why I'm here. When the world spins out of control, we need each other. I thought you might be wanting some company."

"Please come in." Mary opened the door wide. "Would you like some coffee or tea?"

"Coffee sounds good." Luba eyed the pillow and pile of bedding on the floor and gave her daughter a questioning look.

Self-consciously, Mary let her coverlet slip off her shoulders, scooped up the blankets, pushed the bedroom door open with her hip, and deposited the damaging evidence on the bed. She glanced in the mirror. *Now I'll have to explain,* she thought dismally and returned to the front room.

"Where do you keep your cups?" Luba asked, opening a cupboard.

"Right there on the second shelf." Mary picked up a chunk of wood and placed it in the stove. "This house feels cold."

"Would you like some?" Luba asked.

"Yes." Mary approached her mother and cleared her throat. "So . . . I guess you're wondering why there was bedding on the floor."

Luba turned and looked at her daughter. "You may tell me if you like, but your life is your own now." She filled a cup.

Smoothing her skirt, Mary said, "Sean slept there. He . . . he said we won't share a bed because he knows I don't love him."

Luba held out the coffee to her daughter.

Taking it, Mary continued, "I was surprised. It wasn't my idea at all."

Luba smiled. "I knew he was an exceptional man." She took a sip of coffee and grimaced, then asked with a chuckle, "Who made the coffee?"

"Sean. He likes it strong."

Luba held up her hand and sat at the table. "No. Don't bother. It's strong, but I can drink it."

Mary sat across from her mother. Resting her face in her hands, she stared into her mug. Life felt dismal. She was married to a man she didn't love, and there was a war that would probably change her world in ways she couldn't even imagine.

"Do you understand that you've married an uncommon man?" Luba asked.

"Yes. But that doesn't change the fact that I don't love him."

"Love will come."

"And what if it doesn't?" Mary looked directly at her mother.

"Then you will do your duty."

Mary didn't respond but looked at her coffee again. She'd known the answer before she'd asked.

Luba laid a hand over Mary's.

"Mama, I'm afraid. What's going to happen?"

"With you and Sean, or the war?"

"Both."

"I can't say. We just need to leave it all in God's hands."

"But all the men will have to go and fight. I don't love Sean, but I don't want him to go to war and maybe be injured or killed."

"I wish no one had to go." Luba gazed out the window. "Sometimes my father talked about the Civil War. Every time he did I could see that the memories haunted him. I don't know if he ever got over what he witnessed. He didn't like talking about it." Luba looked at Mary. "I'm sorry. This isn't helping." She took a drink of coffee and said resolutely, "We will pray."

"Do you think the men will leave right away?"

"I don't know—probably." Luba looked down the hill at the town. "It is nice having windows. I'd forgotten. It's been so many years since I left Juneau." She sighed. "It will be nice to sit at your kitchen table and enjoy spring flowers and green hillsides."

"I wish spring would get here. It's still awfully cold and wet."

"That's how it always is. It seems as if spring is here, then it turns cold again." Luba straightened and watched the path closely. "Is that Sean? He looks like he's in a hurry."

Sean looked angry as he lumbered toward home. His strides were long and fast, and he stared at the ground as he walked. Uneasiness filled Mary. "I wonder what's wrong."

When Sean reached the house, he didn't come in right away but stood in front of the porch, then sat on the front step. Finally, he stood, knocked the mud from his boots, and stepped inside. His expression veiled, he nodded at Luba and Mary. "Hello, Luba." He stood in front of the stove and held his hands out to it.

"Sean, is something wrong?" Mary asked.

He said nothing for a moment, then with his back still to Mary, he said, "The army won't take me."

"Why?"

"Me hearin'. I'm almost deaf in me left ear."

Mary didn't know what to say. She finally blurted, "Well, that's good. You won't have to go."

"Me hearin' is nothin'," he said, his voice strained.

Luba stood and scooted her chair back. "It's time for me to go home." She walked to Sean and laid a hand on his arm. "Maybe God has something else for you to do."

"Maybe."

Luba looked at Mary. "Thank you for the coffee and the visit," she said and left.

As soon as the door closed, Sean slumped into a chair.

"Why are you so upset? I thought you didn't want to fight."

He looked stricken. "No one wants war, but when ye're needed . . ." He folded his arms over his chest.

"I didn't know you had a bad ear. How did it happen?"

"When I was a kid, a man cuffed me alongside the head. For several days all I could hear was a loud ringin'. When it stopped, I could barely hear. But I do fine." He stared at the floor.

"That's why you tip your head to the right when you're listening to someone."

"I do?"

"Uh-huh." Silence settled over the room. Finally, Mary asked, "Are you hungry? I could make you something to eat. Or maybe you'd like a cup of tea?"

"No thank ye."

"I'm sure there are others who weren't accepted."

Sean said nothing.

Mary searched for something more she could say, something that would help. "I . . . I didn't want you to go anyway."

Sean met Mary's eyes. "Ye don't understand. Ye can't. Ye're not a man." He leaned forward, resting his arms on his legs. "It's not just the honor of defendin' me country. It's the dishonor of not helpin' at all."

"But you can't help it. It's not your fault."

Sean sighed. "No, but when the others leave, I'll stay. The only men left in town will be old or frail, except me."

"You'll be needed here."

"For what?"

Being sympathetic hadn't seemed to help, so Mary decided to try another tact. She planted her hands on her hips. "Sean Calhoun, you're feeling sorry for yourself. And you're being foolish. Sometimes there are things in life that can't be changed. And it's a waste of our time feeling sorry for ourselves. There are better things to do. This town will need a strong man." Her eyes fell upon the nearly empty wood box. "For example, right now we need more wood."

Looking bruised, Sean stood and walked to the door, and without a word, he left.

Mary watched him trudge down the path, hands shoved into his pockets, eyes on the ground. Shoulders slumped, he looked defeated. Mary felt a pang of sadness and wished there were some way she could help him.

Chapter 6

The boat rolled over the top of a wave, and Sean pulled on the oars. He liked the feel of the sea as it rose and fell beneath him. Michael let the net out gradually as they moved across the water. A large set of waves hit the bow and spray splashed over the sides.

"The seas are running high," Michael said.

Gray gulls and white-breasted Murres soared above the rocky coastline, their cries echoing over the bay. Some skimmed the waters and beaches, then lifted into the air, carrying food to their young. A seagull sailed over the small boat. Catching air beneath its wings, it hung motionless, hoping someone would throw out a tidbit. "Sorry, we've had no luck yet today," Sean said with a smile. The bird remained a few moments longer, then flew toward the beach.

As the boat moved through the chop toward open water, Unalaska grew smaller. Since first arriving in the little town,

Sean had liked living there. But now it had become a place of humiliation, and he wished he didn't have to return at the end of the day.

Over the past months, questions and accusations arose about why Sean had remained in Unalaska while so many other young men had gone to war. Sean often found himself on the defensive. Worse than the open confrontations were the silent accusatory stares. He couldn't answer those.

He'd done what he could to fill the gap left by the would-be soldiers. He fished, worked the cannery, and did odd jobs about town for some of the elderly residents. His mind told him he should feel no shame; yet he struggled to maintain his pride.

Michael let out the last of the net and sat on the bench seat. Sean stopped rowing, and the boat wallowed in the waves.

"Are we goin' to drop the other net further out?" Sean asked.

Michael leaned his forearms on his legs. "Yeah, but I thought we could take a break. You look like you need to talk."

"No. I'm just thinkin' is all." Sean returned to watching the shoreline.

"Son, it's time we talked," Michael said soberly. He watched the waves for a few minutes. "I think I know what's eating at you."

"I'm fine," Sean lied. He knew Michael wouldn't believe him, but how could he explain his shame when he didn't even understand it himself.

Michael raised an eyebrow, grabbed a knee between his hands, and leaned back. "Sharing our troubles makes them lighter."

"All right. You're right. Somethin' is botherin' me." Sean pulled the oars inside the boat. He didn't know how to begin. He watched the birds flock around the boat, floating on the waves and hoping for a handout. Sean looked at Michael. "It's hard stayin' here. People stare at me. I know what they're thinkin', and I feel like some sort of defector."

"You're letting your imagination get the best of you."

"No. It's not my imagination." He folded his arms over his chest.

"The folks I've talked to understand there is nothing you can do. Army regulations are army regulations. No one is going to change them."

Sean watched the birds.

"I know this is painful, but you need to look at the positive side of things. You're able to stay with your wife. You don't have to worry about leaving her a widow. And you're needed here."

"I know what ye're sayin' is true and I ought to be grateful, but I'm embarrassed. I can't help it."

Michael took a piece of dried fish out of his front pocket. Tearing off a chunk, he gave it to Sean, then took a bite of his own. He chewed slowly. "I know what it's like to be the one who doesn't fit. I grew up in a village where boys were expected to become hunters and fishermen like their fathers. But I wanted to go to school and teach one day. The elders and even my own family didn't understand. They wouldn't accept it. I was expected to do as my ancestors had always done. Wanting something else made me look peculiar and arrogant to the people in the village."

Tearing off a piece of fish with his teeth, Michael chewed the salty meat. "I tried to find my own way, but many times I nearly changed my mind and did as people expected. But each time I decided to give up my dream of going to school, I'd think about how life would be for me, and I couldn't do it. So I left the village and did the only thing I could.

When I finished college and returned, the people didn't trust me. They didn't understand the outside world and feared it. In the beginning I had no students, then a few. Some people avoided me, but others couldn't hide their thoughts. Their eyes said what was in their hearts. To them I'd become an outsider and couldn't be trusted. It was a difficult time, but gradually more and more students came to the school. Finally people realized I was there to help, and in time they developed faith in me."

"Why don't ye teach any more?"

"When Luba and I left the village to live here in Unalaska, there were already enough teachers. I wasn't needed, although I do some substitute teaching. But I must admit that as I grow older, I've become more interested in the ways of my ancestors. So I've been learning some of the old ways." He smiled. "It feels good."

"Do ye miss teaching?"

"Yes. I miss the children. But I'm happy." Michael stripped away some of the crusty skin of the fish and dropped it in his mouth. His gaze wandered to the horizon, and the wind caught at his hair. "There are many things we can do in this life. Sometimes plans change, but that doesn't mean we quit living."

Sean tore off a piece of fish and threw it to the birds. Several dived for it. One came up with the tidbit and fought to keep it, finally flying away with his prize. "It's hard for me, knowin' people are thinkin' and sayin' things that aren't true."

"What do you think people are saying?"

"That I'm a coward, that I don't love me country enough to fight for it, that I made up an excuse so I didn't have to go."

Michael nodded slowly. "I suppose some are saying those things. But the ones who know you know better." He looked at his son-in-law. "You're a fine, honorable man, Sean, and you can't let the small-minded rob you of life's joy."

"I don't know how honorable I am. Sometimes I'm just plain mad, but ye're right about not letting it bother me. Some days are easier than others. I'd like to move away for awhile."

"I know." Michael pulled a water jug out from under the seat, twisted open the lid, and took a long drink. Wiping his mouth, he said, "The salt in the fish always makes me thirsty."

"Me too. I could use some of that." Sean took the jug, gulped down several mouthfuls, and replaced the lid.

"Do you mind telling me what happened to your hearing?" Michael asked.

"When I was a boy livin' in New York, times were tough. So me and a couple of me buddies would rummage through trash left behind stores and restaurants. Sometimes we'd find good stuff. We weren't doin' anyone any harm, but that's not the way Mr. Baldovino saw it. He owned an Italian restaurant and more than once had warned us to stay away from his place. But that wasn't easy; there was always good stuff in his trash, so we'd chance it. Anyway, one night he came out and caught us. Me friends got away, but before I knew it, he had a hold of the back of me shirt." Sean chuckled. "He was a big man. I was hangin' three feet off the ground and scared to death." Laying his hand over his left ear he continued, "Mr. Baldovino was real mad and cuffed me up alongside the head. I remember me ear was ringin' for days, and after that I couldn't hear too good. I didn't give it much thought, though." He frowned. "It never kept me from doin' anythin' I wanted to do."

"Sean, have you ever thought that maybe you're not supposed to fight?"

"Yeah, I thought of that. I hate war, but I want to help me country. And from what I'm hearing, the army can use every man it can get." Shaking his head, he pulled up on the oars and slipped them back into the water. "What am I goin' to do until the war is over?"

"There's never a shortage of work. The fishing hasn't been good, but you can fish with me. I need a good oarsman." He grinned.

"I know there's work, but somehow it doesn't feel like enough." Sean lifted his hat, smoothed back his hair, then resettled the cap on his head. "I was thinkin' about goin' to work in the copper mines in Cordova. There's good money to be made. But Mary told me how her grandfather was killed in a mine, and she seemed scared about the whole thing. She asked me not to go." Sounding dejected, he continued, "I told her I'd stay."

"Luba will be happy to hear you won't be working in a mine." Michael met Sean's eyes. "God knows what's best. Have you asked him what you should do?"

Sean studied Michael, then looked out across the waves. Clouds were building on the horizon. "I'm not sure God has anythin' to do with this."

"Of course he does. He cares about every detail of our lives."

"That's what I hear, but a lot of the time it doesn't seem as if he's payin' attention. Anyway, he doesn't talk to me."

Michael stared at Sean a moment, then said gently, "You were raised in the church weren't you, son?"

"Oh, yes. Mama wouldn't have allowed us to miss church." He grinned. "Even if she had to use a switch to get us there." He looked directly at Michael. "I went every Sunday, faithfully, but it never seemed like much to me."

"Oh," Michael said soberly. "Well then, maybe God is talking to you, but you're not listening?"

"I s'pose that could be."

"Sean, he wants you to know him. He wants to spend time with you."

"Maybe, but I just don't see it."

Michael picked up the end of a net. "Well, let's get this one set out."

Dipping the oars into the water, Sean turned the boat, and they headed toward the mouth of the bay.

Mary stepped out of the mercantile, a large basket filled with goods slung over her arm. Cold wind caught at her skirt and tossed her hair about wildly. Suppressing a shiver, she hugged her basket against her. Gazing at dark clouds that had gathered over the distant hillsides, she sighed. *Summer's nearly gone. Soon winter's darkness will settle over us. I wish summer would go on a little longer.* The clouds looked as if they were swirling in from the north. *This could be a bad one,* she thought. *I hope Sean and Daddy don't get caught in it.*

She frowned as she considered her husband. He'd seemed troubled, but she could only guess at what was wrong. Their relationship remained strained, and neither of them shared their inner feelings with the other. *How can we even have a marriage?* she wondered.

"Mary!" Strong arms wrapped themselves around the small woman and pressed her back against a broad chest. With a deep laugh, the arms turned her around.

Mary's eyes locked onto dark brown ones, and she sucked in her breath. Her legs felt weak and her head whirled.

"Aren't you happy to see me?" the native man asked.

"Paul," she whispered.

He pulled Mary closer and kissed her. "I just got off the ship and came looking for you." He smoothed back her hair. "I've missed you. Oh, how I've missed you!"

Mary pressed her cheek against his broad chest and closed her eyes. Sean's face flashed through her mind, then Paul's betrayal swept over her. "No!" she cried and pushed against him, nearly stumbling as she stepped back. "No!"

"Mary, what's wrong? I thought you'd be happy to see me."

Anger quickly replaced shock and Mary tried to think. "Happy? To see you? The man who betrayed me? You lied to me!"

"What are you talking about?" He reached for her.

Mary moved out of reach. "Don't touch me!"

Paul dropped his arms to his sides. "What did I do?"

"That woman . . ."

"Woman? What woman?"

"Don't lie to me. I'm no fool."

His eyes slid away, and he watched a boat move into the harbor. "How do you know about her?" He looked at Mary.

"This is a small town," she said derisively.

"She is nothing. It didn't mean anything."

"That is supposed to make me feel better?"

"Mary, I'd had too much to drink. She threw herself at me."

With her jaw set and arms folded over her chest, Mary glared at Paul.

"One thing led to another. It wasn't planned. She means nothing to me. I love you. All these months at sea, all I could think about was you." He took a step toward her.

Again, Mary moved back. "Stay away from me." Anger seeped away and hurt replaced it. She fought tears. "How could you do such a thing? I loved you. I trusted you."

"I'm sorry. Nothing like that will ever happen again. I promise."

"You're right. It won't." Mary turned and walked away.

Paul followed and grabbed her. "You can't just leave like this." Gripping her upper arms, he turned her so she faced him. "You have to forgive me. I'm going overseas. I want to marry you before I leave."

Mary studied the handsome man. All she'd ever wanted was to marry him; now it was too late. And why did he want to marry her now? He would only leave her again.

Worry creased Paul's face. "You look white as a ghost. Are you all right?"

"No! I'm not all right! I'll never be all right!" Mary wrenched herself free and ran toward home.

———

Anguish pressed down on Mary. She paced, then picked up an afghan from the back of a chair, shook it, smoothed it, then replaced the coverlet. The painting of wildflowers on the wall needed straightening and so did the delicate china cup and saucer on the shelf. She swept the already clean floor, then paced again. Finally, she stopped and stood in front of the window. Unable to restrain her misery any longer, she dropped onto the sofa and wept. *I love him. How can I still love him?*

Banging shook the door and Mary jumped, but she didn't move from the couch.

"Mary, it's me. I know you're in there. I need to talk to you."

Mary remained where she was. She glanced at the window and watched wind-driven rain beat the glass.

"Mary, I'm not leaving," Paul said, resuming his knocking as if to reinforce his words.

Wiping her eyes with shaking hands, Mary stood and walked to the door. She opened it only a little, and a finger of icy wind swept inside.

Paul stood on the porch, hunkered inside his coat. "Are you going to let me in or leave me out here to freeze?"

"You may come in, but only for a few minutes." Mary opened the door and stepped aside.

Looking puffed up and angry, Paul stepped inside and slid off his hood. Brushing black hair away from his face, he looked at Mary. "We need to talk."

Closing the door, Mary asked, "What do you want?"

"You. I want you."

"Since you found your way here, you know I'm married. I'm not free. I belong to someone else now."

Paul scanned the room. "Looks like you've come up in the world." He turned an angry gaze on Mary. "Is that why you married him?"

"How can you say that?"

"How could you marry someone else while I was gone?" He took a step toward Mary.

"How could I marry? You're the one who betrayed me. You left me no choice."

"You don't love him. You love me."

"How do you know what I feel?" Mary glared at Paul. "You've been gone and know nothing about me. Even when you were here, everything was always about you."

"Mary, I told you I was sorry."

Her tone icy, she said, "What good does that do now?" She turned her back on Paul and walked to the window. "Sean loves me. He is loyal and kind, . . . and I'm happy."

Paul joined Mary and stood close behind her. He rested his hands on her shoulders and pressed his face against her hair. "I don't believe you. I know you still love me."

Mary struggled to maintain composure, but her chin trembled and tears burned her eyes. "He's a good man," is all she managed to say.

Paul turned her around to face him. Taking her hands in his, he said tenderly, "You still love me. I can see it in your eyes." He pressed his lips against her palms. "Please, come away with me. We can still have a life together."

For an instant Mary entertained the idea. If only it could be the way it was. *No! I'm a married woman!* she cried inwardly and stepped away, yanking her hands out of his. "Please leave now," she said as calmly as she could.

Disbelief, then rage filled Paul's face. "You're mine. No one else's."

Keeping her face a mask of calm, Mary walked to the door and opened it. "Please leave."

Through clenched teeth, he said, "You didn't have to marry him. You chose to." Paul stepped onto the porch. "You'll never be happy," he threw at her before storming off.

With counterfeit calm Mary closed the door and pressed her back against the wood. It was over. Paul was gone.

Tears wetting her cheeks, she stoked the fire and prepared dinner for her husband.

The storm grew fierce. When Sean and her father didn't return, fear gnawed at Mary. She knew how bad the seas could be in foul weather. She sat on the sofa and tried to occupy herself by embroidering a pillowcase, but with each gust of wind and pelting rain upon the window, she tensed.

Finally, the storm quieted. A short time later, she heard the familiar stomp of Sean's boots against the porch as he freed them of mud. Knowing he must be cold and hungry, Mary set her sewing aside. Going to the cupboard, she took down bowls and cups.

The door opened, and Sean, wet and red-faced, stepped inside. He shrugged out of his wet coat and hung it beside the door, then crossed to the stove. Holding his hands out to the heat, he glanced at Mary. "It was a rough day. I'm glad to be home."

"I was afraid you and Daddy were caught out in the storm." Mary ladled fish chowder into the bowls. "I kept this hot," she said, setting the soup on the table.

"If I'd been alone, I would have been in real trouble. Yer father knows every cove there is for waitin' out storms. We stayed tucked away until the wind let up, then hustled back." He washed in the sink, then sat at the table.

Mary set butter and sliced bread out, poured coffee into their cups, then sat across from Sean. "How was the fishing?"

"Not good. The storm came in fast, and we had to pull in the nets before the rough water shredded them." Sean tore off a piece of bread, dunked it in his soup, and ate it. Keeping his eyes on his bowl, he stirred his chowder. "When we docked, an old friend of yers met us."

Mary's stomach dropped.

Sean dipped out a spoon of soup, then drizzled it back into the bowl. "Paul said he talked to ye. He wants ye back, and according to him, ye want the same thing."

Mary stared at Sean. "You believed him?"

"I don't know what to believe."

Anger welled up in Mary. "He had no right to speak to you."

"Was he tellin' the truth? Do ye want to go to him?"

"I never said that. I told him I was married and asked him to leave this house."

Sean nodded slowly. "Well, that's settled then."

Mary stared at her cup. "He's very persistent when it comes to getting his way. I don't think he'll leave us alone."

"Is there a reason we should care what he wants?"

Mary pushed her soup aside and folded her hands on the table in front of her. "I don't know what he'll do, but he'll keep on until something happens."

"Mary, ye don't need to be afraid." Sean took her hands in his. "I love ye. I'll watch over ye."

Mary didn't know how to respond. She didn't love Sean. "Please, this is very hard for me. You know how I feel." She pulled her hands free, pushed her chair back, and walked to the stove. Picking up a chunk of wood, she shoved it into the fire. "When I took my vows, I meant them. I won't leave you, but that doesn't change anything."

Sean pushed away from the table and walked to Mary. He stood close but didn't touch her. "Please give this marriage a chance. Allow yerself to love me."

Unable to meet his eyes, Mary said, "I will keep your house and cook for you, and I will not leave you, but that is all I can promise."

Sean's shoulders drooped. "We're nearly out of wood. I'll get more," he said somberly and walked out.

Mary stared at the door and remembered the time her brother had captured a baby fox. He'd loved the animal and had taken good care of it, but the fox had been kept in a cage. When she watched the fox pace the borders of its pen, she'd hurt inside a little. And now she hurt even more, for she understood how he'd felt.

Chapter 7

*W*earing a smile, Sean tramped into the house without closing the front door.

Mary stood at the stove stirring a pot of beans. She tapped a wooden spoon against the rim of the kettle, replaced the lid, and turned to face her husband. "You look happy. What's happened?"

Sean didn't answer immediately. He turned and seeing the door was open, closed it, then shoved his hands in his pockets and glanced out the window.

"What is it?" Mary pressed.

With a sheepish grin, Sean took a deep breath and said, "I had to take it. But I think ye'll be happy. Anyway, I hope ye are."

Mary set the wooden spoon on the stove and stared at her husband.

"I took a job today. It's perfect." He combed his hand through his hair. "I'll be overseeing a fox island for the winter."

Mary felt as if she'd been hit. Caretaking a fox island meant long, lonely months of isolation and danger. Putting on an outward calm, she waited for Sean to explain.

"Nick Berens was lookin' for someone to harvest his fox this winter and to keep poachers out. He posted an ad at the store, but with so many men gone, he couldn't find anyone. I've been thinkin' on it, and I know it's what I need. So today I talked to him. It pays good and ye can come with me."

How can he think spending the winter on an isolated island with him can make me happy? Careful to keep her voice calm, she asked, "Where is the island?"

"It's called Unalga. It's one of the Andreanof Islands."

"You mean beyond Tanaga?"

Sean studied his hands. "Yes, but not as far as Kiska."

Mary's heart sank. Unalga was at the extreme western end of the Aleutian Chain. A person couldn't get much farther from civilization. "Sean, that's hundreds of miles from here."

"I know."

Turning her back to her husband, Mary fought tears. She envisioned what a lonely winter spent on a desolate island would be like with only her and Sean.

"I know it's a long way from here, but it's just for one season. Nick said there's a cabin, and the island isn't very big, so settin' out traps and checkin' the traplines won't keep me away from home much."

Careful to keep her emotions in check, Mary turned and faced her husband. "Sean, I don't want to go. It's too far, too dangerous. Anything could happen, and there would only be the two of us."

Sean's face crumpled into disappointment. "I can go alone. Lots of men do."

"No. That would be worse. If you get hurt or sick, who would help you?" She returned to stirring the beans. "Why do you have to go? You have work here."

"Why? I thought ye understood how hard it is for me here. People stare and judge. They think I'm a coward for not goin' to war." He set his jaw. "And there's Paul. Do ye know he watches the house, just hopin' to catch a glimpse of ye?"

Involuntarily, Mary glanced out the window. She knew.

"And he says things about us, about me."

"He'll be leaving soon. He's enlisted."

"Oh, yes, the brave one who goes to war," Sean said sarcastically.

Mary looked at her husband. "People who know you know the truth."

Sean stared at a cup sitting on the table. "I already told him I'd do it."

Mary knew he would never go back on his word. With a sigh of resignation, she asked, "When do we leave?"

"Nick needs someone right away, and the weather is turnin' cold, so he hoped we could be out of here by the end of the week."

"That's only four days!" *I need more time,* Mary thought, struggling against rising panic. *How can I leave with him?* She closed her eyes and took a slow deep breath, then another. She didn't want to leave home or the people she loved, and she didn't want to go to Unalga with a man she'd known only a few months. She looked at Sean. "We must go?"

"Yes. I gave me word."

The following morning, Mary followed the trail from her home to her family's barabara. She stopped on a rise and gazed at the harbor. Cold wind whipped her legs and snatched at her clothing. Winter would be here soon. Whitecaps danced across waves that broke against fingerlings of land reaching into the bay.

As Mary considered the open waters beyond, her stomach knotted. She and Sean would travel west to Unalga. It would take many days to reach the island, and once there, they'd be left alone. There would be no one she could talk to, no one to share her troubles or insights with, no one to remind her she wasn't alone. She shivered and pulled her cloak tighter.

Heavy, black clouds tumbled inland. Mary thought she smelled snow and was reminded of the heavy coats she'd seen on the marten, fox, and even the rabbits. It promised to be a harsh winter.

She turned and headed for her parents' house. She approached the barabara, which looked like a mound of earth in the tall grass. It was much different from her new home. Stepping down into the stairwell, the pungent odor of dirt and grass came from the earthen walls. When she'd lived here she'd never noticed the smell, but now it jarred her at each visit. She was no longer used to living in a barabara.

She knocked and walked in. The odor of smoke and sweat greeted her. There were no windows to replace stale air, so the smell of bodies, burning oil lamps, and cooking food were trapped indoors.

She remembered how, at first, she'd felt unprotected and exposed in her wood house. Now she appreciated the light and the fresh air allowed in through the windows and doubted she'd ever want to return to living in a barabara. Her father had told her that one winter in a house made with lumber would change her mind. She smiled, thinking, *He may be right, but I doubt it.*

"Mary!" Luba said as she spotted her daughter. "It is good that you are here. Come in, come in."

Mary closed the door and stepped into the dimly lit room. After the cold, it felt almost too warm indoors. She took off her cloak and hung it on a hook near the door.

"Would you like some chia?" Luba asked.

"Yes. It's been a while. Sean likes coffee." She sat at the kitchen table. "It's turned cold. A storm is moving in. I think it might snow."

"It's still October, a little early."

"Maybe," Mary said with a shrug.

Luba filled two cups with tea. "If it comes early, we're ready. The larder is packed." She smiled. "This winter the vegetables and fruits will taste good. And although the fishing has been off, our smoke house is full. We will not be hungry this year."

"I'm ready too. When I look at the shelves of jars in the pantry, I feel good." But as she said this, Mary felt a twinge of regret. She knew that most of it would be left behind when she traveled to Unalga. Her eyes wandered around the barabara. The hut was dark, but her mother had worked hard to add life to it. Seal and fox furs hung on the walls, and religious icons with candles burning in their holders illuminated reverent saints. A few scattered shelves held knickknacks. Some items were of native origin—hand-carved sea animals made from walrus tusk and whale bone, and a bone doll. There were also items from outside—delicate cups and saucers, a vase, and a mantle clock. In the corner of the room stood her mother's most cherished possession, a sewing machine. Mary hoped to have one, one day.

Luba set one cup of tea in front of Mary and kept the other. She sat across from her daughter. Observing Mary, she took a sip. "Is something troubling you? Have there been more reports that some of our boys have been injured or killed in the war?"

"No." Mary stirred sugar into her tea, then tasted it. "This is good." She set her cup in front of her and stared at the honey-colored drink. "But, there is something . . ." She took a deep breath. "Last night Sean came home with news."

Luba took another drink of tea.

"He has a new job."

"That's good news. Why does it trouble you?"

"It is good news." Mary hesitated. "But the job is on a fox island."

Luba carefully set her cup on its saucer. "Which island?"

"Unalga. It's near Kiska, almost at the end of the chain."

"Hmm, that is a long way."

Mary grabbed her mother's hand. "It's so far, Mama. There is no one out there. I . . . I'll be alone."

"You'll have Sean." Luba squeezed Mary's hand. "But I will miss you."

"Mama, I still don't know Sean. We don't talk. Even though we've lived in the same house for five months, we are like strangers. On Unalga I will feel all alone."

A sparkle lit Luba's eyes. "Maybe being just the two of you is exactly what you need." She patted Mary's hand. "Trust God. He'll watch over you both."

Mary removed her hand, picked up her tea, and sat very straight in her chair. "You do not care if I go so far away?"

"Yes. But Unalga is not the end of the world. Our people have been traveling these islands for centuries. Often there are times of separation, but they are not forever. When spring returns, so will you and Sean." A soft smile touched her lips and she looked at Mary. "Do you remember the story of how your grandmother Anna met your grandfather?"

"Yes, but please tell me again."

"After your grandmother's village was destroyed by a giant wave, she and her sister, Iya, were the only ones left alive. A stranger named Eric was also on the island. Your grandmother didn't trust him. He was an outsider. It took a lot of convincing to get her to go with your grandfather, but finally she accepted his offer of help, and she and Iya left their home in search of a new one. They had only an umiak, but it was all they needed. They traveled a few days, and a storm forced them to put in on another island. Eric found a walrus tooth necklace there." Luba touched the necklace she always wore. "This one. He gave it to your grandmother."

"Why do you never take it off?" Mary asked.

"It reminds me of my heritage and of your grandmother. I miss her." Luba looked at the smooth, yellowed walrus tooth. "Your grandfather and grandmother traveled hundreds of miles together. When they began their journey, they were strangers. But as the miles passed, they learned to trust and depend upon each other and on God. They finally found a village, but by that time they loved each other. Your grandfather couldn't leave your grandmother, so they were married."

"Mama, I love that story, but with me and Sean it's different. I don't love him."

"Did God take good care of your grandmother?"

"Yes, but . . ."

"Mary, there is no but." She leaned back, folded her arms over her chest, and eyed her daughter. "Either you trust God or you don't."

Mary ran her finger along the ridge of her cup. "Mama, you know I don't feel the same about God as you."

"It takes only a little faith. God doesn't ask a great deal of us."

"It's easier for you than for me."

Luba took Mary's hands and squeezed them affectionately. "God has given this job to your husband, and I think it will be good for both of you. You know how difficult it has been for him since the war began. And with Paul always lurking about—do you think it is easy for Sean to face him every day when he believes you're going to leave your husband for him?" She fixed a stern look on her daughter. "It is time for you to grow up. You must think about someone other than yourself. Think about your husband."

"I have . . ." Mary began, but she knew her mother spoke the truth and closed her mouth. Swallowing her pride, she said, "You're right."

Luba picked up her cup. "When will you leave?"

"In three days." Mary stared into her tea. It no longer appealed to her.

"Then you have much to do. You'll have to gather supplies enough for the winter and . . ."

"Sean said Nick Berens, the man who hired him, would take care of the supplies. All we need to take are our personal things. And there's a cabin on the island."

Luba cocked one eyebrow. "Are you certain he will do as he says?"

Mary shrugged. "That's what Sean said."

"I've known Mr. Berens a long time. He's a good man, but sometimes things don't turn out the way he has planned."

———————————

The night before they were to leave, Mary lay awake thinking of the journey and the distance that would lie between her and the people she loved. Sadness blanketed her as she waited for morning light. The hours dragged, and finally, unable to remain horizontal a moment longer, she threw back the covers, sat up, and dropped her legs over the side of the bed. She lit the lantern, then set her feet on the cold floor and walked to the bureau. Stripping to the waist, she washed her upper body and face with cold water from the basin. Gooseflesh covered her torso, and she shivered as she quickly towel dried. She pulled on a pair of long underwear, wool pants, a heavy cotton shirt, and wool socks, then brushed her black hair free of snarls and plaited it into a thick braid.

When she finished, it was still black outside the window. Looking into the mirror, she studied her image in the lantern light. The skin beneath her eyes looked dark and her eyes mournful. She felt weary. It would be difficult to conceal her unhappiness. She pinched her cheeks, trying to brighten her color. It did little good.

She could hear Sean moving about. Opening the door, she peeked out. He was already dressed and sat on a chair lacing a boot. He glanced up at her and smiled. His eyes looked animated. Clearly, he was anticipating this adventure. *That is so like a man,* Mary thought in frustration.

"Good mornin'." He glanced at his makeshift bed. "I'll get that."

"I'll do it." Taking short, quick steps she crossed the room and scooped up the blankets. With the bundle in her arms, she hesitated, "Do you think we'll need these?"

Sean thought a moment. "I guess it wouldn't hurt to have a few extras. Set them on the sofa and I'll pack them."

Mary folded the bedding, placed it on the davenport, then went to the kitchen. After starting a fire in the stove, she set a pot of coffee and two frying pans on the cooktop. She melted butter in one and cracked eggs into it, then sliced bread, buttered it, and laid it in the other skillet.

"I think we should take some spices," she said as she sprinkled the eggs with salt.

"That's a good idea," Sean said.

Mary flipped the toast, then glanced out the window. A smudge of light touched the clouds above the hills. A rush of apprehension coursed through Mary. *We'll leave soon.*

"I'm starved," Sean said. "Those eggs smell wonderful!" He took a cup from the cupboard. "How long til' the coffee's ready?"

"A few more minutes."

He sat at the table. "Have ye been out to sea much?"

"Some. My father and brothers always did the fishing. The only time I've gone beyond the bay is when I visited the village."

"Have ye ever been seasick?"

"Not exactly. A few times I felt a little queasy."

"Well, then, ye might want to eat lightly."

Mary looked at the eggs, and her stomach quailed. *I don't want to eat at all,* she thought. Aloud she said, "I'll be fine."

"I'd hate to have ye get sick."

"I said I'll be fine." With a flip of the spatula, she scooped eggs onto a plate, then toast. She set them in front of her husband. *There are more important things to worry about than getting seasick,* she thought and placed the last of the eggs and one slice of toast on her plate.

"Ye look upset. What did I say?"

"Nothing. I'm fine," Mary said crisply.

"Ye look kind of upset."

Her mouth fixed, Mary set her plate on the table, then took the coffee from the stove and filled their cups.

"I know goin' off to an island with me and bein' so far from home isn't easy for ye. I remember when I first set out from Seattle. I was scared. I didn't know what I'd find up here."

Mary replaced the coffeepot on the stove. "I'll be fine." She sat at the table and speared her eggs, then stared at them. They didn't look appealing. She forced them into her mouth and chewed.

Sean frowned and stared at Mary, then visibly forcing himself to relax, he said, "This is more than a job. It's an adventure."

"Men are always looking for adventures," Mary said caustically.

"Maybe, but this one is a necessity."

They finished the rest of their breakfast in silence.

_____

Mary washed the dishes and tidied the kitchen. "I'll get my bag," she said and walked to her room where she hefted the duffel bag off the floor. Resting it against her thigh, she lugged it into the living room and dropped it next to the door. Then she set a box of spices and a few canned goods beside it.

"Did ye get everything ye need?" Sean asked.

Mary gritted her teeth. "Yes, of course."

While Sean hauled their belongings to the dock, Mary finished cleaning the house and making certain everything was secure. Sean returned for the last of the bags. "It's time to go."

I've barely had time to adjust to living here, Mary thought as she let her eyes wander over the kitchen and front room. She sighed. *I will appreciate it more when we return.*

Michael, Luba, Erik, and Alex waited at the wharf. Although they'd said good-bye the night before, Mary was happy to see them.

While Sean handed the bag to Nick, Mary stepped into her mother's embrace. The two held each other tightly. "Mama, I'm glad you're here." She couldn't stop her tears. "I'll miss you."

Luba kissed her daughter's cheek. "And I'll miss you. We'll pray for you every day."

"Try not to worry, Nick will get you safely to Unalga," Michael said too cheerfully. "His boat is the best in Unalaska, and he knows these waters."

"It's not the trip I'm afraid of."

"I know. I know," Luba said in a reassuring voice. "Even though you can't see it yet, this is an exciting and amazing time for you and Sean."

Mary nodded half-heartedly.

"You won't be gone so long. It's already October, and spring will be here before you know it."

Mary gazed beyond the bay, as if trying to see the tiny island so far to the west. "It's a long way."

"We'd better get going," Nick called from the boat. The big German bit off the end of a cigar and spat it into the water. He lit the end of the stogy and took a long drag.

Sean shook Michael's hand, then stepped on board.

Mary studied the boat captain. His coat stretched over a rotund belly, its buttons looking as if they might pop off at any moment. He'd pulled his hat down tightly over his balding head. She'd never cared much for the blustery man and wished Sean had gone to work for someone else.

"It's time to go, Mary." Sean held out a hand to her.

She gave her brothers and Michael a quick hug, then turned to Luba. "Spring. I will see you in the spring," she said and hugged her mother again.

"God goes with you," Luba said and released her daughter.

Taking Sean's hand, Mary stepped onto the boat. It dipped slightly as she joined her husband.

"Untie us," Nick called as he started the engines and took his place at the wheel.

The steam engine chugged to life and the smell of burning coal assaulted Mary. She gave the boat a quick perusal. It needed a good cleaning and was small. They would be living in close quarters on this trek.

Sean stood with his arm draped over wife's shoulders. He saluted Michael and waved at Luba and the boys as they pulled away from the dock.

The boat rolled, forcing Mary to lean against him. Tears blurred her vision as she waved to her family. All too quickly, the small hamlet of Unalaska disappeared as they headed toward open water and Unalga.

Chapter 8

The boat cut through untamed waves. Mary watched for Unalga, eager to be free of the cramped vessel. Standing at the rail, she peered through mists, searching for the horizon and feeling as if she might never be free of the rolling deck, the smell of burning coal, or the fish stink rising from the vessel's hold.

A large island appeared behind the haze, and Mary's discontent dissolved. Her attention was now focused on lush green hills spotted with vivid reds and yellows and dappled by sunshine and shadows.

Mr. Berens sucked hard on a cigar as he kept the boat on course.

"Is this it? Is this Unalga?" Mary yelled over the engines.

"No."

Unable to conceal her disappointment, Mary folded her arms over her chest, stared at the vision a moment longer, then turned her back to it and leaned against the railing. "I can't stand another day on this boat."

Eating the last of a sandwich, Sean joined her. "Don't get discouraged. It won't be much longer." He pointed to a cliff where hundreds of seabirds circled craggy peaks and cried to others sunning themselves on the rocks. "I'll never get tired of nature. Mary, look. It's an incredible sight."

"I've seen birds before," Mary said irritably. As their cries carried over the waves, she fought the temptation to look. Giving in, she glanced at the winged pageant and couldn't conceal a smile as she watched their clamoring exaltations.

A half dozen gulls flew above the boat, hovering as they inspected the interlopers. "Do ye s'pose even here, they're lookin' for a handout?" Sean asked and threw a piece of bread into the air. The birds ignored the offering until it dropped into the water. One dove down, snatched it up, and quickly devoured it. Puffins with flat, pudgy faces and splashes of blazing orange over their beaks bobbed in the boat's wake. They seemed little interested in outsiders.

Mary couldn't resist and leaned out over the railing to get a better look. "I love puffins. They're beautiful and comical all at the same time." She glanced at Sean and discovered he was staring at her. His gaze was intense, and it felt as if he could see within, to her core. Mary felt her cheeks heat up and turned her attention back to the birds.

Later that day, when the sun rested just above the edge of the sea, a tiny island appeared.

"That's Unalga," Nick said, pointing at the small, green scrap of land.

Mary's heart sank. It was tiny. Barely a speck in the vast ocean.

As they approached, it looked like many of the islands in the Aleutians. Steep cliffs rose above dark beaches, and dense vegetation crowded the island. Soon the snows would come and cover the green, locking her and Sean on the tiny piece of frozen rock.

Mary felt trapped. She searched the ocean as if she might discover an escape but found only endless water. Maybe she could return to Unalaska with Mr. Berens. The moment the idea entered her mind, she dismissed it, knowing she must stay. Closing her eyes, Mary took a steadying breath and slowly let it out. Slightly calmer, she looked at the island that would be home for the next several months.

"It's small," Sean said.

"That it is," Nick offered, chewing on the butt of a cigar. "But it's a good place for fox. They've got access to the beach. They're pretty good at hunting birds." He grinned. "There's plenty here, so they stay fat and happy." He took his stogy from his mouth and tapped ashes into the water. "You shouldn't have any trouble snaring them. I spent several months here last year and brought back enough furs to keep me comfortable." He grinned at Sean. "You do a good job for me, and I might be inclined to give you a bonus."

Sean nodded.

Nick steered the boat into a small inlet on the northeast side of the island. There were no cliffs, only an open beach bordered by grasses and jagged boulders. He ran the boat in close to the beach and dropped anchor. "Good thing the tide's in or you'd have a long walk through the mud." He squinted against the setting sun and pointed at a grassy knoll on the south side of the inlet. "The house is up there. It's hard to see because of the deep grass, but it's there. There's a shed too."

"We might as well get unloaded," Sean said and leaped over the side, splashing into the water. "Mary, let me carry ye in, then I'll come back for the supplies."

Mary didn't relish the idea of getting wet but wasn't about to let Sean carry her. "I'll be fine," she said and swung her legs over the side of the boat and dropped into the water. Her feet immediately sank into thick, heavy mud. And she'd forgotten to account for the height difference between herself and Sean, so unexpectedly the frigid water came up to her chest. She sucked in her breath. A set of small waves toppled her facefirst into the bay.

Immediately, Sean grabbed hold of the back of her coat and pulled her upright. Mary gulped down air and wiped wet hair out of her face, then lifted one leg, trying to free herself from the mud.

"Ye should have let me carry ye," Sean teased.

Mary pushed away from him. "Thank you, but I'm fine." Holding her arms above the water, she trudged toward shore.

Nick threw two bags to Sean. "I'll haul up some of your trapping gear." He disappeared inside the cabin.

Sean waded to the beach and dropped the bags on the pebbled shore. His boots were encased in mud.

Mary stripped out of her coat and wrung water from her blouse, then tried to pull the clinging material away from her body. Finally giving up, she grabbed a bag. "I'll take this up to the house," she said and turned in the direction Nick had said the cabin lay.

Nick Berens stood on the boat and held up more gear. "You'll need these."

"Wait and we'll go together," Sean said, wading back to the boat. "I don't suppose ye're goin' to give me a hand with any of this?" he asked Nick.

"I've done this enough times. Today, it's your turn," the German said with a grin and handed several leghold traps to Sean. "Be careful with these. They cost me plenty."

Sean nodded and hauled them to shore. When he returned to the boat, Nick handed him a box and said, "That's the last of it."

Holding the box out of the water, Sean asked, "This is all? There isn't enough here to see us through more than a few weeks, let alone an entire winter."

"I thought I'd told you. There wasn't enough room to carry all the supplies with the two of you, your baggage, plus the gear. Besides, the store in Unalaska was out of some of the things you'll need. I had to order them." He glanced out at the sea. "I'll be back before you run out of food." He revved the engine. "I better get out before the tide changes. See you in a couple of weeks."

"But," Sean began to object, then closed his mouth. Nick was already headed out, and Sean's voice couldn't be heard over the engine.

Mary climbed a little way up the beach. Sitting on a sandy knoll, she watched the boat as it headed away from the island and disappeared. Now, she and Sean were alone.

With the box tucked under one arm, Sean walked up the beach and stopped at the mound of provisions. "Ye just gonna sit there all day or ye goin' to help carry some of this stuff up to the house?" he teased.

Mary looked at the small pile of supplies. "There isn't much to carry. How will that see us through the winter?"

"It won't. Nick said he'd be back with the rest in a couple weeks."

A sharp blast of cold air cut through Mary's wet clothing, and she looked at the breakwater at the mouth of the bay. Mists obscured any further view. She'd never felt so alone. Pushing herself to her feet, she brushed sand from her pants and headed toward Sean.

"After we haul this to the house, we can get into some dry clothes." He hefted a bag and headed up the hill.

Mary sighed and lifted a suitcase and some traps, then followed her husband.

At the top of the knoll, the promised cabin emerged from its hiding place among the grasses. Sean had stopped and stood gazing at the house. Mary joined him, set down her bag, and stared at the dilapidated building. It was nothing like she'd envisioned.

Tiny and square, it looked as if it might collapse into a pile of rubble at the slightest wind. It had been made of driftwood and packed with mud, but over time some of the chinking had disintegrated, leaving gaps in the wall. A driftwood door hung at an angle beneath an overabundant grass roof, and a grimy but intact glass window peered at them.

"It doesn't look like much on the outside. Maybe it's better inside," Sean said hopefully and walked on.

Picking up her bag, Mary followed.

Sean yanked open the door and propped it with a rock, then stepped inside. Mary followed and stood in the middle of the single room dwelling. Her eyes moved over uneven beams bracing the ceiling and walls. She stared at one especially large hole left by broken chinking.

"We can plug the holes with fresh mud," Sean said. He lifted a shirt that had been thrown casually over the back of a chair. "What's this?" He searched the pockets. They were empty. Still holding the shirt, his attention was drawn to a wooden shelf stocked with canned goods. He touched the top of the wood cookstove. "It's warm. Looks like someone's been livin' here."

Mary felt a prickle of fear and glanced over her shoulder at the propped door. "Someone is on the island with us?" Her eyes searched the tiny room. A pair of worn boots rested beside the stove, and a shaving brush and straight razor sat beside a wash bowl on the countertop that represented the kitchen.

A leather traveling bag rested against the far wall. Sean crossed to it, knelt down, and opened it. Rifling the contents, he found socks, long johns, another shirt, and a pair of denim jeans, all carefully folded. He set them on the floor, then removed a gold pocket watch. He opened the face, studied the timepiece, then set it beside the clothes. Next he picked up a harmonica, boxes of cartridges, tobacco and cigarette papers and laid them on the floor. When he came across a photo, he stared at it, then handed the picture to Mary. "What do ye think of this?"

She studied the photograph of a man and woman probably in their early forties. Stylishly dressed, they stood stiffly side by side. The man looked peacockish, the woman snooty. Mary shrugged and returned the picture. "They don't look very friendly."

A revolver lay at the bottom of the bag. Sean lifted it out, turned it over in his hands, then snapped open the chamber. It was loaded. He emptied the shells into his hand and closed the chamber. Dropping the cartridges into his coat pocket, he said, "We have an intruder. And I don't trust someone who leaves a loaded pistol hidden away." He carefully replaced the items, including the emptied gun, and closed the bag.

"Why would someone be here?" Mary asked.

Sean shrugged. "A guess there's lots of reasons. I just hope he's not a poacher." He stepped out the door and studied the closest hills. "No tellin' where he is, but he'll be back sooner or later." He continued to scrutinize the fields. "You stay here while I get the rest of the supplies. Keep the door locked." Sean inspected the broken latch. "I'll have to fix this."

"You go ahead. I'll be fine."

As Mary watched Sean stroll down the trail toward the beach, she wished she hadn't told him to go. She didn't like the idea of a stranger being on the island. The wind gusted, bending the deep grasses and raising goose bumps on Mary's arms. Her clothes were still wet. She'd nearly forgotten. "I better change," she said, the sound of her voice comforting.

———————

Trent Parker knelt beside the dead fox and removed it from his trap. He brushed the gray-blue fur free of dirt, then took a knife out of his belt and cut off the animal's feet and expertly slid his knife between the skin and hide. Working his fingers beneath the pelt, he pulled, tearing it forward to the shoulders. He made two deep cuts at the ears and two more around the eyes, then cut around the teeth on both sides and finally straight through the nose cartilage, then pulled the pelt over the animal's head. Shoving his knife back in its sheath, he carelessly discarded the carcass. With a satisfied grin, he turned the fur right side out and held it up. "Not bad for this early in the season. Nice blue color."

He walked to the edge of the lake and dipped the pelt in the icy water, swirling it back and forth. Blood eddied around the fur. He lifted it out, allowed it to drip a few moments, wrung it free of excess water, then wiped it with a rag before adding it to the others tied to his belt.

Kneeling on the bank, he washed blood from his hands, then washed them again and dried them on his pant legs. Standing, he surveyed the small lake and surrounding marsh with disdain. "I'll be glad to leave this God-forsaken place." He smirked. "Soon. And thanks to whoever planted the fox, I'll be rich . . . for a while anyway."

He walked back to the trap, smoothed the hole it sat in, pressed it against a clump of grass, and reset the spring with the jaws open. That done, he baited it with a piece of over-ripe fowl and sifted dirt and grass over the leghold trap. *Maybe I'll get myself some fancy new duds and visit my parents. Wouldn't they be surprised.* He compressed his lips into a tight line. His parents had never had time for him; they never thought he'd amount to anything. *I didn't disappoint them,* he thought, blaming their lack of nurturing for his failure. Bitterness swelled within him, spreading up from his gut and into his chest. As he considered his childhood, rage infused his venom.

Standing, he forced back the memories and headed for the cabin. Tall, stiff grasses nearly shoulder high brushed against his body, and a brisk wind lashed his face. He was cold and looked forward to a hot fire and rabbit stew.

Going directly to the shed, he unhooked the pelts and hung them from hooks on the wall. "I'll flesh these out and stretch them after I get something to eat," he told himself. Stomach growling, he strode outside and to the cabin. He pulled open the door and a gust of wind nearly wrenched it out of his hands. He could feel the hinges loosen. "One more good blow and this place is liable to collapse," he muttered and stepped inside.

Mary gasped, clutching her open bodice closed. Her eyes wide, she stared at the stranger.

Still gripping the door, Trent stared back. "What the . . . ?" He glanced around the room. "Where did you come from?"

"Me? Who are you?"

Trent didn't answer. He knew he didn't belong here. Fox islands were leased from the federal government, then stocked with fox. He hadn't done either of those things. He was simply taking advantage of someone else's hard work. He pasted a smile on his face. "I'm sorry for startling you. I didn't expect to find anyone here." He casually adjusted his cap. "Where did you say you're from?"

Mary didn't respond but tightened her grip on her blouse.

Trent felt a surge of excitement at the high color in the woman's cheeks and the fear emanating from her. And he liked her looks—dark, defiant eyes, brown hair, tawny skin. She was very striking. He let his eyes travel to her throat and the blouse she had bunched in her hands.

Mary did up her buttons and grabbed a blanket, throwing it around her shoulders. "What are you doing in my house?"

Trent leaned casually against the door frame. "Your house? I was here first." He grinned, counting on his good looks to charm this stranger.

Mary met his eyes. "My husband was hired to take care of the fox on this island. And to keep out poachers," she added deliberately.

"Well, I'm no poacher. I can assure you of that." Trent pushed open the door a bit and peered outside. "Where is your husband?"

"He's getting the rest of our supplies. He'll be back any minute." Mary's voice trembled slightly.

"Good. I'd like to meet him," Trent said benevolently as he let the door close. He reached out his hand. "My name is Trent Parker."

Mary ignored his attempt to be sociable.

"Just because you didn't expect to find me here doesn't mean I can't be trusted," Trent said, sounding hurt. Withdrawing his hand, he dropped onto a wooden chair and leaned back, lifting its front legs off the floor.

Mary glanced at the door. "I would like you to leave."

"You want to send me out into a gale? The wind's really picking up." He took off his fur cap and dropped it on the table. "Ma'am, I don't mean you any harm. I'm just traveling the world. Left the states a few months ago hoping to see places I've only read about in books."

"This is a long way from the rest of the world."

"That's why I'm here."

The door opened and Sean stepped inside carrying a box. Trent didn't move but watched the newcomer.

"Looks like a powerful storm . . ." Sean began, then saw Trent. He looked from the stranger to his wife. "Ye all right, Mary?"

"Yes."

Keeping his eyes on the intruder, he knelt and set the box on the floor. "Who are ye?"

Trent stood and held out his hand. "Trent Parker. It feels good to talk with people again. I've been traveling a long while and was beginning to feel lonely."

Tentatively, Sean took the man's hand. "Sean Calhoun. Obviously ye've met me wife, Mary."

"Not exactly." Trent tipped his head slightly toward Mary.

"What are ye doin' on Unalga?" Sean asked.

"Like I told your lovely wife, I'm traveling, seeing a little of the world."

Sean eyed the man suspiciously. "Why here?"

"I'd heard Alaska was a beautiful place. My uncle visited once, and he said a man hasn't lived until he's seen Alaska. And he was especially fond of the Aleutians." With a sidewise grin, he continued, "Well, I'm not the kind of man who just takes a person's word for something. I have to see it myself."

Sean nodded. "Winter's about to set in. It would be wise if ye found yer way back to the mainland."

"I've been thinking on that, but I'm not sure I'm ready to leave just yet."

Chapter 9

$\mathcal{M}$ary studied Trent Parker but couldn't decide his age. He held his tall lean frame with the self-assurance often seen in the mature, but his clean-shaven face and short-cropped hair gave him a youthful appearance. *He can't be much over twenty,* she thought. And, if not for the darkness concealed behind his eyes, she would have considered him handsome.

"It's probably not a good idea for ye to stay," Sean said. "Sometimes winter comes creepin' in and ye have ample warnin', but there are years it arrives with an arctic blast that doesn't let loose until spring. Ye could get stuck here."

"I know what you're saying is true, but I haven't seen all I want yet." Trent's eyes settled on Mary. "So I'll take my chances and spend a few extra days."

Mary's inner alarm flared, and like a serpent, wariness coiled itself within her. "This is a small island," she said. "There can't be much to see."

"Do ye have a boat?" Sean asked. "I didn't see one when we set to shore."

"It's on the other side of the island."

Mary joined Sean and linked arms.

Sean's eyebrows raised, but he quickly accepted the uncharacteristic gesture and patted her hand affectionately.

Mary smiled at her husband, then turned her attention back to their unwanted guest. "There was a lot of talk in Unalaska about how we should expect a hard winter and an early one. I wouldn't wait if I were you."

"You're not me," Trent said evenly.

A wind gust hit the house, sweeping through the cracks in the walls and under the door, chilling the room. "We can talk this through later. Right now we need some heat." Sean lifted the lid on the stove and added kindling and paper. "This storm's coming in from the north, and I'll bet ye it's goin' to be a cold one." He looked at the nearly empty wood box, then at Trent. "Where's the wood stacked?"

Trent straightened his relaxed stance. "I'll get some. It's just outside in the shed." Before Sean could object, he walked to the door and stepped outside.

———————————

"I've got to get the furs out of here," Trent muttered as he marched toward the shed. "If anyone sees them, I'm finished here." *What am I going to do with them?* he wondered to himself as his eyes scanned the hillsides. *And how am I going to get in more trapping?* Anger surged through the poacher. *I'd counted on more time to set myself up for the coming year.*

He stepped inside the dark shed. *Most men wait for colder weather when the furs are heavier,* he reasoned. *I can still do a little more trapping. Sean won't even set out his snares until after I'm gone.* He relaxed a little. *All I have to do is hide these pelts.* He lifted one that had already been fleshed and stretched. *I'll have to stash them in the boat. There's no reason for anyone to wander down there. I'll do it first thing tomorrow.*

He piled driftwood in his arms, grabbed a rabbit he'd been saving for dinner off a hook, and headed back to the cabin. When he stepped inside, Mary abruptly stopped speaking. "What's this? You talking about me?" he teased, but there was no jest in the set of his mouth or the hard look of his eyes.

Sean and Mary said nothing.

Trent walked across the room and dropped the wood into a box. "That should last us awhile. I'll get more later if we need it."

Howling like a lonely wolf, wind rattled the window. Cold shivered in through the disintegrating walls. "It's going to take a lot more than a little fire to warm up this house," Sean said. "First thing tomorrow we'd be wise to patch up this place." He glanced in the direction of the bay. "And until this storm passes, I guess ye have no choice but to stay put. I hope Nick's all right."

Trent shoved two pieces of wood into the small fire. "Seems like a fool for taking off in such bad weather."

Mary huddled beneath her blanket. "It wasn't bad when he left."

"Mary, ye need to get into dry clothes," Sean said.

She gazed around the room. "Where? There's no private place."

"I can fix that." Sean grabbed a piece of rope, a hammer, and two nails from a pack. He fastened the rope to one end of the cabin, ran it across the back corner, and hooked it to the opposite wall. Taking two blankets, he draped them over it. "I'm glad we brought extras," he said with a grin and pulled back one side. "This should work."

"Thank you," Mary said, picking up her bag and stepping behind the makeshift wall.

"I'll make some coffee," Sean offered.

"Sounds good," Trent said. "There's some on the shelf there."

Mary was grateful for Sean's cheerful attitude. Without it, she knew she'd be tempted to languish in angry self-pity. She stripped off her wet clothing, and nearly blue with cold, pulled on a wool shirt and pants, then stuck her feet into dry socks. She pulled on her boots. The laces felt stiff in her shaking hands as she struggled to tie them.

When she stepped from behind the drape, Trent stared at her. "You look good, even in that getup."

Sean gave Trent a sidelong glance, then lit his pipe.

Ignoring his comment, Mary walked across the room and picked up the rabbit Trent had left on the countertop. "I'll cook this up with some fried bread."

"You ought to appreciate that rabbit. They're not easy to come by. Too many fox on this island."

"There's supposed to be fox here. It's a fox island," Sean said dryly.

"Yeah, I figured."

Mary scooped lard out of a bucket and dropped it into a skillet sitting on the stove. While it was heating, she cut up the rabbit and tossed it into the hot fat. The meat sizzled and spit, then settled into a steady simmer. Next she blended flour, sugar, salt, and water in a bowl, then divided the firm dough into round balls, which she flattened between her palms and set aside. The coffee boiled and she poured them each a cup of the hot brew, then sat at the wobbly table, mug between her hands. As she sipped the drink, it warmed her insides and she began to feel less cold. "Ah, that's good," she said, glancing up and finding Trent watching her. He always seemed to be looking at her. She didn't like it, and before she could bite back her words, she asked, "Why are you staring at me?"

Trent smiled, then said as smoothly as soft butter, "I'm sorry. It's just that you're so beautiful. It's been a long while since I've seen a woman, let alone one as pretty as you."

Mary didn't know what she'd expected to hear from him, but it hadn't been charming words. "Well, thank you for the compliment, but I wish you wouldn't," she said stiffly.

"Listen to the woman." Sean took a drink of his coffee, cleared his throat, and leaned forward on his arms. Looking directly at Trent, he said, "When we first got here and discovered someone was stayin' in the cabin, I went through yer bag." He waited, but Trent said nothing. "I found a loaded revolver. Why would ye keep a loaded gun in yer satchel?"

Trent's mouth turned up in an insolent grin. "What good is an empty one?"

"I don't see a reason to keep it loaded." Sean reached into his pocket, pulled out the shells, then held his hand out palm up. "So I emptied it. I'd feel better if ye left it that way."

Trent snatched the cartridges. "I'd appreciate it if you'd leave my stuff alone," he said, his voice stone-cold. He pushed himself away from the table, walked to his bag, and placed the shells inside. "And I'll decide if my guns are loaded. Not you."

Mary didn't realize she'd been holding her breath until she let it out. *At least he didn't reload,* she thought and pushed away from the table. She returned to the stove and checked the rabbit, turning it. *While our dinner's cooking, I might as well get our supplies unpacked,* she thought. Going to the shelf, she moved Trent's scanty collection of canned goods to one end, then put their couple dozen cans of fruits and vegetables beside them. She also added a bag of flour, another of sugar, a small bag of salt, and finally a large can of coffee. Lifting out a salt pork and smoked fish, she said, "These will keep fine inside for tonight. I'll put them in the shed tomorrow."

Finally, she set her box of spices and several cans of milk with the other food, stepped back, placed her hands on her hips, and surveyed the provisions. "It's not much. I'll feel better when Mr. Berens returns with the rest of our supplies." A strong blast of wind shook the house, peppering the window with ice particles. "The storm's getting worse."

Trent jumped up and walked to the door. Yanking it open, he leaned out. "It's snowing. It's really coming down." He stayed like that a moment longer, then closed the door. He looked shaken. "It's piling up. And it's gotten a lot colder."

"That's not good, to be sure," Sean said. He looked at Mary. "I haven't lived in this part of the world as long as ye have. Is it possible winter could set in this early and stay?"

Her stomach churning, Mary stared at the window. She didn't want to believe it was possible, but she knew it was. "It happens," she said quietly. "But it's awfully early. This will probably pass soon, and the temperatures will warm up again." She took a deep breath. "If it doesn't, though, we're in trouble." Her eyes moved to the shelf.

Trent sat down and in a high-pitched voice, asked, "Are you saying this could be it? That winter is here?"

"Probably not. But here the weather has a mind of its own."

"But if it is, then what happens?"

Mary didn't answer. She didn't want to think of the consequences.

"I asked you a question. What happens to us?" Trent repeated sharply.

Mary leveled a steady gaze on the stranger. "We will probably die," she said evenly.

Trent stood and paced in front of the window. Throwing his arms away from his body, he said, "Well, I, I've got to get out of here. There's no way I can stay."

Sean chuckled. "Calm down. This storm will probably pass by tomorrow just like Mary said. And it seems to me that just a few minutes ago ye said ye didn't mind stayin' on. And there's nothin' to be done about it. We'll just have to wait." He patted his stomach. "But right now, all I want is some dinner. It smells good."

"Yeah? Well, if we're stuck here, there won't be any food for dinners," Trent ranted.

Sean crossed to the young man. "Trent, we're not stuck just yet. Storms come and go. When this one is done with us, ye can leave." He rested a hand on the younger man's shoulder. "Now, let's sit down, drink our coffee, and have some dinner."

Trent allowed himself to be steered to a chair.

Sean refilled his cup. "This will sturdy ye up."

Mary speared rabbit onto a plate, then dropped flat bread one piece at a time into the hot grease. It sank, then sizzled and floated. As soon as one side browned, Mary turned it. When both sides were golden, she placed the bread on a plate. When all the fried bread was done, she set it on the table beside the rabbit and refilled each of the cups.

"It looks good, Mary. Thank ye," Sean said, stabbing a piece of meat.

Trent took a chunk. Using a knife and fork, he cut off a piece, placed it in his mouth, and chewed. "Not bad." He tore off a bite of bread.

Silence fell over the threesome, the only sound being the raging storm. When Mary finished, she cleared away the dishes and utensils, setting them in a large pot. Taking a kettle off the stove, she poured hot water over them. "I'll need more water," she said.

"There's a wooden barrel just outside the door," Trent explained, tilting his chair back.

"I'll get it," Sean said, taking the kettle and stepping outside. He returned a few moments later, water splashing over the container's sides. "Do ye want me to pour this over the dishes?"

"No. I'll need it for rinsing. Just set it on the stove, please." Mary gingerly settled her hands into the hot water.

Sean set the kettle back on the stove. "I think I'll see if I can find somethin' to patch up some of the gaps in the wall." He headed for the door.

Trent scrambled out of his chair and stepped in front of him. "Why bother tonight? It's late and dark. You can't see anything out there. It's better to wait until morning. We can just bundle up tonight. Besides, it's starting to warm up in here."

Mary didn't agree but said nothing.

"I suppose it can wait until tomorrow," Sean conceded and looked at Mary. "I guess I'd better make ye . . ." he started, then corrected himself, "us a warm bed." He dug into their supplies and hauled out several blankets and pillows. "I'll put us behind the partition," he said and disappeared between the two suspended blankets.

Trent picked up his cup and ambled toward Mary. "Here's another dish for you," he said, dipping the mug in the water and allowing his hand to rest on Mary's. A lazy smile touched his lips, but his eyes blazed with lust.

Mary snatched her hand away, splashing water down her front.

"I'm not going to bite," he whispered before walking back to the table and nonchalantly sitting down.

Sean emerged from behind the blanket. "We should be snug." He looked at the frosted window.

Following his gaze, Trent said, "The storm's getting worse."

Mary set the last dish on the counter and dried her hands on a towel. "I think I'll go to bed. I'm cold and tired."

"Well, I guess I might as well go on to bed too." Sean glanced at Mary and his cheeks pinked slightly. She gave him a small nod and disappeared behind the draping.

"Well, good night to ye, Trent." Sean followed Mary.

"Good night. I'll be fine out here."

Still wearing her clothes and coat, Mary lay on the thin bedding and pulled the blankets over her.

"I'm sorry there's no bed," Sean said, lying beside his wife, careful not to touch her. He dragged the covers up.

"That's all right. Most of my life I slept on a pallet on the floor. I'm used to sleeping on a hard surface."

Sean and Mary lay on their backs, blankets tucked under their chins, and stared at the ceiling. Trent blew out the lantern and the room turned black. For a long while the couple lay side by side, silent and rigid. Trent snored softly.

"Mary," Sean whispered. "Are ye awake?"

"Yes."

"I hope ye know I have no intentions of . . . I mean I won't . . . I'm sleeping here to protect ye," he finally finished.

"I know."

"I've seen how Trent looks at ye. I wouldn't want him to get any ideas."

"I understand. Thank you." Mary nearly told Sean she felt comforted by his presence but decided it best to keep such feelings to herself. Exhausted, she closed her eyes and slept.

The blizzard locked Unalga and its visitors in an icy prison for three days. Finally, the morning of the fourth, Mary woke to soft light and quiet. The wind had stopped. She peered around the draping and smiled as her eyes rested on the sparkling window. Sunlight shimmered through crystalline frost and splintered into a kaleidoscope of colors.

She looked at the place where Trent had been sleeping. He was gone. Careful not to waken Sean, she climbed from beneath her blankets. Cold penetrated her clothes and sent spikes into her feet. She pulled on socks and threw a blanket over her shoulders. Walking to the door, she yanked it open. The edges were encrusted with ice. Frigid air spilled into the cabin along with a whisper of snow. Footprints led to the shed, and another set headed away from the cabin.

Why would Trent be wandering around the island? Mary wondered.

She closed the door, wishing Sean had fixed the lock. She knew it was unrealistic, but she couldn't help thinking how much better she would feel if the door could be bolted, locking Trent outside. During their unwelcome confinement, her dislike for the man had grown. He worked too little, ate too much, and always seemed to be watching her.

"Trent's gone?" Sean asked.

Mary startled. Pressing her hand to her throat, she turned and faced her husband. "You scared me."

"Sorry," he said with a smile.

"Yeah, he's gone. What do you think he's doing?"

"I wish I knew," Sean said thoughtfully. "I'll be glad when it's just the two of us again." He rubbed his hands together. "It's cold. I'll stoke up the fire."

"I'll make breakfast."

The fire warmed the cabin, and coffee warmed Sean and Mary's spirits. Bundled in coats, they sat across from each other at the small table. Sean ate the last of a biscuit. "I wouldn't have guessed we'd have such a fierce storm so early in the season."

"Do you think Mr. Berens is all right?"

"Sure. He's had a lot of experience in these waters. Besides, we don't know if it was this bad all over. Sometimes the brunt of storms hit only the farthest western islands."

"Our supplies won't last long, especially with Trent eating so much of . . ."

"Nick will be back, Mary. And we'll be fine."

"But if the bad weather keeps up, how can he make it back?"

"He wouldn't leave us here without supplies," Sean tried to reassure Mary. "It pains me to see ye worryin' so."

"I'm trying not to, but I can't help it."

———————————

"Michael, are you going to talk to Nick this morning?" Luba asked her husband as he walked into the kitchen.

"Yes. All I need is a cup of coffee, and I'm on my way."

"Do you think he meant it when he said he wouldn't go back for Mary and Sean if the weather stays bad?" She filled a cup with coffee. "We've had a long spell of it, and you know how it can be. Once winter's here, it stays." She handed him the cup. "Michael, he has to go back for them. He has to."

Looking into his wife's eyes, Michael cupped her face in one hand and kissed her. "All this worrying isn't going to help. Nick will do the right thing."

———————————

Michael knocked at Nick's door and waited several moments before the big man answered. As usual, he had a cigar between his teeth. When he saw Michael, his expression turned stormy. Taking the stogy out of his mouth, he said, "I told you I'm not going back until the weather changes."

Michael breathed slowly, calming himself. He knew better than to go on the attack. Angry charges would only aggravate Nick. "Please, just hear me out." Nick stared at Michael but didn't respond. "Please, may I come in?"

Grudgingly, Nick opened the door. "I've got some coffee on. You want some?"

"Sounds good. It's cold." Michael stepped inside. He settled himself on a rickety wooden chair while Nick poured a cup of black brew. The odors of cigar and wood smoke mingled in the air. It smelled almost pleasant.

Nick handed the coffee to the younger man, then eased himself into an overlarge, cushioned chair with broad armrests and hand-carved wooden legs. It fit the stout man perfectly.

Michael tasted his coffee. It was strong. Searching his mind for the right words, he took another sip, then looked squarely at his neighbor. "Nick, I know you said you couldn't venture out until the weather changes, but you know as well as I that it might not change. If you wait, Mary and Sean will die."

"Maybe. But one thing I know for certain is that any man who travels that far out on the chain in this weather is a fool. You're asking me to be that fool and risk my life for theirs." He sucked on his cigar, held the smoke in his mouth a moment, then slowly released it. "I'll be honest with you. I hate to think of them stranded out there, but there's nothing I can do."

"I've seen you go out in bad weather before."

"Yes, but not so far and not during the winter." He stood, putting an end to the discussion. "I'm sorry, Michael, but I've said all I'm going to."

"Then let me take your boat. I'll go after them."

"You'd be the fool, then." Nick thought a moment. "I can't let you do it. That boat is my living. I won't risk losing it. If those two use their heads, they'll make it."

Michael clenched his jaw and did his best to check the outrage boiling inside. He set his cup down hard on the table and stood. His voice bitter, he said, "Nick Berens, you're a hard man, and you'll answer to God for this. You'll answer to God."

His face empty and hard as stone, Nick walked to the door and opened it. "When the weather changes, I'll go. Not before."

Chapter 10

The days passed. Winds and snow continued to lash the cabin. The greater turmoil, however, brewed within the walls. Tensions grew as the likelihood of Nick's return diminished, and the three stranded travelers' fear and frustration grew.

Carrying the coffeepot to the table, Mary set it down hard. "It's been five weeks, and except for an occasional sunny break, the weather is still bad." She filled three cups. "Nick's not coming back."

Sean tipped back his chair, stared at the pot, and said nothing.

"So, what're we gonna' do?" Trent whined. "We've got to do something."

Mary looked at Sean. "What can we do?"

Sean rocked his chair forward, resting its front legs firmly on the floor. He glanced at Mary. "I don't know for sure. I suppose we need to think of the best way to survive." He looked at Trent.

Trent raised his hands, palm out. "Don't look at me. I only know the basics, nothing about finding food or whatever else it takes to survive. I grew up in a house where I had everything I needed. I never had to know how to do much of anything."

Sean turned to Mary. "Ye grew up in the village."

"That was years ago. I was a little girl. I don't remember much."

"I thought ye said ye visit all the time."

"I go about four times a year, but that's not enough to know how to survive."

Sean rocked back in his chair. "Me father was a good provider. We never wanted for anythin' after comin' out West. Before that I was a city kid. We used to rob garbage pails." He grinned, then shrugged. "If ye give me a fishin' net, I can do some fishin', but right now I don't think we'll find much in the bay. I can trap, but what is there on this island to trap that we can eat?"

"Rabbits?" Mary asked.

"There are almost none," Trent said. "The fox eat them as fast as they can reproduce."

Quiet settled over the room.

"Me mother would have prayed," Sean said softly.

"Oh, that'll do a lot of good," Trent mocked.

Sean shot him a angry glance. "It served me mother well. Do ye have any other suggestions?"

Trent pursed his lips and didn't answer.

"I don't see meself as any better then me mother." Sean pushed away from the table, crossed the room to his pack, and dug through his belongings. "I have me Bible." He held it up. "All the years Mama made me go to church, I never paid heed to the priest's words. Now I wish I had."

Mary dropped into a chair. "How is that going to help?"

"Well, I was always told God speaks to us through this book. If he's God, then he'll know what we should do. Maybe he will tell us."

Mary propped her arm up on an elbow and rested her chin in her hand. "I don't believe in the Bible. It never made sense to me."

Sean sat down and placed the black book on the table in front of him. "What do ye believe, Mary?"

"I don't know for sure. Like you, I went to church with my family. And the priest used to speak, but I didn't understand what he was talking about, and I didn't see God there. My parents tried to help me understand, but . . ." She shrugged. "At the village I was interested in the old beliefs of the medicine man, Norutuk. He always seemed wise. And there was power in his medicine." She glanced out the window. "But even he believed in one great God who ruled over smaller gods. Norutuk was a powerful man. He used to pray and make remedies, and people got well. Sometimes it felt as if there were magic within him." She slowly shook her head. "But I don't know what he considered to be truth or where he got his power. I was very young. I wish I knew how he did it." She glanced at the Bible. "I don't think *that's* going to help."

"All this God talk isn't gonna' do any good," Trent said. "If you're gonna' spend time searching through that book, you're wasting your time." He stood, leaned his hands on the window-sill, and stared outside. "It's snowing again." Wearing a sneer, he turned and looked at Sean. "Tell me how reading that book is going to change the weather and get us off this island. Or do you think God can just rain down food for us?"

Sean rested his hands on the Bible's leather cover. "Maybe. Me mother used to say God could do anything." He tentatively opened the first page and began leafing through the book, then looked at Mary. "I don't know where to begin."

"Well," Mary said uncertainly, "I guess you read it like any other book . . ."

"You start at the beginning!" snapped Trent. "But why read it at all? It's nothing but a bunch of lies and fairy tales. I've seen how people use that thing. They're heartless. They have no love. Oh, they spout off words they say are God's, but I thought he taught forgiveness and love. That's not what I saw. And if what they did pleased God . . ." Trent searched for his next thought. "Then if there is a God, he's cruel and I don't want to have anything to do with him." He slammed his hat on his head. "And he won't help us. In fact, he's probably laughing right now, enjoying our situation."

Shocked at his words, Mary and Sean stared at Trent. They'd never seen him so angry, and he'd never mentioned any church background before. "I suppose people could misuse the Bible, but I'd say we have nothin' to lose," Sean said. "There are a lot of people who believe in God. Me father and mother did. And they were never cruel."

"Yeah, me father and mother believed too," Trent taunted.

Resolutely, Sean turned to the front of the book. "We'll start at the beginnin'." He began to read from the Book of Genesis, chapter one. *"In the beginning God created the heaven and the earth. . . ."*

"I'm not going to stay around and listen to this drivel," Trent said, pulling on his coat and walking out of the cabin.

Sean didn't look up but continued to read about how God made all creation, using nothing but his voice to speak it into existence. Although the words were familiar, they felt as if he were reading them for the very first time. When he came to the part where God created man in his own image, Sean stopped, thinking on the meaning a moment before continuing. After finishing the first chapter, he said, "It's very comfortin' to think that God created everything. And especially that he created us." He looked at Mary. "Do ye think he really cares about us?"

"I don't even know if I believe in God, but if you believe what's written there, I guess you'd have to say he cares. He said that what he created was good."

Sean smiled. "I guess the next time we wander outside we ought to think some about how God made everything that surrounds us and that he loved what he made."

"I suppose," Mary said, but she didn't really care much what God may or may not have made. She was more interested in how they were going to feed themselves in the months to come. She refilled her cup, then held out the coffeepot. "You want some?"

"No."

Setting it back on the table, she picked up her mug and cradled it between her hands. "What I do know is we're nearly out of food. I've been hungry so long, I can hardly remember what it feels like to have a full stomach. I hate to agree with Trent, but we have to do something. We won't be going back to Unalaska before spring." She sipped her coffee. Looking at the Bible, she added, "I wish I believed in God, but I don't." She stared at the window and the frost sparkling beneath the slanting sunlight. "Even when the snow stops, it's only for a day or two, then it begins again." Turning her eyes on Sean, she said, "I'm scared. I don't know what to do."

Sean closed the Bible and rested his hands on top of it. His voice barely more than a whisper, he said, "I think we should pray."

Mary shot him a look of disbelief.

"It can't hurt."

"All right. But you'll have to do it. I don't like praying."

"Well, it can't be that hard. Lots of people do it." Clearing his throat, he bowed his head and closed his eyes. "Dear God," he began, "I know it's been a long while since I talked to ye. Ye knew me mother very well. She used to talk to ye all the time. Anyway, she used to tell me ye loved everyone and cared about everyone. And as I was readin' yer book just now it seems ye love beautiful things or ye wouldn't have created them. And it also says ye made a man and a woman. So I guess ye must have liked them too." He paused. "Well, if ye're real and watchin' over us, we need yer help. We're in a bad way here and need ye to show us what to do. And God, it seems I heard before that ye sometimes do miracles for people. It would be all right with us if ye did one now. And God, I don't believe what Trent said. Amen," he ended abruptly.

Mary held up her cup. "I hope that if there is a God he heard you because the only thing we have plenty of is coffee, and even that isn't going to last. We'll have to start reusing the grounds."

"I'd better check me traplines. That's why I'm here in the first place. Anyway, it helps to keep busy."

"I've been thinking. I do remember some things from the village. The women taught me about gathering wild plants. We collected a lot of wild foods—different kinds of seaweed and green plants, berries, and shellfish. And although the women weren't supposed to hunt, I watched the men. I remember some of it.

"The cold came on us in an awful hurry; there might still be frozen berries buried beneath the snow." The pitch of Mary's voice rose as she contemplated the possibilities. "And there are probably mussels on the rocks. And I can show you how to make a fishing pole. At the beach it's too cold to fish, but there's the lake. There should be fish in it."

Sean grinned. "Looks like me prayer is already workin'."

Mary gave him a quizzical look. "I don't think that's what this is. These are things I've known. I just didn't think of them before."

"It seems strange you remember so much only after we prayed," Sean teased.

"I didn't have time to think when you asked. And I haven't been making plans because I thought Nick would bring supplies."

Sean grinned and nodded knowingly. "Nick might still show up. We can't give up hope. If I shoot a sea lion, we'll have lots of meat." Sean frowned. "But I haven't seen any."

"The only animals on this island are fox, the rodents they eat, and birds. You could shoot the birds."

"They're puny, and a shotgun will just fill them with BBs."

"What about a snare?" Mary asked. "My brothers used to use one."

"I can try it, but a mouthful of meat is all ye'll get. They're mostly feathers and bones."

"A mouthful is better than nothing." Mary stood. "I'll show you how to make one."

"All right then. We'll do it." Sean jumped up. "Tonight, it's fresh meat for dinner!"

Chapter 11

*W*hile enjoying the meager warmth of the winter sun, Mary helped Sean assemble a snare and showed him how to set it. When she left him, he waited, hidden behind snow-piled grasses, and she began her search for hidden berry bushes.

She knocked the plants free of snow and happily discovered frozen berries still clinging to the branches. Picking as fast as she could, the bottom of her basket was soon covered with small hard fruits. She sighed, knowing it would take many hours in the cold to glean the fall leftovers.

When she thought she had enough for a couple of meals, she made her way to the beach. For a long while she walked the rocks, searching tide pools for edible seaweed. It grew in abundance, but she harvested only a little, knowing they weren't hungry enough yet to eat much of it. Although, when it was dried, it was crispy, and its salty flavor was satisfying.

Growing cold, she considered returning to the house, but she knew they would need mussels if Trent and Sean weren't successful. She set her basket on the top of a jagged boulder, stripped off her gloves, and waded into the icy water. Shaking with cold, she ran her hand over encrusted rocks. Just below the waterline, her fingers found a clump of rough, tear-drop shaped shells. Shivering, she took her knife from its sheath, wedged the blade beneath a mussel, and pried at it until it fell into her other hand.

Next time I'll watch the snare, she promised herself through gritted teeth. Her fingers burned as she went after more mussels. She only managed to pry off half a dozen more before aching numbness in her hands and feet drove her out of the water. Shivering hard, she dried her hands on her shirt, pulled on her gloves, and huddled beside a rock, shielded from the sea breezes. She knew she needed to get back to the cabin and warm up but didn't have the energy to move.

She stared at distant breaking waves. *How did I get into this trouble?* she wondered as Paul's handsome face filled her mind. She clenched her jaw. *This wouldn't have happened to me if you'd been an honorable man,* she thought. *More like Sean.* The idea stunned her. She'd never compared the two and felt uncomfortable as she considered the differences between the men. Everything Paul wasn't, Sean was. Paul was deceitful; Sean was honest. Paul was corrupt; Sean was good. Paul was agitated; Sean was calm. *No! I won't compare the two. Anyway, it doesn't matter anymore.*

The last she'd heard, Paul had joined the army and was being sent off to war. The thought of a war raging in a far-off country made her feel strange. She knew it was happening, but it felt unreal, probably because it was so far away.

She closed her eyes and tipped her face up, trying to catch more of the sun's rays. It failed to warm her chilled body and a strong shiver spread through her. She felt anxious and alone. *I wonder if this is how Nana felt when the tidal wave destroyed her village? She'd had to find a way to survive just like us.*

Mary smiled. Nana and Grandpa Engstrom had lived the kind of adventure written of in books. Many times Luba had told Mary the story of how Anna and Eric had met. Her grandfather and grandmother had been young when they were thrown into their unexpected adventure. Grandpa Engstrom had been an outsider and had watched the tidal wave destroy her grandmother's village. Anna and her sister Iya had been left orphaned, and Eric offered to help them find a home. Neither Eric nor Anna had expected to fall in love, but they did. Their life together had not been easy, but Nana always talked of the past with fondness.

Cold penetrated Mary's musings and she said aloud, "I better get back." Still shivering, she walked down the beach the way she'd come.

When Sean saw her, he stood and waved.

"Did you get anything?" she asked.

He held up an empty snare. "I think they're smarter than me. Maybe I should look for rabbits instead. The only trouble is, I haven't seen any. I s'pose Trent's right; the fox have been takin' a lot of them."

Mary nodded and held up her basket. "I found a few mussels. I could have gotten more, but the water was too cold. I couldn't stay in any longer."

"Ye be careful. It doesn't take long for hypothermia to set in, in these waters. If a man were to fall in, he wouldn't last long."

"I don't plan on swimming," Mary said derisively. She glanced toward the cabin. "Have you seen Trent?"

"Yes. A little while ago. He said he knew how to rig up a fishing line and that he'd be fishin' at the lake. I hope he catches somethin'. Me stomach's been rumblin' all mornin'." He peered into Mary's basket. "And those aren't goin' to be nearly enough to fill me up."

"I'm sorry. I'll do better tomorrow," Mary said as she shuddered.

"I'll help ye next time. But now, we need to get ye into warm, dry clothes." As he started toward the cabin, several gulls flew overhead. "I wish I could use me shotgun on them, but I hate to use the ammunition on so little meat, especially when we'll need the shells for ducks and geese come spring. Now, if I were to come across a sea lion, I could use me rifle. Maybe I ought to start carryin' it."

"Mmm. Sea lion. Just thinking about it makes my mouth water." Mary smiled. "It would be such a treat. But they're not easy to hunt. It could be dangerous." She shrugged. "For now, I guess we'll have to make due with mussels and fish, that is, if Trent catches one. Tomorrow I'll see if I can find more berries and some seaweed."

Sean grimaced. "Seaweed doesn't sound very appealing. But I'll do me best to find somethin' to go with it." After walking in silence for several minutes, Sean slowed his steps. Keeping his eyes on the ground, he said, "I'm sorry, Mary."

"For what?"

"I got us into this mess. If I'd kept me pride in check, we wouldn't be here."

"It's not your fault. You thought you were doing what was best. Providing for a family is a serious thing."

Sean kicked at a dead leaf lying on top of the snow. "I wish that's how it was, but it's not. What I wanted most was to get away from me shame. I was embarrassed that I couldn't join the army with the other men." He gave his wife a sidelong glance. "Plus, I wanted to get away from Paul. I was thinkin' about me, not us." Sean stopped and took Mary's hands in his. "I'm so sorry."

Mary was touched by Sean's regret and his willingness to share his failure, but holding hands felt too intimate. She wasn't ready for that and pulled free. Continuing on, she said, "Sean, I accept your apology, but I understand why you did what you did."

When they approached the cabin, Trent was sitting on a log alongside the house. He'd cleared away the snow and now sat whittling a piece of driftwood. He glanced up but said nothing.

Seeing the young man reminded Mary of her uneasiness around him. Quietly she asked Sean, "Could you teach me to shoot the rifle? I've never actually fired one."

"I s'pose it wouldn't hurt for ye to know. When do ye want yer first lesson?"

"Right now? I'm awful hungry." She looked inside her basket. "But if we wait, we can go to bed less hungry. I'll change into dry clothes; then we can go back to the beach."

"All right." As they came closer to Trent, Sean asked, "Did ye have any luck with yer fishin'?"

"Yeah. Caught two. Enough for a meal." He didn't look up but kept whittling. "Left them on the counter."

"Good. I'm hungry."

Mary hurried inside and changed into warm, dry clothing. As she was leaving, she glanced at the mussels on the shelf and was tempted to plunk them into boiling water, and when the shells opened, to pick out the delectable meats inside. Instead, she told herself they would taste even better if she waited and stepped outside.

She'd never been interested in knowing how to shoot a gun, but now it seemed important—not just because of their need to hunt, but because of the unsettled feeling Trent gave her. She didn't trust him. It would be good to know how to defend herself if she needed to.

Sean leaned against the cabin and watched Trent's efforts. "That's a good looking kayak," he said.

"I think it's a baidarka," Mary corrected.

"She's right," Trent said and kept whittling.

Sean looked at Mary. "Well, are ye ready for your first lesson in firearms?"

"I am."

Trent's knife stopped momentarily, but he said nothing, then continued working.

Sean and Mary walked toward the bay. When they were out of earshot, Mary said, "Trent makes me nervous. He's odd."

"I'll have to admit he's an odd one, but he's probably all right. I'm sure we have nothin' to worry about." He grinned. "And he can't be too bad. He caught our dinner—two fish. Me mouth is ready for that."

———————————

When they reached the cove, Sean handed Mary the rifle and some shells. "Hold these," he said and trudged down the beach across a mix of ice, melting snow, and sand. It crunched beneath his boots. He bent and pulled a piece of flat driftwood out of the snow, then stood it on its edge and pressed it into the half frozen ground. Then he walked back to Mary. "Let's see if you can hit that." He took the gun, snapped up the bolt on the right side, dropped a shell into the magazine, and closed it.

Mary watched carefully, doing her best to remember all the steps so she could duplicate them. "Let me try to load it." Sean discharged the bullet and handed the Remington to her. "I push up on this lever?"

Sean nodded.

Mary pushed it forward, but it didn't budge. She tried again. Still it wouldn't slide open. Frustrated, she looked at Sean. "What am I doing wrong?"

"You have to lift it up, not push it forward, then slide it back," Sean said smiling.

"Oh." She did as instructed and the bolt popped up and easily slid open. She dropped in a cartridge, snapped the chamber shut, and smiled at her success.

Sean stepped behind Mary, and wrapping his arms around her upper body, took hold of the gun.

Mary felt awkward at his closeness but didn't dislike it altogether. However, she wasn't about to admit this, not even to herself.

"All right, now ye rest the butt of the gun against yer right shoulder." Taking her hands, he placed the left one on the barrel and the right one on the stock, making sure it was pressed firmly against her shoulder. "Ye need to aim carefully. It won't do ye much good if ye don't hit what ye're shootin' at. See those little nubs on the barrel—one at each end. Ye'll need to line them up with what ye're aimin' at."

"What? These?" Mary asked, pointing at the two sights.

"That's right. Tighten yer grip a bit and press the butt of that gun firm against yer shoulder so it doesn't jump so hard when it's fired."

Mary tightened her hold. "Now what?"

"Take a deep breath, hold it, and squeeze the trigger nice and smooth, makin' sure to keep yer target in the sights." He stepped back. "Now, try to hit the center of that driftwood."

Mists swirled over the ice-encrusted sand, momentarily concealing the target. Mary waited for it to appear again, took a breath, and squeezed the trigger. The gun blast hit her ears, reverberating through her head. The stalk bashed her shoulder and knocked her backwards, forcing the rifle barrel upward and spoiling her shot. When the remnants of the blast cleared her head, she let the gun rest in her arms. "That was awful. I didn't hit anything."

Sean chuckled. "Don't get yer dander up. It was yer first try. Do it again, and I bet next time ye'll do better."

Mary reloaded, lined up the rifle, and squeezed the trigger. This time, she managed to keep the barrel almost still and her feet planted. And although the end of the stock still rammed her shoulder, she hit her target. "I did it!" she yelled.

Sean jogged down the beach where he bent and examined the driftwood. Straightening, he raised an arm in victory. "Good shot! Not in the center, but good." He started walking back toward Mary. "Do it again."

Mary loaded the gun, placed it against her shoulder, and

pointed it at the wood. Sean ducked to the side. "Wait a minute. I'm not the target. If ye're not careful, ye'll have me off me feet."

Immediately, Mary lowered the rifle. "I'm sorry. I wasn't going to shoot it. I was just getting the target in my sights." She laughed. "I wouldn't have shot you."

Sean stopped walking and stared at Mary in amazement. "Ye know, I think that's the first time I've heard ye laugh since . . . well, since it was decided we should get married."

Mary hadn't thought about whether she'd laughed or not, but now that Sean had mentioned it, she realized she hadn't felt much like it for a very long time. She also realized it felt good. She smiled and leveled the rifle. "You better move. I'm in a hurry to continue my lesson."

Sean trotted back and stood beside Mary. She fired and hit the driftwood again, this time much closer to the center.

"Ye're a good shot. Ye sure ye haven't done this before?"

"No," Mary said with a sense of satisfaction. She handed back the gun. "I'm hungry. It's time I cooked dinner." She headed toward the cabin, and for the first time in weeks, felt an expectancy about her future. And most surprising of all, she felt happy.

Chapter 12

$\mathcal{M}$emories from Sean's boyhood drifted through his mind as he walked the edge of the frozen pond. He and his family had often visited his uncle's farm in the countryside just outside New York City. Sean had always enjoyed the winter visits most. Maybe that's why he'd ended up in Alaska.

The hillsides of New York would be mounded with snow, creating a perfect playground for sledders. And he could usually count on the pond in the back pasture being frozen. After tumbling down snow-covered hills, he and his two cousins would head for the ice. He could almost hear Tom and Jake's cries and laughter echoing over the pond as they chased him down. They'd sweep past, shoving and doing their best to trip him up. Too often the pranksters succeeded and Sean found himself on his backside, the cold sending chills through his clothing. In turn, he'd jump up and take after them.

Sean smiled. *Those were good days.*

The neighbors would join in the fun until the chill drove them to shore where they'd sip hot chocolate and warm themselves at a bonfire. It was there that he'd met Jessica Louise Adams. She was the prettiest girl in town and, like most young men, he did all he could to attract her attention. Sean grinned as he remembered the brazen young man who'd glided past Jessica as fast as he could, then kicked up ice shavings with his blades to show off his skating prowess.

Jessica did notice Sean, and it didn't take long for the young couple to become a twosome whenever Sean visited. Jessica had never been good at concealing her feelings, so each time she looked at Sean her eyes radiated devotion. Jessica's family moved west the summer before Sean's did and he never saw her after that.

Sean stepped out of his snowshoes, and with a fishing pole under one arm and a saw under the other, cautiously stepped onto the ice. He took a practice slide, then another and another until he plowed into a pile of snow. He turned and slid back the way he'd come. It wasn't skating, but it was as close as he was going to get to it. His growling stomach reminded him he was a grown man with work to do. He needed to check his traps, then do some fishing. "Stop bein' silly and get on to yer work," he told himself matter-of-factly.

As he walked back to the bank, Jessica's face came to mind. She'd had dark hair and eyes like Mary. *I wish Mary would look at me the way Jessica used to,* Sean thought sadly. *Most likely, she never will. Maybe it was a mistake to marry her.*

If she only would really see how I feel. I wish I could do something for her, he thought as he walked away from the pond. *I know. As a surprise for Mary, I can try to make her some skates.*

He knelt beside a trap that held a dead fox. It's body had stiffened, but the fur was dense and soft. Setting his pole and saw aside, he released the animal and ran his hand over the blue, gray fur. *This is the last time I caretake a fox island,* he thought. He detested the grisly work. He hated collecting the corpses of these beautiful animals, then skinning them. It was alright in moderation. A man did what he must, but running a trapline was too much. He was grateful that Mary often helped him flesh out the skins. She was good at it. In fact, she was good at almost every survival skill. *I don't know if I could make it without her help,* he thought. His mind moved on to Trent. *He's worthless—too busy whittling or sleeping to be of any help,* he thought with disgust. "Or he's staring at me wife," he said out loud.

Sean glanced in the direction of the cabin. He'd left Mary alone with Trent. *I hate leavin' them for too long. There's somethin' peculiar about that man. It's almost as if his life is a masquerade. I don't think he ever shows us the real Trent Parker.*

I'll be glad when we're not trapped on this island with him. He said he had a boat, but I've never seen it. I wonder . . . Sean stood and peered at the hill that blocked the far side of the island from view. Curiosity needled him. There might be something on the boat that would provide a truer picture of the man.

The question whether to investigate Trent unsettled his mind as he knelt and skinned the fox. By the time he'd added the pelt to the others hanging from his belt, he'd decided to take a look at Trent's boat.

Sean lashed on his snowshoes, and with snow crunching under his feet and cold air searing his lungs, trudged up the hillside. He was thankful for his wool socks and the fur lining in his boots. As the slope grew steeper, he breathed hard. His breath fogged the air and ice crystals collected above his upper lip.

I'm bein' foolish. The boat is certainly buried beneath the snow. And even if I can find it, what could I discover that would help me understand Trent? He considered turning back but walked on, driven by curiosity and a sense that the boat held something important.

Cresting the hill, he stopped to catch his breath. He leaned over, pressed his hands on his thighs, and gulped in air as he studied a small cove. Tall cliffs, encrusted with ice and snow hedged it in on both sides. Turning sideways, he cautiously descended.

When he reached the water's edge, he scanned the shoreline. Small waves broke against the icy beach, and even in the cold the pungent odor of shellfish, sand, and sea was strong. He saw no sign of a boat. *Where could it be?* he asked himself as his eyes swept every bump on the shoreline, knowing it was certainly buried and out of sight. His eyes stopped at a dark hollow place in the white landscape.

Making his way across the base of the hill, his snowshoe tracks intersected with a well-worn fox trail leading to the recess. *It's probably just a den,* he thought, but followed the footmarks. They ended abruptly, disappearing into a dark hole that was clearly not a den. It was Trent's boat. The fox had burrowed through the snow and into the bow.

That's odd, Sean thought as he dug away some of the snow, revealing a pile of metal and chains. "What the . . . ?" Sean exploded, snatching up a trap. "He's a poacher! He's a blasted poacher!" Sean hurled the snare away from the boat, then grabbed another and flung it into the snow. Digging further, he discovered a bundle of furs. Dragging them free of their hiding place, he held the pelts out at arm's length, anger percolating. Obviously Trent had been very busy before he and Mary arrived on Unalga.

"I'd like to see you explain this, Mr. Parker," Sean seethed as he grabbed out another bundle of furs and a pair of traps. He tromped back up the hill, heading for the cabin. As he approached the snow-laden cabin, all he could think about was confronting Trent Parker, the thief.

Moving as fast as his snowshoes would allow, he marched down the trail. He stopped in front of the door, untied the lacings on his snowshoes and kicked them off, then yanked open the door and stepped inside,

Trent was complaining, "I'm sick of fish. It's all we eat. It's about time we had some real food." He turned and faced an angry Sean. His eyes went to what Sean carried, and the color drained from his face.

Sean closed the door hard. "It seems the fox sniffed out yer bait."

"So, what you got there?" Trent asked, in a light tone.

"What do ye think?"

Trent didn't answer.

"Sean, what is it?" Mary asked.

"He's a poacher." Sean held up the traps and furs. "I found these in his boat." He looked at Trent. "I got this feelin' today that I ought to go down and see if I could find out more about ye. Well, the fox showed me just what kind of man ye are." He tossed the furs and traps at Trent's feet. "All this time we've been helpin' ye and we believed yer story about just bein' a traveler." He shook his head. "Out. Get out of this house."

"You can't do that. I'll die out there." Trent swiped his hand back over his brow and through his hair. "I was just trying to make a living. Life is harder in Alaska than I expected. I went through my cash and this was the only way I could survive." Trent stood. "I've never done anything like this in my life. You have to believe me. I'm sorry. When I started harvesting furs, I didn't know you. And I didn't take any more after you came." Helplessly, he looked from Mary to Sean.

"Sean, we can't put him out," Mary said quietly. "That would be murder."

He turned an angry look on Trent and silently contemplated Mary's remark. "Ye can stay, but from now on ye'll start doin' yer share of the work, and ye'll get the rest of the furs out of yer boat and add them to ones in the shed."

"But that's all the valuables I have in the world. Those furs are my only way of living when I get off this island."

"They're not yers. They never were. They belong to Nick Berens."

"Who's probably dead," Trent retorted. "Have you forgotten the big storm that trapped us here just after he left? He's dead and won't miss the furs. We could divide up what we have."

Sean stared at the corrupt man, unable to disguise his disgust. "The pelts don't belong to us. I don't steal. And I don't believe Nick is dead. He'll be back in the spring."

"You're more of a fool than I thought you were."

Sean clenched his teeth, holding back scornful words. "This discussion is over. Ye obviously don't have a conscience."

"I have a conscience. I do what's best for me. And what's best for me is what's right."

That night, when Sean crawled in beside his wife, he placed his rifle on the floor beside him. There would be no more trusting Trent. As always he was careful not to touch Mary. He knew she wasn't ready. He wondered if she would ever be. *And what will I do if she never loves me?* he wondered, longing to love her more completely.

"I don't know if I'll be able to sleep after finding out how Trent's mind works," Mary whispered. "He's frightening."

"I know," Sean said, catching his breath as Mary's body accidentally touched his. "Maybe we can work out a way he can sleep in the shed."

"I don't see how. There's no heat, and that shack has more holes in it than this one did. I want him out, but I don't see how we can do that. And besides, he might do something crazy. I don't think he's very far from it now."

"I'll have to think on it." Sean trapped his arms over his chest and stared at the ceiling. He wanted to reach for Mary, to hold her and comfort her the way a husband should, but he dared not. *If only she'd turn to me,* he thought. *Maybe Christmas will stir somethin' within her.* He'd forgotten to tell her and since she'd never mentioned it, she obviously didn't care about the holiday. Turning to her, he said, "Ye know Christmas is tomorrow."

"It is? I'd forgotten." Mary rolled onto her side, and facing Sean, rested her hands under her cheek. "I can't believe I forgot. My family is busy baking and making gifts. In our house, Christmas is a special time. I'll miss it."

"Me too. We used to have a big family celebration. Me mother would bake for days ahead, and there were always secrets to be kept. On Christmas mornin' me father would read from his Bible, then hand out gifts." He closed his eyes. "Me father could be a stern man, but not on Christmas. He'd laugh and even sing." Sean sighed. "We nearly forgot it was Christmas, and it may be our last."

Mary tentatively placed her hand on Sean's arm. "It won't be. We'll survive." She rolled onto her back and said softly, "Good night."

The next morning, Sean left the house, hoping to find something special for Christmas dinner. His family had always had goose. He knew there were none of those to be had, but he longed for something more substantial than fish or mussels. He searched and searched but found nothing. Finally, in exasperation he sawed a hole in the lake and dropped in a line. "Well, fish it will be," he said as he sat and waited for a bite. The wind picked up and cold penetrated his clothing. Soon he was shivering.

Out of the corner of his eye, he thought he saw something dart across the front of the bank. Sean's head jerked around and he searched the snow. At first, he saw nothing. Then a pair of dark eyes appeared and an animal hopped forward. It was a rabbit! Slowly, so not to startle him, Sean lowered his pole and reached for his rifle. *It's not a goose, but it will do.*

Raising the gun to his shoulder, he aimed and fired. The rabbit jumped and squealed, then lay dead. Sean ran and grabbed it, holding it in the air. "Rabbit for Christmas dinner," he cheered, before returning to his fishing hole. He'd still have to fish, but at least there would be something special for this night.

At the end of the day, Sean walked back to the cabin with three fish and a rabbit to show for his efforts. When he opened the door, the aroma of baking greeted him. "What's that I smell?" he asked cheerfully, holding the rabbit behind him.

Mary turned away from the stove. "I had a little flour and sugar left so I thought I'd see if I could make a berry cobbler to go with our fish. It was the last of the flour and sugar, but it's Christmas."

Sean grinned. "I know." He held up the rabbit.

"Oh, Sean, how wonderful!"

Mary nibbled the last bite of meat off the bone. "I never thought I'd like rabbit so much," she said with a smile. "And I can use the bones to make soup."

"It was a puny rabbit," Trent griped.

"Well, since ye're so unhappy about the fare, ye can do the huntin' tomorrow," Sean said. "I'll concentrate on fleshing out the new hides."

Trent sneered.

Sean pushed back his chair and walked across the room to the shelf where he kept his Bible. "Since it's Christmas, I think we should read from the Bible. Do ye mind?"

"Forgive me if I don't stay," Trent said, shoving himself away from the table. He grabbed his tobacco and cigarette papers off the shelf and disappeared out the door.

"I don't mind," Mary said as she cleared away the dishes and returned with the coffeepot. "Would you like more coffee? I'm sorry but it's reused grounds."

"It'll taste perfect with some of that cobbler you made. We can eat it while I read."

"All right." Mary served the cobbler then sat at the table.

"Mmm. Looks good," Sean said as he cut into his. He scooped a bite of the confection onto his fork and placed it on his tongue. Closing his eyes, he chewed. A smile emerged and he looked at Mary. "It's delicious. The best I've tasted." He took another bite and again chewed slowly, savoring the morsel.

Mary cut into hers and dropped it in her mouth. "Mmm. It is good."

Sean leafed through his Bible. "Me father always read about Jesus' birth from the Book of Luke. Is that all right with ye?"

Mary nodded.

Taking another bite of cobbler, Sean began reading. His voice was calm and strong as he read the account of Jesus' birth.

When he finished, Mary said, "I've heard the story so many times, but I've never been able to believe it. How can God come to earth in the form of a baby? And if there are angels, why don't they visit us now?"

"Me mom said angels do visit. We just don't know they're angels." Sean shrugged. "I wish I understood it all." He thumbed through the pages. "Do you mind if I read more?"

"No. Go ahead."

"Here's somethin' me mother marked. It's in the Book of Psalms. It says, *'The heavens declare the glory of God; and the firmanent sheweth his handywork. Day unto day uttereth speech, and night unto night sheweth knowledge.'"* Thoughtfully, he set the Bible down.

"What does that mean, 'the heavens declare the glory of God, and the firmanent sheweth his handywork'?" Mary asked.

"I'm not sure. Maybe the writer is talking about when we see the heavens we see God. And that God made the heavens."

"My parents have been reading the Bible to me for years and the priests teach us, but I've never understood it."

"Maybe we need to be persistent in trying to understand? And if we keep seekin', he'll show us."

"I don't think God will show me anything. He never has. And according to the priest at the church at home, I'm a sinner."

"Me mother used to quote a verse about that. She would say we're all sinners, but God loves even sinners and shows himself to everyone."

"It just confuses me," Mary said and stood. "Thank you for the rabbit and the Bible reading. It was a little like the Christmas I've always had at home." She headed toward their bed.

Sean searched his mind for a way to spend more time with her. After all, this was Christmas. He'd hoped something special would happen between them. "Wait," he said. Mary stopped and looked at him. "Uh, do you have to go to bed so soon? Maybe we could enjoy the night sky for a few minutes. It's clear, and the Northern Lights can be seen this time of year."

Mary smiled. "All right. That would be nice." She pulled on her coat, hat, and gloves, then walked to the door. Sean was right behind her.

As he stepped into the night air, it burned his cheeks and lungs, but it's sharpness felt good. Snow crunched beneath their boots as they followed a path leading away from the cabin. Lantern light lit up the shed. "Trent must be hidin' out in there," Sean said, as he circled his arm around Mary's waist and escorted her up the slight hill to the beach overlook.

Mary hesitated at the close contact but decided she didn't mind so much and continued on.

Small waves frolicked beneath moonlight, shimmering with life and reflecting the light of the glowing orb. "It's beautiful," Mary said. She sighed. "Tonight, I think I miss home more than I ever have."

"Me too." Sean gazed at the sky. Its blackness was broken up by thousands of burning stars and a butter-yellow moon.

Unexpectedly, lights lit up the dark canopy. Streaks of color leaped from one part of the sky to another, then flashed and writhed in ghost-like formations. Abruptly the heavens went black except for the stars and moon.

"That was beautiful!" Mary exclaimed.

"I've only seen them once before." Sean took a slow, even breath as he thought. "It's like the Bible said about the heavens declaring God. Watching something like this makes you believe there must be a God. How else could it exist? I mean, how does somethin' like this just happen?"

Mary said nothing.

Again, the sky brightened and the lights danced. For a time they stretched out in great arcs and streaks, then like a giant, colorful blanket they overlaid the heavens with color.

Sean and Mary stood side by side silently embracing the beauty. Sean placed his arm over Mary's shoulders and she didn't draw away. "Maybe this is our Christmas gift from God. Maybe he's sayin' he hasn't forgotten us."

Chapter 13

$\mathcal{M}$ary hummed "In the Good Old Summer Time" as she poked a needle into the toe of a sock. Pulling the thread through, her mind meandered toward spring when the storms would quiet, the sun would warm the island, and she could return home. *It will be wonderful not to be hungry,* she thought as she pushed the needle through the material and into her finger.

"Ouch! I need to pay more attention to what I'm doing," she sputtered and put her fingertip to her mouth to stanch the flow of blood.

When the puncture stopped bleeding, she held up the threadbare sock and studied it. Shaking her head, she wondered, *How will this sock ever make it until spring?*

Pale sunlight nuzzled the window and bathed the room with its soft glow. Mary knotted the thread, then broke off the extra. After pushing the needle into a pin cushion, she set the sock in her lap and stretched her arms over her head. Her eyes returned to the window. The light invited her outside. *Sean is checking traplines, and Trent is fishing. I might as well be outside too,* she decided, returning the sock to Sean's clothing pile.

After stuffing extra wood into the stove, she grabbed her coat and pulled it on, tying the hood tightly about her face. After pulling on gloves, she stepped outside into the cold pallid sunlight and powder snow. Taking the last pair of snowshoes off the hook beside the door, she strapped them on and set out, following tracks left by Sean and Trent.

The path veered toward the lake, but she decided to make a new trail and headed for the cove on the far side of the island. With each step, energy coursed through her, sunshine and fresh air feeding her spirit.

The sun had warmed the earth just enough to melt the frozen crystals lying on the snow's surface, making it slippery going. Mary headed up a slope, carefully placing her feet so she wouldn't slip. Snow crunched beneath her snowshoes, making a squeaking sound with each step. When she reached the top of the bluff, she was breathing hard, the cold air stabbing her lungs. Chilly winds buffeted her. They were stronger here than on the other side of the island. Resting, she gazed at the small cove bordered on two sides by steep cliffs. A wide stretch of beach and water lay between the headlands.

Making her way down the hillside was difficult. Slippery snow and ice threatened to topple her, so Mary turned her body sideways and planted her feet deliberately and cautiously. By the time she reached the beach, she labored for breath.

She wiped snow off a rock and sat, ignoring the cold that penetrated her wool pants. Just like the rest of the island, it was white here, except for the open cliff faces. Even the choppy water was topped by whitecaps. Brisk breezes splashed ocean mists against the cliffs, leaving heavy and intricate ice formations clinging to the rocks. The frosty air pushed Mary deeper into her coat. Her cheeks and nose felt numb, and she knew her dark complexion had turned ruddy. It always did in the cold.

Barks and throaty roars echoed over the water, drawing Mary's eyes to an outcropping of rocks. Sea lions lounged atop a tiny island; some contended for the best position by nipping and prodding, while others napped contentedly. Mary's thoughts wandered home, and she remembered how her father and brothers had hunted sea lions. The large bulls and lactating cows could be quite aggressive. One time she'd convinced her father to take her along. It had been a frightening and bloody experience. Her brother had nearly fallen prey to an angry bull, and when the eventual killing and butchering took place, she was repulsed. It was not an experience she wanted to repeat.

A pang of regret swept over her as she remembered how Paul had often bragged about his hunting skills. In the village where he'd grown up, the people depended almost solely on the food offered by the sea. There had been very little help or interference from the outside. Mary could picture the broad-shouldered man standing in the bow of a boat, ready to thrust his spear into a fleeing whale. While attending the Chemawa School in Oregon, he'd often talked about how he missed village life and would one day return to it. *I hope he's all right,* she thought, knowing that by now he was fighting a war.

A strong windy gust swept across the water and snatched at Mary's hood, making her eyes water. She closed them, trying to remember Paul the way he'd looked the last time she'd seen him. He'd been angry and hurt. As she considered the man, she realized how little she'd thought of him lately. And when her mind wandered over memories, the hurt she'd once felt was gone. *Maybe I didn't love him. When you love someone, you never stop loving him.* Paul's handsome face filled her thoughts, but she felt only a little sadness over what had happened. She sighed and pulled her knees up close to her chest.

Snow crunched behind Mary. She turned and found Trent stepping toward her. Wariness pressed down on her.

Wearing his usual taunting half smile, he asked, "You're a long way from home, aren't you?"

"Not so far. I was bored and needed to get out. I decided a walk would be good."

"A walk?" Trent placed a foot on the rock where Mary sat and leaned over her. "You're an odd one. I've never known anyone who considered a mile hike in deep snow just a walk."

"You're here," she said soberly. "And like I said . . ."

"I know. You were bored." He stared at Mary.

Forcing herself not to flinch, Mary wished he'd look elsewhere. She hated how his dark blue eyes probed her. He kept staring, and finally she asked, "What are you looking at?"

"You. What else?" He straightened slightly. "You're very pretty, you know."

"Thank you, but please don't stare. It's impolite."

"Impolite?" Trent chuckled. "Well, I'd hate to be impolite." He gazed at her a moment longer, then turned his eyes to the bay. Keeping his gaze on the water, he said calmly, "I could do anything I wanted to you right now. Sean's busy with his traps. It's just you and me." He gave her a lascivious smile.

Mary felt as if she'd been hit. Filled with revulsion, she stared at his insulting smile. "Stay away from me." She forced herself to remain still and not scan the hillside for Sean, knowing her fear would only tantalize Trent.

"I didn't say I was going to do anything," Trent said coldly. "I only said I could if I wanted to. And I don't." He removed his foot from her rock and stuffed his hands in his pockets. Staring at the pod of seals, he asked, "What's out there?"

"Sea lions." Mary stood and started for the cabin.

"Where you going?"

"Home. I'm cold."

Trent looked back at the sea lions. "Can you eat them?"

"Yes. The meat is good."

"Well, I say we ought to shoot one. I'm sick of fish, mussels, and that filthy seaweed. It's time for some real meat."

"It can be dangerous and very difficult."

"Ah, it can't be that hard. They're just lying out there. All we need is a rifle and a boat. I've got both." He started up the beach. "Get your husband."

Mary didn't move. "Trent, you don't know how to hunt them. And if you do shoot one, how are you going to get it back here?"

Trent stopped, turned to look at Mary, and said through clenched teeth, "I'll take care of it. Just get Sean."

Mary knew that arguing with Trent would accomplish nothing, so she asked, "Where is he?"

"Just beyond the lake on the west side. Hurry, before the sea lions leave."

Sucking in cold air, Mary trudged up the hill, then plod-ded around the tiny lake and down a shallow slope where she found Sean.

"What are ye doin' out here?" he asked.

"Trent sent me. He wants you to help him kill a sea lion."

"Where?"

"In the cove where he left his boat. There are some in the bay."

"Hmm, I've never hunted them, but real meat would be great. This sounds like a good idea."

"It's not easy to kill them. My brothers and father hunted for many years and still got into trouble. It's dangerous and takes time to learn. If you're not careful, you could get washed up on the rocks or a bull might . . ."

Sean rested his hands on Mary's shoulders. His eyes bright, he said, "Meat, Mary. Think of that. Real meat." He smiled. "Nothin' we've done since we got here has been easy. I'm goin' to try." He started toward the bay, and Mary joined him.

By the time they arrived, Trent had freed the boat of snow and ice and had maneuvered it to the water's edge. "What took you so long?" he shouted over a rising wind. "It's gonna' be dark soon, and those animals could leave at any moment."

"I couldn't find Sean right away," Mary explained, but Trent ignored her as he pushed the boat into deeper water.

Sean unlaced his snowshoes, stepped out of them, and grabbed hold of the side of the boat. Nodding at the pod of seals, he said, "It doesn't look too far."

Mary studied black clouds tumbling in from the sea and somehow knew catastrophe waited for the two men. "Sean, please, don't. The weather is turning bad. It's too dangerous."

"Shut up! I've heard enough out of you," Trent bellowed.

"Trent! That's enough. Ye'll not talk to her that way."

Trent's eyes locked on to Sean's; then he smiled. "I'm sorry, just a bit anxious to get started." He slapped his gun. "I'm ready. I'll shoot one and we can haul it back here. Mary, you better get that stove heated up. We're going to need it."

The boat bobbed and washed toward shore as a wave swept under it, then as the water receded, the dory moved away from shore. Trent grabbed it and laid his gun inside. Sean held the boat steady while Trent climbed in, then quickly followed.

His legs braced against the roll of waves, Trent stood in the bow while Sean settled on the center seat and dipped the oars into the water. Mary watched as they headed out, her trepidation growing with each pass of the oars.

Swells lifted the boat, then dropped it into dark, wet valleys. They slowly approached the rocks. Mary could hear the uproar from the sea lions as they recognized danger and began diving off their haven and into the sea. Trent raised his gun to his shoulder. A rifle blast echoed over the bay, then another.

"I got one!" Trent shouted and jumped, nearly falling into the water. He regained his balance and pointed at the floating animal. "It fell in on the other side of the rocks. Over there. It's over there. Get this boat moving before the tide carries it away!" Red tainted the water as the animal's blood seeped into the bay. "It's heading out! Come on! Hurry! We'll lose it!" Trent's voice was high and tight.

Sean pulled hard on the oars. He wanted the meat as much as Trent did. He worked his way around the rocks, but the wind pushed him back and the animal remained out of reach.

"We're going to lose him!" Trent screamed, leaning out over the water and straining toward the animal. It bobbed in the waves as if taunting him. "I'm going in after it," Trent said, stripping off his coat and boots.

"Ye're crazy. The water is ice-cold. Ye can't stay in for long. It'll kill ye."

"I'm not about to let it just float away! I'll grab it and swim right back." Without another word Trent dove in, his body disappearing beneath the waves. When he broke the surface, he let out a howl and treaded water, then remembering his mission, he headed for the animal. Soon his strong strokes turned weak and ineffective, his hands splashed the surface, looking like those of a drowning man. His head disappeared beneath the waves. When his face came out of the water, he cried, "Help! Help me!"

"I told ye not to go," Sean muttered as he steered toward Trent. "I'm comin'! Hang on!" When he was a few feet away, he stood, grabbed the oar out of its bracket, and held it out to Trent. "Grab hold." Trent didn't seem to hear and disappeared beneath the water. "Trent! Grab hold!" Sean yelled. He searched the water's surface but didn't see the man. "Trent!" he screamed. "Trent!"

Pulling off his coat and boots, he grabbed a rope and tied it around his waist, then secured it to a hook inside the boat before diving in. The cold hit him, and he felt as if he'd dived into ice. The shock of it knocked the wind out of him, and he fought for the surface. As he broke free, he sucked in air. He searched for Trent but couldn't find him, so he reached below the water and began to seek the man with his fingers. He found nothing. Knowing he had only seconds before the cold robbed him of strength, he dove beneath the waves, his hands searching the dark waters. *God, if ye're here, help me now.* Almost immediately he felt a piece of cloth. *It must be Trent's shirt,* he thought and hauled on it. Whatever he'd grabbed felt heavy. Sean pulled and kicked for the surface. Effects from the icy water were beginning to set in. His arms were heavy, his fingers were quickly losing feeling. *What am I doin'? Why should I die for a man like this?* Although he knew it made no sense, Sean held on and pulled Trent to the surface. Trent didn't move as Sean dragged him toward the boat. The cold consumed Sean's strength. He pulled himself along the rope, kicking numbed legs. *I'm goin' to die. We're not goin' to make it.*

Struggling the last few feet, he grabbed hold of the boat. Knowing there was no way he could push Trent into the boat from the water, he snagged the man's shirt on a grapple, scrambled in, then using the last of his energy, he hauled Trent over the side. Falling to the bottom of the boat, he lay on his back, arms outstretched, lungs heaving, and his body shaking. *I've got to get us to shore or we'll die.*

Exhaustion overwhelming him, Sean fought for strength. He pushed himself onto hands and knees, grabbed Trent's coat and draped it over the man, then shoved numbed arms into his own. Wind hastened freezing. Ice already encased his clothing and cracked when he moved. He climbed onto the wooden bench. His hands feeling like lifeless stumps, he struggled to pick up the loose oar. He dropped it, then tried again, and this time managed to snap the oar into place. Trusting his frozen hands to hang on, he pulled on both oars and turned toward the shore.

Trent lay silently on the bottom of the boat, eyes closed, lips tinged blue. At first Sean thought he was dead, but after a moment saw his chest rise and fall. *Thank God he's alive.*

He rowed harder, watching the paddles to make certain they were pushing against the water. Sometimes they flailed uselessly and sometimes they dug in, propelling them forward. Slowly the beach came closer.

Mary waded in and met the boat.

"We both nearly drowned. And we may still freeze to death." Sean jumped into the shallows, and together he and Mary pulled the boat onto the beach. Trembling so hard he could barely speak, he said, "We've got to get warm." He reached over the side of the boat and pulled Trent upright, shaking him. "Trent? Trent? Are ye all right? I need ye to wake up. Come on."

Trent opened his eyes and stared at Sean.

"Ye've got to help us. Can ye sit up?" Trent nodded and pushed himself upright.

Sean grabbed hold of one arm and pulled. "Come on now, we've got to get back to the house." Trent tried to stand but was too weak.

Mary climbed into the boat and helped support him. "We'd better hurry. He's really cold." She glanced at Sean. "And so are you," she added, hefting Trent.

Sean nodded. "I'm past bein' cold. I can't feel me legs or arms."

Their breath fogging the air, Mary and Sean dragged the young man out of the boat, then headed up the hill hauling him between them. "He's too heavy," Mary finally said, letting him slide to the ground.

"Trent!" Sean shouted. "Ye've got to help. Walk or ye'll die right here."

"I thought I was going to die," Trent mumbled as he struggled to his feet. "I . . . I thought I was dead." He looked at Sean soberly, then gazed up the hill. "I can make it." He shuffled forward.

Without their catch, the three stumbled up the hill toward home.

Trent's shakes had quieted, and he silently sipped his coffee.

Mary set a platter of fried fish on the table. Dividing the small bit of food into three portions, she served the two larger pieces to Sean and Trent and kept the smaller one for herself.

Trent looked at her. "Thank you."

Mary couldn't ever remember him thanking anyone. "You're welcome. Do you want more coffee? It's weak but hot."

He held up his cup.

"I'd like some of that too," Sean said with a smile. "I'm still not warm all the way through." He pulled his quilt closer.

Mary refilled their cups and poured one for herself, then sat at the table. She took a bite of fish. "A sea lion isn't worth your lives. You were foolish to go after them."

"We know," Sean said. "We know."

"You don't understand. I'm angry. I stood and watched, and there was nothing I could do. I . . ."

"You saved my life," Trent said to Sean. "Why?"

"Why?" Sean shrugged. "I don't know. It was the right thing to do. To watch a man die when ye can help is inhuman.

We might not be friends, but I do respect yer life." He smiled. "Maybe it's time we mended our relationship a bit. What do ye say?" He held out his hand.

Trent looked at Sean's hand. "I thank you for my life, but I have no friends." He scooted his chair away from the table, walked to his bedding and sat, then proceeded to roll a cigarette.

Chapter 14

*W*ith a fleshing board pressed against his abdomen, Sean ran a broad, flat blade across the inside of a hide. In spite of the cold, moisture gathered on his forehead and trickled into his eyes. Blinking, he wiped away the sweat with the back of his hand. Fleshing was hard, tedious work, but important. Remnants of fat or flesh left on the hide would spoil and ruin the pelt.

He studied the growing pile of finished furs plus the ones still on stretchers. *Nick knew what he was doin',* he thought as he calculated the number of fox still to be taken this season. *There was real money to be made. There are enough furs here to see him through several seasons. He's a smart man.*

Sean tried to envision himself as a fox farmer, but as he considered the hundreds of animals he'd have to slaughter, he knew it wasn't something he wanted to do. There were other ways to make a living. *Maybe the fishin' will pick up, and I can get a boat of me own,* he thought.

The shed door creaked open and Trent stood just outside, handle in hand. "Thought I'd see how your work was going," he said cordially and stepped inside.

Sean was immediately suspicious. Unless Trent had an objective, he was seldom friendly. He nodded.

Trent studied the pile of pelts. "Looks like you've got a lot of furs there." He half smiled. "Course I helped some."

"I wouldn't call poachin' helpin'." Sean continued scraping the inside of the hide.

"I explained all that to you." Trent sat on a stump. "You know, I'm not such a bad guy. But you won't even give me a chance. It's true I was trapping here. But how was I supposed to know the fox belonged to someone else?"

Sean threw him an incredulous look.

Undaunted, Trent continued, "Like everyone else, I was just trying to make a living. It's beautiful country up here, but there aren't many ways to make money."

"Yes, but there are other options besides poachin'."

"Like I said, I didn't know . . ."

"What? Do ye think I'm cracked? Don't give me that story. Ye knew what ye was doin'."

"Well, not everyone has the means to buy fox and start an operation or the money to pay rent to a greedy government. The government doesn't give two hoots about this tiny island. Why should it charge someone to use it?"

"Don't make excuses for yerself. Ye had other options besides stealin' from another."

Trent's eyes flamed. He clenched his jaw and stared at a

fur on the far wall. Finally, he continued, "I suppose you're right, but times are tough and . . ."

"Not tough enough to make thievery acceptable," Sean cut in without missing a stroke. A rush of wind shook the hut. Sean studied the ceiling. "Sounds like another storm is movin' in."

"It's picking up all right." Trent stood and casually ambled across the room to the pile of furs. He rifled through them. "Good quality." The door rattled with another icy blast. "Mind if I give you a hand?"

Sean stopped his blade midstroke and met Trent's eyes. "A little out of character for ye, isn't it?"

Trent forced a grin. "I won't pretend I like work, but I've had about as much inactivity as I can stand. I'll be glad when winter moves on."

"I guess it would be foolish to decline offered help." Nodding toward the far corner, he said, "The tools are over there."

Trent crossed the room casually, dragged out a fleshing board and set it up, then grabbed a flat-bladed knife and a fresh pelt. He stretched the fur out on the wood planking and secured it, bracing one end of the board against the floor and the other against his belly. With the expertise that comes with experience, he scraped the underside of the hide.

For a long while, he worked in silence. Then clearing his throat, he asked, "How much you think these pelts are worth?"

"Can't say. I've never paid much attention. Me job is to trap and skin them, not price 'em."

"There must be enough to keep a person comfortable for a good long while," Trent pressed.

Sean kept working.

"These could give a man a good start. Someone like you. You've got yourself a pretty little wife in there, and soon you'll have children. Seems to me a nice nest egg could give you security."

Sean let his knife rest on the skin and stared at Trent. "Stop jumpin' about and be straight with me. What are ye tryin' to say?"

"I was just thinking, you and me could split these pelts and make a fresh start for ourselves. This man, Nick, must have a lot of money. He won't miss it."

Sean's anger simmered. He clenched his jaw, then said evenly, "Ye come in here offerin' to help, and all ye want is to sweet-talk me into givin' ye somethin' that doesn't belong to ye. Ye're quite a case, Trent Parker. If I was ye, I'd be embarrassed to open me mouth. Have ye no decency?"

"I should have known this is all I'd get from you. I had you pegged right. What is it about you people? Do you think reading the Bible gives you the right to judge everyone else?" He spat the word Bible as if just a taste of it burned his tongue. "You can't tell me you've never done things you've been ashamed of."

"I'm not judgin'. And, yes, I've done plenty, but not this."

"You're just like every other self-righteous Christian I've ever known."

"I don't know anything about the Christians ye've known, but just because someone thinks stealin' is wrong doesn't make the person self-righteous. Everyone knows it's wrong." He returned to fleshing. "At least I thought everyone did," he said under his breath.

His anger boiling over, Trent slammed his hand against his fleshing board. The board fell sideways, crashing to the floor. "I know about stealing! And what matters isn't that the poor steal from the rich. They have to fill their needs where they can, and sometimes it means stealing. The real thieves are the rich who filch from the poor, using their uppity manners and smooth talk." He paced the floor. "I know. I watched it all my life. My parents and their pious friends were good at it, real good. The people they robbed weren't educated and didn't know when they were being taken. Oh, everything was presented as just good business practice, but I knew the truth."

His lip curled up. "On Sundays my parents went to church. They'd sit up straight and proud in the pew, looking pure and humble. But they didn't care about anything but their money—not even their son. They make me sick." He shoved his hat down tighter on his head. "Well, now I'm a poor man, and I'm not about to let the rich get it over on me."

"Not everyone is like that. I grew up in church and there were lots of good, kind folks."

"You were blind, then, only seeing what you wanted. People are people, and when they walk into church, they put on masks." He wore a sickening grin. "And all those years people like you bought it."

Sean had never felt sorry for Trent, but now as he looked at the young man with his warped perspective, he felt sick inside. "I know there are people who say they're good and who aren't, but not everyone is that way."

Trent hooked the top button of his coat. "You want to know where those wonderful people were when trouble found me? They were so busy scrambling up onto their sacred pedestals and pointing fingers at me that they had no comfort or help for me. Not one of them. They couldn't stand the stink of me because I reminded them of their own humanness. They booted me out of the church without a second thought." Trent walked to the door. "Some kind of compassion, don't you think? I decided then never to depend on anyone again. I take care of myself. I don't need counterfeit friends or a false god who doesn't care about the people he's supposed to have created."

"No one is trying to convince you to trust in God. I don't even know how I feel. But all of us need friends. Even you."

"I don't need friends."

"I'm sorry to hear ye say that, but I can't convince ye about any of this. It's yer choice." Another blast of wind hit the shed, and the rafters clacked like sick geese. "Sounds like a bad one's comin' in. I need to check the traplines, but I suppose it can wait until the storm passes."

Trent said nothing for a moment, then as if their previous argument hadn't happened, he said smoothly, "I don't know if I'd wait. If it comes and stays, you'll have dead fox out there for days. Besides, these storms usually take their time coming ashore. And it's not bad yet. You can probably check the traps and be back before the storm actually gets here."

"Yeah, I suppose ye're right." Sean set his knife on a shelf and laid the board against the shed wall. "I'll check the closest line, and then, if the storm's not so bad, I'll look over the rest." He pulled his hood over his head. "Tell Mary I'll be back in time for supper."

"Right."

As Sean opened the door, the wind caught it, nearly yanking it out of his hands. Icy wind stabbed at his face and burned his eyes. But the snow hadn't started to fall yet, so he headed out.

As Sean trudged toward the next trap, the storm pushed from behind. Snow fell in a white swathe, the brilliant white tempest stealing Sean's vision. He stared into the spiraling curtain of crystals. He'd lost all sense of direction and was forced to stop.

Panic swept over him like a deadly specter. He knew his life was in jeopardy, but he didn't know what to do to save himself. Throwing his arms out, he turned and took a step, then not knowing which way to go, he turned again and took several steps in another direction. *What am I going to do? I don't know which way to go!*

Fighting terror, Sean struggled to clear his thinking. He closed his eyes and forced his breathing to slow. His heart hammered as if a dozen horses were tramping through his chest, and the cold burned his lungs. He tried to recall the verses he'd read from the Book of Psalms that morning. The words tumbled through his mind as he tried to grab on to them. He could remember pieces. *God Most High will shelter me under his wings of protection,* he remembered. *He will provide a dwelling place of safety and no harm will come to me.* Sean knew there was more. He thought hard, trying to get hold of it. *A condition, there was a condition.* And as the words, *Because he has set his love upon me I will deliver him,* fear renewed itself in his heart. He didn't know what it meant to set his love upon God, to love God. He'd never believed in making last-minute deals just to save oneself, but now he prayed, *God, I need yer help. I want to know what it means to love ye, and if ye'll save me life, I'll try me hardest. I must live. What will happen to Mary if I'm gone and she's here alone with Trent? Ye know what he's like. Please help me.*

He opened his eyes, hoping the storm would have cleared enough for him to see, but all that surrounded him was a sea of white flakes. He turned. *Which way? Which way?* he asked, then headed in the direction that felt right.

The temperature continued to drop, and the wind grew stronger, pushing the white curtain sideways. Still, Sean trudged on, knowing he needed to find shelter or lose his life. Pulling his hood close about his face, he cupped his hands over his mouth and blew his breath against his freezing skin. *Show me what to do,* he prayed. *Show me.*

He needed shelter, any kind of shelter. *I'll build a snow cave,* he decided and began searching for an embankment to build it against. He moved forward cautiously, feeling for any rise in elevation. His foot slipped; then slipped again, and he knew he was climbing uphill. He stopped there and began scooping snow away from the bank, gradually forming a small cave. He pressed the snow flat between his hands inside and out, building sturdy walls. When he thought it was just big enough, he scrambled inside, scooping snow from the outside to close off the entrance. He left a small opening for air, then huddled down to wait out the storm.

Icy walls muffled the screaming wind. Sean wrapped his arms about his knees and pulled his legs against his chest. Shivers shook his body so hard he feared he'd shake down his newly constructed walls. *It will warm up soon,* he told himself. *Ye'll make it.*

He leaned against the wall and closed his eyes. *Father, yer book says that ye hear our prayers. It also says ye never leave us. I pray it is true. I need ye now. I pray ye will keep me safe. I don't ask so much for meself but for Mary. She'll need me. Ye can't leave her alone with Trent.*

The cave felt a little less dark and maybe even warmer as Sean felt sleep overtake him.

Mary wrung water out of a pair of wool pants, then draped them over a rope strung across the room. As she returned to the water and a dirty shirt that waited to be washed, she looked out the window hoping to find Sean at the door. But all she could see was the white storm. She scrubbed the shirt and the rest of the dirty laundry, but still Sean didn't come. Hours passed and her fear grew. Like a beast, it threatened to devour her until she paced, unable to rest. *Where are you, Sean? Where are you?*

"Hey, why don't you sit down. You're gonna' wear a hole in the floor," Trent griped.

"You should have stopped him. It's crazy for anyone to go out in a storm like this."

"What makes you think I didn't try? I told him it was dangerous, but he wouldn't listen. You know how he is . . . always wanting to be the he-man."

Mary opened the door. She knew Sean could be stubborn, but he wasn't usually careless. Stinging snow lashed her face. Pushing the door closed against the gale, she shivered and huddled deeper into her coat. "Do you think he's all right?" she asked, wondering why she would even ask Trent. He certainly didn't care. In fact, he'd been wearing a satisfied grin all after-noon. *He's probably happy Sean's out in the storm.*

Trent walked to the shelf and picked up a partially carved miniature totem. Taking his knife out of its sheath, he faced Mary. "How should I know if he's all right? It's fierce out there. Anything could happen." Pressing the tip of his knife against a hideous face carved in the center of the totem, he chipped out a piece of wood. "I have to admit, it's not so awful thinking of him out there." He smirked. "He might never return." Raising an eyebrow, he said pointedly, "That would leave just you and me. Can't say I'd mind that."

Mary's stomach turned. *Sean has to come back,* she thought. Ignoring Trent's comment, she walked to the stove and poured herself a cup of coffee. As she set the pot back on the burner, she felt hands on her shoulders. Fearful, she jumped and then spun around.

Trent's twisted smile was only inches from her face. "What, did I scare you?"

Revulsion filled Mary. She wanted to spit into his grinning face but knew that would be going too far. Instead she pressed her hands flat against his chest and pushed hard. "Get away from me!"

Trent's grin disappeared momentarily. He replaced it quickly with an insipid smile. "Just you and me, Mary. It would be just you and me."

Resting her hand against her queasy stomach, Mary said as boldly as she could, "Don't ever touch me again." She squared her shoulders. "Sean *will* be back." She remembered the rifle and wondered if it were loaded. *I'll use it if I have to,* she told herself.

Trent sat in a chair, leaned his forearms on his thighs, and chiseled on his totem. "I'm making this for you."

"Don't bother. It's hideous."

Feigning hurt, he held it up. "You don't like it? I think it's quite . . . well . . . quite distinctive. And very authentic."

"Yes, if you're an Indian waging war."

"Well, warring I am," Trent said flippantly and returned to carving.

Mary leaned against the counter, picked up her cup, and wrapped her free arm about her waist. *Sean, come home. Please come home. God, watch over him.* Before she'd even finished the plea, Mary was stunned at the prayer. She hadn't talked to God since she was a child, before she'd decided she didn't believe. It made no sense to ask someone you didn't believe in for something. And yet, she repeated, *God, please watch over Sean.*

Chapter 15

*M*ary slept little that night. Each time she'd drift off, alarming images captured her thoughts. One terrifying picture lodged in her mind, then played over and over. Sean lay injured, and she stood by helplessly. He looked at her and cried out for help, then struggled to drag himself toward her. His arms had no strength, and after moving only inches, he stopped and lay panting. Mary tried to go to him, but her legs felt as if heavy weights had been strapped to them and they refused to budge. She looked at her feet to see if they were weighted but found nothing unusual.

When she looked back at Sean, he lay stiff and still as a dead man, a world of white whirling around him, burying him. Mary tried to scream, but she couldn't utter a sound. *I have to help him. He'll be buried alive.*

Suffocated by despair and feeling as if she were swimming through mud, Mary struggled toward consciousness. *It's only a dream,* she told herself. *He's here beside me. Wake up! Wake up!*

She forced her eyes open and stared into blackness. Her heart hammered against her ribs. The dream was still close. Had it been real? She reached out and touched the bedding beside her. Sean wasn't there. Catching her breath, she remembered, *He's out in the storm.* The torment of the dream reclaimed her.

Hoping to put it behind her, she tried to focus on the gale pounding the island. Wind moaned and howled, and the house shook with each powerful barrage. Still, Trent's snoring could be heard above the roar. Mary felt momentary relief as she realized he was asleep.

Since her encounter with Trent at the cove, she hated being alone with him. The tone of his voice and the look in his eyes that day had shaken her. She could no longer look at him without seeing his depravity. He'd made it clear he'd do exactly as he wished, no matter how evil or base the desire.

With Sean gone, her anxiety had only increased. *Trent might do anything,* she thought, fear spiking through her. Although she'd tried to convince herself he'd only been bluffing and had simply wanted to frighten her, she couldn't brush aside his indifferent and heartless spirit. She'd seen no conscience in him, no tenderness. And now in the darkness, alone with the man, fear pursued her.

A burst of wind shouted the storm's dominance, and ice and snow pelted the small house, reminding Mary of the real enemy. Ashamed at her cowardice, she pulled the blankets up tightly under her chin. *Sean is out there, alone. He's the one in trouble,* she thought, recoiling from the image of his death in her dream. The horrifying sensations from her nightmare returned.

She squeezed her eyes closed. *No. He's all right. He found shelter. That's where he is now.* She rolled onto her side. The realization that she cared more deeply for Sean than she'd thought possible nudged her. What other explanation was there for her extreme anxiety? Loving someone was not what she wanted. She'd loved once and had been betrayed. *No,* she told herself, dismissing her emotions. *There's nothing unusual about my being upset. He's a good man and my friend. I'd feel this way about anyone I cared for. This is nothing more than concern for a friend.*

She threw back her blankets and sat up. *I don't love him. He's a fine man, and I like and respect him, but it's nothing more,* she thought, still trying to convince herself. Sadness settled over her as she remembered how things had once been between her and Paul. *Love hurt too much. She never wanted to love anyone again.*

Mary couldn't stay in bed. Shivering against the cold, she pulled on her shoes, draped a quilt over her shoulders, and stood. She dared not light the lantern for fear of waking Trent, so she fumbled toward the window in the dark. She stared at it, knowing ice had formed inside. It always did when the temperature turned cold. She touched the frozen crystals, and running a finger over the ice formations, followed their swirling patterns.

The storm paused, and quiet settled over the house. Mary stared through the glass at distant hills. Against the blackness of early morning, the snow's brilliance illuminated the outline of white bluffs. Sean was out there somewhere. *Please be all right,* Mary thought as an impulse to search for her husband caught hold of her. She looked at the door. *You're thinking foolishness,* she told herself. *You must wait. There's nothing you can do now. Wait.*

No matter how firmly she told herself to stay put, the urge to find Sean needled her. Trying to distract herself by doing something, she shuffled to the stove, quietly lifted the lid of the firebox, and added wood to the hot embers. After placing the half-full coffee pot on a back burner, she sat at the table. *Sean will need something hot when he gets home,* she told herself, as if saying it would make it so.

Mary's exhausted body yearned for sleep, but her troubled mind wouldn't allow it. Instead of returning to a warm bed, she sat with her quilt bundled tightly about her, and when she could no longer sit, she paced and waited for daylight.

"What are you up to?" Trent grumbled from the darkness.

His voice startled Mary. She looked at his sleeping place but couldn't see him in the dark. "Nothing. I can't sleep. I didn't mean to wake you." She heard the sound of a match being struck, and a tiny flame illuminated Trent's sleepy and surly face. *It's amazing how his boyish features have changed,* Mary thought, remembering their first meeting. He'd looked so young.

He held the flame to a lantern, and the room brightened. Holding the light away from his body, he peered at Mary. "What're you doing walking around in the dark?"

"I didn't want to disturb you."

"Well, you did." Trent ran his free hand over his face.

"I'm worried about Sean. I've decided to go after him when it's light outside."

The house shuddered and wind whistled through the cracks around the door as the storm brought a fresh assault. "You crazy? Can't you hear that? It's wicked out there."

"It's better than it was. The wind isn't as strong. I think the worst is over." She walked to the door and rested her hand on the knob. "I can't sit here doing nothing. He might need help."

"I didn't know natives were so witless. Or is it just you?"

Mary ignored Trent's comment.

"Do you really think that by putting yourself in danger you can help Sean?" He sneered. "Well, leave me out of it. I'm not risking my neck."

Tightness and pain rose in Mary's chest and settled at the base of her throat as she fought tears. She let go of the door. Trent was right. It would be foolish. *But how can I do nothing?* Keeping her face turned away from Trent so he wouldn't see her tears, she again puzzled over her feelings for Sean. Why was she reacting so strongly? She didn't want to care. *I can't worry about any of that now,* she told herself. *I need to concentrate on finding a way to help him.*

"Isn't this a pretty picture of eternal love," Trent taunted. "The little wife, willing to put her life in danger for her husband. Ugh. You're a fool." Trent extinguished the light and laid down. "Go back to bed, would ya'. I need my sleep."

With a sigh, Mary went to her bed. There was nothing she could do for now. She might as well try to rest. Fatigue prevailed, and Mary fell into a fitful sleep.

"Hey! Get up, ye lazy sods," someone called.

A cold blast of wind swept through the cabin and Mary pried open her eyes. She sat up. "Sean? Is that you?" The door banged closed.

"It's me all right—cold and hungry."

Joy and relief pulsed through Mary. "Sean!" She sprang out of bed and pulled back the curtain. Her husband stood just inside the door, arms bundled across his chest, his flushed face peering out of an ice-encrusted hood. His rigid frame shook. Mary took a step toward him. "Are you all right?"

Sean's face creased into a smile. "Yes. I'm fine, just cold. The storm let up some, so I took a chance."

Happiness vanquished the last remnants of Mary's reserve, and she ran to Sean, throwing her arms around his neck. "I'm so glad you're all right! I was so afraid." She held him a long time before stepping back. Keeping her hands on his arms, she studied his face. "I knew you'd find a way."

"It wasn't me," Sean said, his hazel eyes bright. "It was God. I prayed and he showed me what to do."

His words shocked Mary, and she felt as if she'd been doused with cold water. "What do you mean, God showed you what to do?" Suddenly feeling too close, she stepped away.

"Well, just that. He saved me. I would have died without him. I was lost in that horrible storm and didn't know what I should do." He grinned and held out his arms, palms up. "God saved me."

"So glad you're back," Trent muttered. "But please stop jabbering on about God." He pushed himself up from his bed on the floor. "I for one am more interested in breakfast. Being stuck inside made it impossible to find any food yesterday, and dinner wasn't much."

"I saved some fish for you," Mary said. "I'll warm it up." She walked to the stove and put the small piece in a pan. "The coffee is hot." She filled a cup and handed it to Sean.

"Thank ye." His hands shaking, Sean put the cup to his

mouth. Coffee splashed over the sides, but he ignored the spillage and drained half of it. Smiling, he said, "That's better."

"You need some warm clothes." Mary stripped off his gloves and hat, then held out her hand. "If you'll give me your coat, I'll hang it up."

"Gladly." Sean handed her the coat.

Mary hung the wet articles on hooks near the door, then grabbed dry pants, a shirt, long underwear, and socks off the clothesline. "I washed these yesterday," she said, handing them to Sean.

"Thanks." With the items pressed against his chest, Sean disappeared behind the curtain. "It will feel good to get into somethin' dry and warm." A few minutes later he emerged, still shivering, but definitely on his way to recovering. "That's much better," he said and sat at the table.

Mary refilled his cup with the weak coffee and set a plate with the fish in front of him. "I wish there were more, but like Trent said, we couldn't get out."

"This will be fine." Sean took a bite.

Mary sat across from Sean and silently watched him eat, wishing there were more fish to quiet her own empty stomach. She chastised herself for thinking about herself before her husband. There would be plenty of time for eating. Now she needed to concentrate on Sean. Finally, she said quietly, "I was afraid . . . afraid you might not come back."

Trent filled a cup with coffee and leaned against the counter. "I thought we'd gotten rid of you."

Sean ignored the comment.

Biting back a retort, Mary said, "Trent, we need wood. Could you please get some?"

"Yeah. I'll get it." Wearing his usual scowl, Trent pulled on his boots, shrugged into his coat, and stomped out of the house.

"What happened to you, Sean?" Mary asked.

"I went out to check one set of traps, but the storm came in fast, and before I knew it, I couldn't see. I headed in the direction I thought the house was, but I got all turned around, and pretty soon I didn't know which way to go. I knew my chances of stumbling across the cabin were almost none, and if I kept wandering about out there, I'd freeze to death." He ate his last bite of fish, chewed it slowly, then drained his cup. "Tasted good, but there wasn't enough of it," he said with a grin. "I'll do some fishin' later today."

His expression turned serious. "I've been readin' me Bible a lot lately, Mary, and it says we can depend on God to help us, that he's always with us. When I realized I was lost, I prayed. Then the idea of makin' a snow cave came to me." He reached across the table and captured Mary's hand under his. "I'll tell ye, I was scared. It was bad." He hesitated. "I didn't think I'd see ye again."

Mary glanced at his hand and was tempted to slide hers out from under his but decided that to do so would be too great an insult, so she did nothing. "I'm glad you're safe."

"I can thank only God for me life. I haven't made a snow house since I was a boy. I was fightin' panic and couldn't think. Again, I asked God for help, and all of a sudden, it came back to me."

Apprehension fell over Mary. When he'd started reading his Bible every day, she'd had qualms, but he'd kept most of what he'd read to himself. But now, he was talking like a . . .

a Christian. And she didn't want to hear it. "Sean, you're not going to get all religious are you?"

"What do ye mean? Just because I believe in God?"

"I've seen this before. People believe God has saved them from some calamity, or they have what they think is a spiritual experience, and they change. They read their Bibles all the time and start spouting off verses that are supposed to help people, and then they insist everyone should have a special encounter with God."

"Mary, it *was* God. When I lost me way, I prayed and he showed me where to go," Sean said gently. "He led me to the proper place to build a shelter, then reminded me how to do it. And once I was bundled up inside, he kept me from freezin'. I know it was him." He squeezed Mary's hand. "I talked to him. I met God last night. Now I understand how me mother felt about him." He looked into Mary's eyes. "I'm not the same as I was."

Mary braced herself for what was coming. She slipped her hand free of his and straightened. "Sean, you're not different. You look the same. You are the same."

He smiled. "I'm not talkin' about the outside. It's the inside that's changed—me heart. It's hard to explain. I feel alive inside. I have this joy bubblin' up in me. I want ye to know what I'm feelin'. I want ye to have it for yerself."

Wishing she could shut out his words, Mary stood, walked to the stove, and refilled her cup. "Sean, this doesn't have anything to do with God. You're just happy to be alive. Anyone would feel the same."

"No. It's more than that. I know God." Pushing his chair back, Sean walked to the shelf and grabbed his Bible. "I've been thinkin' about some of the things I've been readin'. I think

I understand some of it now." He opened the Bible and read silently. His face was alight like that of a young boy's.

"Listen to this: *'Therefore, if any man be in Christ, he is a new Creature: old things are passed away; behold, all things are become new.'*" He sat down. "That's it! I told ye. I'm new!" Sean turned the pages and resumed reading. "Here's somethin' else!"

"No. That's enough." Mary set her cup on the counter. "I don't want to hear any more."

"Just a wee bit more?"

Mary kept her back to him, pressed balled fists down on the counter, and shook her head. "No, Sean. No more."

Sean propelled himself out of his chair and across the room. Taking her arm, he turned her around to face him. "Please give it a chance. It's wonderful! How can ye decide about a thing if ye don't know what it's all about?"

"I do know. I've heard it from my parents for years. And I don't want to hear it from you."

"But, Mary, God has so much for ye."

She held up her hand, palm out. "Please. Stop." She forced a smile. "You need rest."

"But . . ." Sean began. Then his exuberance collapsed, and he said, "All right. I'm sorry. I won't say anythin' more, but please remember the Bible is here if ye want to read it. And if ye ever want to study together . . ."

"Sean . . ."

"All right." Sean offered a smile of surrender. "I'm goin' to bed."

Chapter 16

*W*hile Sean slept, the storm moved on, leaving sunshine and calm, cold air. He awoke to the smell of fish. The cruel winds had ceased and all was quiet. Sean pulled his blankets up under his chin and rolled onto his side. Staring at the wall, his eyes followed the irregular pattern of driftwood. It seemed simply to meander, one piece fitting into the next. He yawned and stretched. His shivering had stopped. *I feel more like meself,* he thought, except for the unusual contentment and peace filling him. He thought over what had happened, his encounter with God and how he'd been saved in the midst of the storm. "Thank ye, Father," he said softly and sat up.

He could hear Mary moving around in the kitchen. He pulled on more clothes and stepped from behind the curtains. He watched Mary flip a piece of fish in the pan, unaware of his perusal. *She's beautiful,* he thought. *I wish she were truly mine, not just in name.*

Mary glanced up. "Oh, I didn't know you were up." She smiled. "You look better." Spooning mussels out of hot water, she placed them on a plate, then added a chunk of fish. "Yesterday while you were sleeping, Trent caught a fish, and I managed to find some mussels." She set the plate on the table. "You need to eat to get your strength back."

Rubbing his stomach, Sean said, "I do feel empty, and that looks good." He nodded to Trent who was already sitting at the table, an empty plate in front of him. Sean sat across from him. Using the tongs of a fork, he dug the meat out of the mussel shell and ate it. "I never thought I'd enjoy mussels so much. They're good."

"This is the third day on the coffee grounds. Do you want some?"

"Sure," he said through a mouthful. Splitting off a piece of fish with his fork, he stuffed it into his mouth. "Even fish tastes good today." He smiled and gazed contentedly out the window. The frosted glass made it difficult to see, but clearly it would be a rare, beautiful day. "It's goin' to be nice. Perfect for skatin'. Do ye like to ice-skate?"

"I used to," Mary said as she set his coffee on the table. "It's been a long time though. I don't think I remember how."

"I never liked skating much. It's a waste of time if ya ask me," Trent said.

"I've been waitin' for a clear day." Sean grinned. "A few weeks back I found a walrus tusk on the beach, and I made two pairs of skates out of it." His grin expanded. "I wanted to surprise ye." He finished off his last mussel and pushed away from the table. "I'll be right back."

Sean disappeared out the door, and a few minutes later returned with a pair of skates dangling from each hand. "They're not fancy, but I think they'll work. The bone is strong, and I sanded it down real smooth, then slicked up the blades with candle wax." He handed a pair to Mary, hoping she would appreciate the gift. "Would ye like to give it a try?"

Mary grinned and nodded. "Yes."

Sean glanced at Trent. "Sorry, but I only made two pair. There wasn't enough bone for more."

Trent smirked. "Suits me fine. Like I said, it's a waste of time." He scooted his chair back and casually crossed the room. Grabbing a totem he'd been working on, he walked to his bedding on the floor, dropped onto it, and leaned against the wall. Taking a knife out of its sheath, he set to work.

"So, ye ready?" Sean asked Mary.

"Are you sure you're feeling up to it?"

"I'm fine. Better than I've ever been."

"You want to go right now?"

"Well, we'd better. There's no tellin' how long the weather will hold. Ye know how it can be."

"I need to finish cleaning in here first."

"All right. I'll go up to the lake and clear away the snow."

Mary smiled. "Skating. It sounds wonderful. It's been too long since I've had any fun."

Sean shoveled and swept snow, gradually clearing a large portion of ice. Occasionally he glanced at the hill, hoping to find Mary making her way to the lake. Instead he found a pale winter sun glistening off the white landscape. The hills looked washed and shimmering. In some way they reminded him of the way the floors at home had looked after his mother had scrubbed and polished them. She'd always taken pride in a tidy house, and a week never passed without a thorough cleaning.

Sean leaned on the broom and considered his home. It had been a good place to grow up. His father had been a strong disciplinarian but had made certain that love and fun were plentiful. Still, it was his mother who'd held the family together. No matter how great the obstacle, she'd face it with confidence and an assurance that God would see them through.

Sean realized how much he missed his parents, and his throat constricted. *Mama would have liked Mary. When we get back to Unalaska, we'll have to make a trip to Seattle,* he decided. *At least Mary can meet me dad. And I need to see him too. It's been too long.*

Mary crested the hill. She stopped and looked down on the lake, then waved and called, "Hello."

Seeing Mary drew Sean back to the present, and feeling like a boy anticipating Christmas, he smiled and waved to her. "Come on. We only have a couple hours before it gets dark." He set the shovel and broom on the bank, then watched her hike down the gradual slope, carefully setting her feet sideways in the snow to keep from slipping. His love for Mary welled up, and like a spring breeze, swept through him. The emotions were almost too powerful to contain. He longed to tell her how he felt, but his mind played the scene for him, and he knew it would only make Mary uncomfortable and spoil the day.

By the time she reached the pond, her cheeks were flushed and she was out of breath. The hair around her face had escaped their pins and softly framed her face. Her smile matched the brightness in her dark eyes. *She's so beautiful,* Sean thought but said as casually as he could, "The ice is ready."

"It's been a long time." Mary studied the frozen lake. "I used to be pretty good, but I don't know if I remember how any more."

"It'll come back to ye. Ye'll see."

"I hope so." Mary sat on a log and examined the skates. "These are nice. You did a good job." She looked at him. "Is there anything you don't know how to do?"

"Lots," Sean said. "If I'd been stuck on this island without ye, I'd be done for. I knew almost nothin' about livin' from what exists around here."

"You'd have done fine," Mary said as she pressed the skate against her boot. She cinched the straps, pulled them tight, and laced them.

Sean did the same, then tentatively stepped onto the ice. His feet slid out from under him almost immediately. He fought to stay upright, but despite his efforts, he landed hard on his backside. Laughing, he said, "It's been a long time for me too." He pushed himself back to his feet, faltered a moment, then steadied himself and held out a hand to Mary.

Skeptically, Mary eyed his hand. "You just fell. How are you going to help me?"

"I'm steady now. I've got me feet. Come on."

Mary still hesitated.

"Come on. I won't let ye fall."

"All right." Mary took his hand and placed one foot on the ice. Setting her other foot beside the first, her skates slipped back and forth while she tottered. She grabbed Sean's other hand. When she regained her balance, she gave him an embarrassed smile. "Maybe I can't skate any more."

"Ye'll get the hang of it. There's nothin' ye can't do. I've seen how determined ye can be." Sean carefully released one of her hands. He pushed off with one foot and led Mary out to the middle of the small lake. Floundering at first, they moved over the frozen water, gradually getting the feel of the skates and ice. Soon they moved more fluidly.

"I think I'm gettin' it!" Sean cried, energy flowing through him. He increased his speed, feeling as if he could actually fly if he tried. Watching Mary's animated smile and bright cheeks, he knew she felt the same.

Mary sped up, let go of Sean's hand, and threw her arms above her head. "This is wonderful! Thank you for thinking of it." Then she crouched low, and swinging her arms from side to side, sped up again. "Catch me!" She called as she hurried over the ice.

"Ye can't outskate me." Sean bent low, pushed hard and fast against the ice, and propelled himself forward. When he caught up to Mary, he grabbed her hand and pulled her along with him. Laughing, they slowed, and Sean placed an arm around Mary's waist. He wanted to pull her closer but was careful to keep a discreet distance between them.

Side by side they glided over the ice. "I've always liked skatin' with a pretty girl," he teased. Mary gazed at him, and for a moment he lost his breath. It was the same look of admiration and affection he'd seen long ago on Jessica Adams's face. For a moment his love for Mary lifted him off the ice, and he spun into a world where he and his wife were truly one.

"Was there a special girl once?" Mary asked, dragging Sean back to reality.

He managed a sidewise grin. "Yes, and she was crazy about me." Wind splashed him with cold as he glided over the frozen water. *Could she love me?* he wondered. He looked down at the small woman. Had he imagined the look? *If only she would love me. She's me wife, but she isn't. God, is it possible for her to love me? Please help her love me.*

Chapter 17

"Yesterday was fun," Mary said as she set her knife blade aside and rubbed her hands.

"When do ye want to go again?" Sean asked.

"Soon. Maybe tomorrow?"

"If the weather holds."

As Mary considered the fun they'd had on the ice, she wished she were skating now rather than fleshing furs. Her hands and back ached. She and Sean had been working for hours, fleshing out the newest hides. Closing her eyes, she rolled her head back, then kneaded her neck muscles with her fingers.

"Ye doin' all right?" Sean asked.

"Yes. Just tired. We've been at this a long time." She smiled. "You've done a good job for Nick. I'm sure he'll be pleased."

"I'd like to take the credit, but it has nothin' to do with me. It's easy pickins here. The fox act as if they want to be

caught. There are so many of them, and it's as if they're linin'
up for the snares. If trappin' were always this easy, a lot more
of us would be doin' it."

"Have you thought about leasing an island of your own
and stocking it? There's obviously good money in it."

"Yeah, I thought about it, but where would we get the
cash to pay the government for the use of an island? Plus, we'd
need extra cash to see us through until the first harvest, and it
costs to hire someone to oversee the fox. I don't have money
for that either. I'd have to do the trappin' meself." He grimaced.
"And I don't much like this work. Killin' and trappin' so many
of them. After a while, it begins to feel unnatural, gruesome."
He ran his hand over the silver blue fur. "They're beautiful animals. It's a shame to be killin' them. It's not like trappin' a few
for personal use."

Mary liked Sean's tender side, and as he spoke, she found
herself drawn to him. Afraid he'd see the affection in her eyes
and misread it, she returned to fleshing. She was fond of Sean
but didn't love him the way he needed her to. She didn't want
him to get the wrong idea.

"I've been thinkin' about maybe doin' more fishin' when
we get back. I could get a bigger boat and really go after it.
There are a lot of fish to be taken, and the cannery is always
needin' more, especially now with the war goin' on and a lot
of the fishermen gone."

"That's a good idea—even if the war is over by the time
we get home."

"I doubt it's over."

"Maybe I can help you. I've done my share of fishing, and
I've always loved the sea."

"Ye do, huh? Seems to me ye were pretty unhappy on our trip out here."

"It wasn't the sea. The boat was small and cramped, and I was leaving my family. And I was going with . . ." Mary stopped. She'd almost told Sean she hated being stuck here with him, but it wasn't true anymore. Over the months she'd grown attached to him.

Although Sean managed a small smile, he was unable to disguise the fresh wound. Gently he said, "Finish what ye were goin' to say."

Mary kept working.

"I think maybe ye need to say somethin'," Sean pressed. "It doesn't work to bottle up our feelin's."

Mary stopped fleshing and looked at Sean. "It was a long time ago. A lot has changed."

Sean nodded encouragement.

"I was with a man . . . you. And I didn't know you real well and . . . it was only going to be the two of us here. . . . I was scared. I'm sorry."

"Why do ye apologize for bein' honest about yer feelin's? I understand." He looked down at the fur. "I didn't then, but I do now. It was wrong for me to bring ye way out here. I should have asked ye first and thought things through more before takin' the job."

"It's all right, Sean. You did what you thought was best and we're surviving. Sometimes I even like it here. If not for Trent, it might be kind of nice, except for being hungry so much of the time." She glanced toward the house, then returned to scraping the fleshy side of the pelt.

"I, too, will be glad not to be hungry one day," Sean said.

After that they labored silently. Mary finished the hide she was working on, then stretched it across a board. Running her hand over the soft fur, she said, "This is a nice pelt. It would make a good ruff for my hood."

"I'll see if I can get Nick to throw it in as a bonus," Sean said with a smile. "Then I'll make ye one."

"You know how to make a ruff?"

"No." Sean grinned. "But I could ask yer mother when we get back."

"By the time we see my mother, I won't need one—not for a while anyway," Mary added with a half smile. She hung the frame on a hook. "I wish the weather would clear long enough so someone could come after us."

"Except for this latest storm, we've had a little more sun and less rain and wind. And there have been some almost warm days."

"Do you think they'll come soon?"

"I doubt they'd chance it yet, but hopefully they won't wait much longer."

Mary sat on a stump. "Soon the birds should begin nesting."

"And that is good?"

"Yes. We can gather their eggs."

"Up on the cliffs?"

"Yes. When I lived in the village, I was allowed to help collect eggs. The first time I was a little scared, but mostly it was fun. Afterwards, we always had a feast, kind of a celebration for the arrival of spring." She clasped a knee between her hands and rocked back slightly. "It isn't hard. The birds lay them right out on the rocks. And they taste good."

"I'll be watchin' the cliffs then." Sean finished off his pelt and removed it from the fleshing board. "Have ye seen Trent?"

"When I came out, he was sitting on the log outside the cabin and whittling. That's about all he does. He's good at it, but I don't like what he makes. I don't understand why he doesn't create something beautiful. All he wants to make are those horrible totems with the beasts on them." She shuddered. "Yesterday he carved a miniature spear and pretended to throw it at me."

"Why don't ye tell me when he torments ye? I'll put a stop to it."

"If I told you every time he did something strange or offensive, there would be no end to the arguments. He'd be angry all the time, and I don't want him mad. He's strange, and he scares me."

Sean set his mouth. "Still, I need to know. Promise me ye'll tell me from now on."

Mary didn't want more conflict, so she said, "All right, I'll tell you." But she knew she wouldn't. In order to keep peace until they were rescued, she'd be quiet about Trent's clandestine abuse. Wanting to talk about something more pleasant, she said, "When we're rescued, the first thing I'm going to do is eat and eat. I'll have some . . ." she laughed. "I almost said fish pie. It used to be my favorite, but I think I've had enough fish for a while." She grimaced, then after a moment's thought, smiled broadly. "I know. I'll have fried chicken with biscuits. And for dessert, blueberry pie."

Sean grinned and joined the game. "Me mother used to make the best Irish stew ye've ever tasted. It's been a long while, but when we get back, I'm gonna make us some. She taught me how when I was a boy. Plus, I'll make some bread and eat it hot out of the oven with lots of butter. I can almost taste it." He grinned. "And I'll eat until I'm stuffed. Then, when I'm already too full, I'm goin' to have a big slab of apple pie with cream drizzled over it."

"My stomach is cramping just thinking about it."

Sean's smile disappeared. "I'm sorry ye're hungry, Mary."

"It's not your fault. You do all you can. You work harder than me or Trent, and you spend more time than anyone in the icy bay gathering mussels and seaweed. I remember when I was picking berries—you kept at it after I was done. And don't forget the rabbit you shot for Christmas dinner. Plus, you spend hours fishing. And besides all that, you gather wood and take care of traplines and the pelts. What more can you do?"

"We wouldn't be in this situation if I'd thought this through before takin' the job." Sean secured the pelt on a stretching board.

"Sean, we just talked about this. Please, I understand why you took the job, and you couldn't have known the weather was going to turn bad. None of this is your fault." Hoping to alleviate more of his guilt, she added, "Anyway, I'm not that hungry. There is food."

"Not enough." Sean's eyes settled on Mary's. "Ye're gettin' thin, and so am I." He turned away and hung the fur on the wall.

Mary couldn't argue with that. She had noticed her clothes were beginning to hang loosely from her small frame. "There are worse things."

Sean leaned against the workbench. "I guess it isn't all bad. I know more about survivin' now. Ye've taught me so much—how to make a snare and where to look for berries in the snow, and I've learned to like mussels, and I don't hate seaweed." He grinned. "But I doubt I'll be eatin' any more of it after we're rescued."

"I promise that when we get back to Unalaska I'll never serve you seaweed again." Mary propped her elbows on her thighs and rested her chin in her hands.

"Sometimes I'm glad to be here. In fact, there have been moments when I've been thoroughly thankful to be here." Sean hesitated, his eyes faltered and moved over the floor before returning to Mary's face. "I'm grateful for the time with ye." He crossed to Mary, taking her hands in his and pulling her to her feet.

Mary felt too close but fought the urge to pull away.

"But I don't think ye feel the same way."

"Sean . . ."

"Wait, let me finish. I've been wantin' to say somethin', but . . . I haven't had the courage." He paused. "I loved ye when I married ye,' and I love ye now even more. It hurts every night lyin' beside ye and not bein' able to reach out and hold ye close. I've been talkin' to God, and he's taken good care of us. He's made sure we haven't starved, and he's kept us sheltered, and he protected me when I was lost in the storm. He even rescued Trent."

"You did that."

"No. I helped, but it was God. And it seems he hears me prayers, except for the one that's most important to me—that ye love me."

Mary felt trapped. How could she respond? She cared deeply for Sean but didn't believe she loved him. How could she tell him what he wanted to hear when she knew it would be a lie? It would only hurt him more in the end. Lying would be worse than the truth. "Sean, you're a good man—kind, honest, and hardworking. I respect you more than any man I've ever known, except for my father." Hope glimmered in Sean's eyes. "But . . ." She stepped closer. "I care for you very much . . . but . . ." Hope became hurt, and it wrenched at Mary, but she had to continue. "I'm glad to be your wife, but I don't have the same feelings you have. I care, but I don't love you. I wish I did, but I can't make myself feel something I don't."

Sean turned away and walked back to the bench. Leaning against it, he said, "It's all right. I knew ye didn't feel the same. I don't expect ye to."

A peculiar chattering began to resonate outside. "What is it?" Mary asked. The noise seemed to come from the sky.

Sean walked to the door and pushed it open. The sound grew louder and more distinct. He stepped outside and looked up. "It's geese! Geese! I need me gun," he said and sprinted for the cabin.

Mary followed. "Isn't it too early for geese?"

"I don't know. Is it?" Sean disappeared inside the house.

"What are you doing?" Trent asked from his place on the bench.

Sean reappeared with his shotgun. "I'm goin' huntin'." He watched the flock sweep toward the lake. "They're goin' to land." Grabbing a pair of snowshoes off a hook, he strapped them on and headed for the lake. "Get the stove good and hot," he called and tramped up the hill.

Sean inched forward on his belly, the coldness of the snow penetrating his coat. When he reached the ridge, he peeked over and looked down on the lake. The soft chatter of geese rose up from the shallow basin. Although still frozen, the lake had become a temporary resting place for the flock. *They won't stay long,* Sean thought, knowing this would be his only chance to shoot one of the big birds.

Cautiously crawling forward, he half burrowed into the snow as he made his way over the crest and moved toward the lake. He kept his breaths shallow and tried to catch the fog from his breathing in the crook of his arm.

Some geese ate grasses hidden beneath the snow along the edge of the lake, others pecked at the ice, and the rest nestled along the shore. Sean sighted in one that was standing on the bank, but he was still too far away. *I need a good shot. As soon as I fire, they'll be in the air. I can't afford to miss.*

The sound of crunching snow came from behind Sean. He turned and saw Trent slushing his way over the top of the hill. *Oh no, he'll scare them.* Sean motioned for him to get down, and Trent immediately dropped onto the snow.

Knowing he had to get his shot before Trent alarmed the flock, Sean quickly crept forward several feet. The cold penetrated his clothes, and he fought off a shiver. He stopped, took a moment to catch his breath, then braced his elbows in the snow. Laying the barrel of his shotgun in his left hand, he pressed the stock against his shoulder and sighted in a large bird, then another. *Maybe if I fire and reload quickly, I can get off two shots before they're gone.* Digging out a second cartridge from his coat pocket, he held it in his hand and aimed the gun. Slowly moving from one bird to the next, he finally set his sights on the largest.

Father, I can't fail. I need yer help to shoot straight, he prayed, then pulled the trigger. He had no time to see if he'd hit the bird as he quickly discharged the empty cartridge, reloaded, and aimed again, picking out another bird in the squawking flock. The geese beat the air with their wings as they scrambled for safety. Sean leveled his sights on one lifting away from the ice and squeezed the trigger. It and another one faltered and fell. By the time he reloaded and aimed again, the birds were too far away. He lowered his gun and watched them disappear.

"Why couldn't you wait for me?" Trent shouted. "You knew I was coming."

"I couldn't wait. Ye were makin' enough noise to wake the dead. They would have been gone by the time ye got into range." Sean pushed himself to his feet. "I know I hit at least two." Feeling euphoric at his luck, he looked at the lake and beyond, and his eyes widened. Instead of two dead birds, he saw four, two on the frozen lake and two more on the bank. "I only took two shots. How can there be four dead geese?"

"You got four with two shots?" Trent repeated dumbly.

Sean tramped down to the lake with Trent following. As he studied the geese, he shook his head in disbelief. "It's not possible." He looked skyward, knowing God was truly his provider. "Thank ye," he said with a laugh, then bent and picked up one of the birds. It was heavy, and as he hefted it, he repeated, "Thank ye!"

Each man carried two birds as they headed back to the cabin. "Mary won't believe this!" Sean said jubilantly. He walked as fast as his snowshoes would allow, eager to see the pleasure and surprise on Mary's face. As he approached the cabin, he called, "Mary! Mary! Look what I've got!"

When Mary stepped out of the cabin, Sean and Trent held

up the game. A smile lit her face, and she raised her hands over head and clapped. "You did it! You did it!"

"We got four!" Sean hollered, then looked at Trent and was surprised to see that even he wore a jubilant smile.

Mary placed her hands together and pressed them against her mouth, then laughed. "I lit the stove."

"I shot four birds with two shots," Sean said as he walked up to Mary.

"How? How did you do that?"

"God. It was God. I only shot twice, but here you see four birds. I have no explanation. I prayed, and . . . here are four geese."

"Well then, thank you, God," Mary said matter-of-factly, as she took one of the birds from Sean.

"I would have shot one if he'd waited for me," Trent whined.

Both Mary and Sean ignored his protest. "Roast goose it is tonight," Sean said.

Mary held up her goose. "Roast goose, thanks to Sean's good aim."

"It wasn't me. I told ye . . ."

"Yeah, yeah, I know. God did it," Trent mumbled.

That night the three sat around the table and feasted on goose. When Sean insisted on saying a prayer of thanks, even Trent didn't complain. And when the young Irishman took Mary's hand during the blessing, she didn't pull away. All agreed they'd never tasted anything as good, and they ate until they were more than full.

Although Trent and Mary didn't believe in miracles, each person who feasted knew a miracle had taken place. They didn't know why or how; they were simply thankful.

Chapter 18

$\mathcal{M}$ary swirled a dishrag over a cup, dipped it into clean rinse water, then set it on the counter to dry. "It's warming up outside," she told Sean. "The snow is beginning to melt. Soon spring will be here and so will our rescuers."

The sound of Sean's chair scraping across the floor told Mary he'd risen from the table, but until she felt his hand on her back, she didn't know he was behind her. His touch sent shivers through her, and she was nearly tempted to lean against his hand, but that was not what she wanted. She couldn't allow herself to fall into an intimate relationship. It would only bring heartache. Instead, she ducked away and whirled around to face him. "What are you doing?"

"Mary, I was watchin' ye work, and I was drawn to ye. I feel close to ye. I would have taken ye into me arms if I thought ye'd not mind. I want us to be more than just cabin mates." He took Mary's hand in his.

She pressed her back against the counter. "Sean, I thought . . . You have your rights . . . but . . ."

"I don't want my 'rights,'" he almost shouted. "I want yer love."

Mary cringed inwardly at her husband's pain. "I'm sorry, Sean. But I don't feel that for you. I don't love you."

"Why? I've been good to ye. We've worked together to make our way here. I thought we were becomin' closer."

"We are."

"What more can I do?"

"Nothing. You've been wonderful, Sean, but I can't create feelings that don't exist."

"Is it Paul? Do ye love him still?"

"No. It's not that." But as Mary said the words, she wasn't at all certain she was telling the truth. She didn't know exactly how she felt about Paul. She knew that once she'd loved him, but now when she thought about him, she felt only a little of the hurt. The wounds were there, but they had changed.

"Ye do still love him," Sean said with disgust.

"I don't know what I feel. Sean, I don't want to hurt you, but I can't turn my feelings off and on whenever I please."

"I've got traplines to check," Sean said abruptly. He walked to the door, grabbed his coat, and tramped out of the house.

Mary watched him go, uneasiness settling over her. How did she feel about him? "I don't know how I feel. I just don't know," she whispered.

"I don't understand women," he muttered. "I've done everything I know to win her over. What more can I do?" Sean's foot slipped on melting snow, and his legs nearly slid out from under him. Clouds hid the sun, but the temperature had warmed enough to begin the melt. Sean replanted his foot and continued up the hill.

As he stepped onto the rise, he saw Trent walking away at a steady gait. It looked as if he were heading for the far side of the island where he'd left his boat. Something about him looked odd. Sean studied the man. "He's carryin' somethin'." He squinted. "What's he up to?" Sean continued to watch him, then realized the load Trent carried was pelts. "He's takin' the furs!" In a half gallop impeded by snowshoes, Sean chased after Trent.

Kicking up snow, Sean gradually closed the distance between himself and Trent. The thief must have heard Sean's pursuit because he turned and looked behind him. Instead of waiting, he hurried his pace.

"Stop!" Sean called.

Trent kept moving.

"Trent! I said stop! Now!" He ignored Sean's command. Sean ran now, kicking up snow with each step. *He's headin' for the boat. He's goin' to take off with the furs.* "Ye'll not get away that easy," he vowed, gulping in air as he continued the chase. His legs felt heavy, picking up snow with each step, but he pushed on, unwilling to slow his pace. "He'll not get away," he vowed.

The weight of the furs slowed Trent. He wouldn't be able to escape. Finally, on a ridge overlooking jagged rocks and white surf, he stopped and faced his pursuer. Trent glared at Sean.

Sean slowed and walked toward Trent.

"You're not getting these," Trent said. "You'd be wise just to go back to the cabin and pretend you never saw me."

"Ye can leave, just not with the furs."

"I didn't take many—just enough to see me through. You owe these to me."

"Owe ye? Why?"

"I've worked with you and Mary all this winter. I . . . I fished for you and helped flesh furs."

"Ye did very little except eat our food, gripe about anything and everything, and whittle. Oh, ye did a bit of fishin', but rarely. And what work ye did with the pelts, ye did for yerself." He kicked out of the snowshoes and took a step toward Trent. "I owe ye nothin'."

"I'm going."

"Ye're welcome to go your way, but leave the furs."

Trent balled his free hand into a fist. "It would give me real pleasure to kill you," he said with a sneer as he lowered the bundle of furs to the ground. Without warning, he lunged at Sean, managing to plant his fist against Sean's jaw.

Sean staggered backward but quickly found his feet and retaliated with a blow of his own.

Trent charged Sean with a bellow, first punching him under the chin, then slamming his body into the smaller man's and pummeling him in the abdomen.

Sean fought to maintain consciousness as darkness closed in around him. He struggled to keep his feet and blinked hard, trying to clear his vision. Sucking in air, he shoved Trent away. Once more clearheaded, he raised his fists and moved in on the younger man, managing to land several short punches to Trent's jaw and stomach.

Bloodied now, Trent pushed against Sean. "You'll pay," he said through gritted teeth. "You'll wish you'd never known me." He hurled several wild punches, his rage overriding reason.

Sean managed to duck the blows, but Trent was relentless, and his fist finally found its mark, grinding itself against Sean's cheek. Sean pitched backwards. Knowing the ledge was close, he glanced back. Less than a foot of ground separated him from the rim. Spiked rocks and untamed breakers waited below. Sean sidestepped, hoping to get around Trent, but the larger man blocked his path.

Sneering, Trent asked, "You afraid of a little water? Seems to me you could use a bath." He straightened. "You sure you want to fight me for the furs?"

"I don't want to fight ye over anythin'," Sean said, "But I'll do what I have to do to keep those furs. They'll be here for Nick when he picks us up."

"You think so?" Trent laughed. "You're such a fool. I could have killed you any time I wanted, then taken the furs and your wife, but I didn't. And now you refuse to be reasonable. Well, don't say I didn't warn you," he hurled himself at Sean, swinging his left fist at Sean's face.

Sean ducked and drove his fist under Trent's jaw. The younger man's head snapped back, and he stumbled, falling to the ground.

Hatred and profanity spewed from Trent. Empowered by his fury, he catapulted himself toward Sean, and with his head down, he grabbed him around the waist. "You won't win this one, you filthy immigrant."

Sean brought a knee up and slammed Trent in the groin.

Trent staggered backwards.

"Ye may be bigger and younger, but ye won't undo me so easily," Sean taunted. "I've had me share of fights. Come on, then." He crouched slightly and took a step backwards.

Trent came after him, throwing punches. His fist connected with the side of Sean's head. Sean took another step back. Trent hit him again.

His adrenaline pumping, Sean forgot about the bluff behind him, and as he prepared for the next assault, he stepped off the ledge. He faltered for a moment, trying to throw himself forward, but it was too late and he fell. Grabbing at grass and earth, Sean tumbled down toward the breakers and rocks. He did his best to propel himself beyond the rocks, but as he hit the water, his head struck a jagged boulder lurking beneath the waves, and the world went black.

Mary didn't know why she'd followed Sean, except that she was compelled to do so. Something outside herself drove her to trail him. When she came upon the fight, she watched in horror. *I have to stop them. Someone is going to be killed,* she thought. She yelled at them to stop, but they didn't hear. She grabbed Trent's arm, but he simply shoved her aside like a rag doll. There was nothing Mary could do. Feeling sick inside and helpless, she watched. When she realized Sean was stepping closer and closer to the ledge, she screamed, "Sean, watch out!" He didn't hear. As he stepped off and tumbled backwards, it seemed to happen in slow motion. Then he was gone.

Her mind shrieking its fear and rage, Mary ran to the cliff and peered down. A wave picked up Sean and sent him crashing against the rocks. He didn't struggle. He looked limp and dead. "Oh, dear God!" She turned to Trent. "Do something! Help him!"

Trent leaned out and gazed down into the water. "He got himself into this. I'm not going down there. It's too late anyway."

"Trent Parker, help him! How can you stand here and do nothing? He saved your life once."

Trent merely gazed at the waves carrying Sean away from the rocks, then said slowly, "I'm not so stupid. A man has to take care of himself."

Knowing she was Sean's only hope, Mary yelled, "May the gods curse you!" Then she started down the embankment.

Trent merely grinned. "You seem to have everything in hand. He's your husband; you save him."

For months Mary had tried to convince herself that Trent wasn't as bad as she'd feared, but now she knew he was evil. There was nothing good in him. She looked down at the sea. Sean was still very close to the rocks. "I'm coming. Please hang on," she said as she scrambled over tufts of grass and boulders. "I can't lose you. I need you."

When she reached the rocks, she unlaced her boots and tossed them against the bank, then shrugged out of her coat, and ran into the water. The cold hit her, feeling as if a hundred icy fists were hitting her body. For a moment she was unable to breathe, and her arms and legs wouldn't obey. Gulping air, she fought to maintain her footing. The waves were carrying Sean away from the shore. Ignoring her own welfare and the painful cold, she plunged into the surf and swam toward him. At any moment she expected her heart to stop from the shock of the freezing water, but she continued to dive through the waves. Her arms and legs began to lose feeling, and she knew she needed to hurry or they would both die. *Don't die,* she thought as she paddled.

When she reached Sean, he felt incredibly cold. She grabbed the back of his coat, but it began to strip away from his body. Struggling to keep herself afloat, she got a hold of his shirt collar and rolled him onto his back. His lips were blue, his face white. "Sean! Sean!" Mary screamed. There was no response. Her own body stiffening, she turned for shore. *Please don't die, please don't die,* she repeated as she swam.

When her feet touched sandy ground, she barely had the strength to stand, but she managed to summon enough energy to keep moving and dragged herself and Sean ashore. She lay on the sand beside his body for a moment, gasping for breath and unable to move. Then she opened her eyes and gazed at him. He wasn't breathing. He looked dead.

Mary sat up. "No, Sean!" she yelled. "You have to live!" She forced herself to her knees and pressed two fingers against his throat. His heart beat, but weakly. She rested her hand on his chest and put her cheek against his mouth. There was no breath. "What do I do?" she cried. "What do I do? Somebody help me!" But there was no one.

Taking a deep breath, she rolled Sean onto his side and pummeled his back, hoping to dislodge any water. "Breathe! Breathe!"

There was no change.

Mary searched her mind for the right thing to do. She didn't know. Closing her eyes, she prayed, "God, I need you. Sean needs you. He believes in you. Please save him." She threw herself across his upper body and wept.

Unexpectedly, Sean coughed. He coughed again and again as water cleared from his lungs. Mary sat back on her heels. "Sean? Sean?"

For several moments, he gulped down air. Finally he opened his eyes, rolled onto his back, and looked at Mary.

She draped herself across his chest, wrapping her arms about him. "Oh, Sean. I thought you were dead."

He laid a weak arm over Mary's back. "No. I'm here." Shivering hard, he coughed. "Me chest hurts."

Shaking with the cold, Mary said, "We've got to get into dry clothes and get warm. Do you think you can stand?"

Sean nodded and sat up slowly. Mary helped him to his feet, and with his arm draped across her shoulder, the two hobbled toward the cabin. Mary watched for Trent. Where had he gone? What would he do now?

At the house, Mary handed Sean dry clothes, then added wood to the fire while he dressed. "Try to drink some of this," she said, offering him coffee.

"Thanks," he said, sitting at the table and taking the drink. He sipped the hot brew, then coughed. "It will take some time to clear me lungs."

Mary dipped a cloth in water and wrung it out. "You're pretty beat up," she said as she crossed over to him. She dabbed at a cut on his cheek. Sean winced. "What was the fight about?" she asked, probing his head where it had hit the rocks.

"Oh, that's sore," Sean said as he sucked air through his teeth. "Trent was stealin' furs. He was headin' for his boat, and I think he was goin' to leave."

"Leave? That would be suicide. The weather can change in an instant."

Sean nodded. "He's never been one for clear thinkin'." His eyes traveled over Mary. "Ye better get changed. Yer soaked too."

Mary finished doctoring Sean, then stepped behind the curtain and stripped off her wet clothes, exchanging them for dry.

"I've got to lie down. Can I come in?" Sean asked.

"Yes." Mary pulled the drapery back.

Laying his rifle on the floor beside him, Sean climbed into their bed.

Mary laid beside him and pulled the blankets up tight about them. "Maybe we can warm each other up," she said, cuddling against him.

Sean smiled weakly. "Thank ye for savin' me life," he said in a whisper, then closed his eyes. Immediately he fell asleep.

"I had no choice," Mary whispered, "because I do love you."

Chapter 19

*T*he door banged shut, and Mary sat up, startled out of sleep. Sean didn't stir. *Trent must be back,* she thought. Barely breathing, she listened for him.

The sound of shuffling feet and something crashing to the floor sent a bolt through Mary that made her jerk. Then she heard an explosion of profanity from Trent followed by another crashing sound. Mary thought he must have kicked whatever he'd tripped over, probably a chair.

Abruptly, it turned quiet again. Mary pulled back the curtain a little and strained to see through inky blackness. *Where is he?* Nerves on edge, she shuddered. *Did he have a gun, or worse, his knife?* A glass shattered in the sink, sending her pulse leaping. Trent let loose with another string of cursing. *I wish he'd just left with the furs,* Mary thought. *He's vicious and has no conscience. He could do anything. Even murder.* As the thought seized her, Mary glanced at Sean in the darkness and wished he would wake up.

She recognized the sound of a match scraping across the stove top. A light glowed. Fear turned to anger as she realized he was making himself at home. *What? He thinks he can just walk back in here as if nothing happened? Sean nearly died because of him!* Rage burned within her, and she considered all she'd like to say to the self-serving coward. *I will tell him,* she decided and stood, taking a blanket with her. She pulled it around her shoulders and stepped out from behind the curtain.

For a long moment, she stood and silently watched Trent rifle through his bag. When he looked up, their eyes met. Mary hoped he saw only wrath and revulsion and not the fear that prickled up her back as his cruel eyes bored into her. He half grinned and purposely moved his hand to the rifle resting against the wall beside him. Anger overriding terror, Mary barely glanced at the weapon and boldly asked, "What are you doing here? How dare you come into this house after what you did!"

"What I did? I'm not the one who started the fight."

"You were stealing. Sean told me what happened. He was only trying to stop you."

"I took a few furs. That friend of yours, uh, Nick, he wouldn't have missed them. Sean's a fool."

"You would have let him drown." Mary gripped the edges of the blanket. "I want you out of this house. Until we leave this island, you'll sleep in the shed."

Cold eyes penetrated Mary's. "I'll sleep where I want." Trent hefted the rifle and held it in both hands. He lifted it to his shoulder and lined up the sights on Mary. "You know, I could shoot you if I wanted. Right here, right now." His mouth set in a hard line.

Determined not to show fear, Mary glared at Trent.

He let the gun fall slightly. "Of course, I don't have to kill you. I could just shoot off a leg."

"Ye won't be doin' no such thing." His rifle aimed at Trent's head, Sean stepped out into the room.

Trent raised a hand in the air and let his weapon fall until it pointed at the floor. "Whoa. Put your rifle down. I wasn't going to shoot her. I was only fooling around."

"That's not what I'd call it." Sean glanced at Mary, then returned to staring at Trent. "Ye have a lot of nerve comin' here after what happened today."

"Nothing happened. We had a fight. . . ."

"Ye were takin' off with furs that didn't belong to ye, and . . ."

"And we had a fight. It isn't the first time men have settled differences with their fists. And it won't be the last."

"You were going to let him drown," Mary charged.

"You didn't need me. I knew you could take care of him. And you did."

"These last months we've given ye the benefit of the doubt," Sean said. "We've been patient and more than fair, but no more. Ye're not welcome here any longer. The weather's warmed up enough. Ye can sleep in the shed from now on. I want all yer stuff out."

Trent glared at Sean, his eyes hot with hatred. "I'll go, but . . ." He stopped and weighed his words. "You need to know that making me mad isn't always a wise thing to do. You should talk to the last man who annoyed me." His malicious smile reappeared. "But you can't. You see, he's dead." Trent's voice was empty, like a grave waiting for a body.

Horror coursed through Mary, and she fought a wave of nausea.

Keeping his rifle aimed at Trent, Sean remained cool. "That's a shame. I'd like to have had a chance to talk with him. I'm sure he'd have had a lot to say."

Trent walked over to the shelf nonchalantly. Taking down one of his totems, he studied the carving and ran a finger over the smooth figure of a grotesque beast. "I'll take my work with me," he said stiffly. He gathered up the rest of his totems, picked up his bedding and bag, and opened the door. "I'm not really out," he said, tipping his hat to Mary.

After the door closed, Mary and Sean watched it for a long moment. Finally Sean walked across the room and made certain it was latched. "I'll put a lock on this tomorrow."

"That won't keep him away from us. We have to go out-doors." Taking a deep breath, Mary blew it out hard. "He won't leave us alone. I'm scared. I think he's crazy."

Sean crossed to Mary and rested a hand on her shoulder. "Ye don't need to be afraid. Trent's just a lot of talk. It gives him some kind of thrill to scare us. I don't think he'll do anything."

"I don't know," Mary said shaking her head. "Yesterday, when you fell into the water, he watched you, and I could tell he truly didn't care what happened to you. You were uncon-scious and would have died. I know he would have let you drown. He's more dangerous than you think."

Sean stared at the door. His voice grave, he said, "He could have shot ye, but he didn't." He placed an arm around

Mary's shoulders. "Let's not think any more about it tonight. We need sleep."

Sean and Mary returned to bed. The night was filled with demons, and they lay awake.

Mary listened to every creak and groan, afraid Trent would return. She thought about Sean and her earlier rush of feelings for him. She tried to explain away the emotions as nothing more than relief that he hadn't drowned. Remembering her profession of love, she hoped Sean hadn't heard. She wasn't at all sure what she felt, but knew she didn't want to love him. Loving was too complicated. *Things are just fine between Sean and me the way they are,* she told herself. *We don't need passion.*

Sean stared at the ceiling, arms folded beneath his head. He worried about how he would protect Mary. He knew Trent was dangerous. *I'll have to keep a better eye out for him,* he decided, trying to figure out how to do that without alarming Mary more than she already was. He glanced at her in the dark. Her breathing was irregular, and he knew she lay awake too. *I wish she would love me,* he thought and closed his eyes.

Morning light came with gratitude, and Mary rose early. She made a breakfast of fish and weak coffee, then roused Sean. After eating their meager meal, Mary cleared away the dishes. She did her best to maintain a routine conversation. "With the weather changing, the birds will be laying soon. It will be good to have something else to eat." She offered Sean a smile. "I'll be glad to climb out on the rocks if it means I can return with eggs. We'll have a feast." She chuckled. "My mother would be amazed to hear me now. During the spring months, she always used to scold me for complaining about eating too many eggs."

"How about some crab?" Sean lifted an eyebrow. "The weather is good, and the waters might have warmed up some. We can use Trent's boat."

"Crab would be wonderful!"

"We have plenty of bait," Sean said. "I've been saving fish heads."

"Trent won't like us using his boat."

"Maybe a little crabmeat will quiet him." Sean grabbed his coat off its hook. "Let's go. It'll feel good to get out on the water again."

Mary left the cabin, her step light. The idea of being out on the bay and feasting on crab afterward lifted her mood. She'd felt panicked when she rose that morning, remembering Trent would still be on the island with them for several days, maybe weeks. How could she live with his threats? It seemed too much to bear.

Carrying two nets and a bag of fish heads, Sean and Mary walked to the other side of the island. The melting snow was slippery and forced them to place their feet carefully. Mary wished they could walk faster. She was anxious to begin crabbing; plus she was certain that Trent was watching them. She scanned the hills many times but didn't see him.

When they reached the boat, Sean and Mary dragged it to the water's edge and floated it. Mary climbed in and settled on the front seat while Sean pushed the dory into deeper water. He jumped in, sitting on the middle seat and dipping the oars into the surf. Shaking his head, he said, "It's hard to imagine a lone man making a trip all the way out here in this, especially an outsider."

"He's either crazy or very determined, or both."

"I'd say very greedy," Sean corrected. "Greed can do awful things to people." Sean pulled hard on the oars and propelled them away from the shore. "I hope the crabs are hungry. I know I am."

"They will be. We'll catch all we want," Mary said with more confidence than she felt.

As they moved into the bay, Sean and Mary couldn't help but scan the hillsides and cliffs looking for Trent. They saw only cliffs and rolling hills with brown blemishes in the white blanket.

When Sean thought he'd gone far enough, he let the oars rest in their metal rings while he set a fish head in the bottom of a net. As he lowered the weighted trap into the water, he said, "We'll set out the next one over there by the rocks, then come back to check this one." Once the net was on the bay's floor, he rowed to the rocks and dropped the second.

"Sean, isn't it possible to take the boat and head for Unalaska? The weather is better now and we've got food we can take."

"We could try . . . but if we stay, we're not going to starve or end up on the bottom of the ocean." Leaning on the oars, he stared at the island. "And I wouldn't want to spend all that time in close quarters with Trent. I don't trust him. But as much as I detest him, I wouldn't feel right leavin' him. His eyes roamed over the shore. "It looks cold and barren from here. Hopefully the sun will stay out and before too many more days it'll turn green."

"It will happen soon." Mary watched seabirds circle craggy cliffs on the far end of the island. "I'm waiting for the eggs," she said with a grin.

"Eggs are good, but I've got me mouth set on crab. It's been a long, cold winter and . . ." Sean stopped and stared hard at a distant rise. His voice tight, he said, "Trent. He's watchin' us."

Mary's heart pulsed, and she looked in the direction Sean stared. A tall thin figure stood like an apparition. Trent had his rifle resting across his chest. Slowly he lowered the gun. Mary's nerves prickled, and she held her breath. He pressed the rifle against his shoulder and pointed the barrel straight at Sean and Mary.

"Get down!" Sean yelled, pulling Mary to the bottom of the boat with him. They waited, but there were no shots. Sean peeked over the edge of the boat, then straightened. "He's gone."

"What do you think he was doing?"

An uncharacteristic sneer crossed Sean's face. "He's tryin' to scare us. It's his form of amusement."

A black fin moved through the water. Another merged with the first, and the two headed straight toward the boat.

"Orcas," Mary said pointing at the whales as another fin appeared and banded with the first two.

Sean stiffened, and with an edge to his voice he said, "They're heading straight for us."

"I've never seen them attack a boat. I'm sure we're safe." Another fin appeared. "There's a whole pod of them. At least four, probably more."

The whales charged swiftly through the water, creating small wakes as they swam past the boat. Circling the dory, they headed for it, then veered off.

"What are they doin'?"

"They're curious," Mary said.

The whales swam closer and closer. With each pass they appeared more aggressive. One animal bumped the boat, then another hit it hard enough to rock them. Mary and Sean grabbed hold of the sides.

"I don't like this," Sean said.

"I don't know what they're doing. I've never heard of them actually attacking a boat." Mary's voice had a purposeful calm quality. "Sit very still. They'll probably get bored with us and leave."

Careful to keep his hands inside, Sean sat silent while the black Orcas squealed and chirped. They cut through the water, circled, and rammed the dory. Finally, seeming to tire of the sport, the whales abandoned their assault and headed back to sea.

"I'm glad to see them go," Sean said with a relieved smile and a big breath. "I was beginnin' to worry they'd sink us."

"Their behavior was odd. I've heard native stories about angry whales who avenge the deaths of their brothers, but I always thought they were just legends."

Sean dipped the oars into the water. "We'll be gone before they come back. Let's check the nets, then go in." Rowing hard, he steered them to the nearest float. Pulling on the rope, he said, "It's heavy. That's a good sign."

The net broke the surface, and sea water spilled out while crabs scrambled in search of freedom. Sean hauled them into the boat. "Would ye look at this! It's a feast we'll be havin' tonight. It might even calm Trent's nerves. Just like the story in the Bible. Some fishermen were fishin' but didn't catch anythin'. When God told them where to throw their nets, they did as he said and the nets came up full. God blessed them just like he's blessing us now."

Mary said nothing. She didn't want to get into a religious discussion.

Sean dropped the crabs into a bucket, set the net in the bottom of the boat, and rowed to the next float. It had only two crabs, but added with the others, they would truly have a feast.

"I must say, I hate to share with Trent," Sean quipped.

Mary studied their haul. "He didn't help catch them." She looked at Sean. "I guess we can't exclude him. Besides, if we don't feed him, he might shoot us," she added with a laugh, but her try at humor only fell flat. It was too close to the truth to be funny.

Chapter 20

*A*ngry murres and kittiwakes bombarded Mary as she crawled onto the ledge. Their screeches and squawks grated, but they were worth tolerating for the prize Mary would receive for her efforts. She glanced at the white spray hurtling itself over the rocks far below. Momentarily dizzied by the height, she huddled against the cliff face. *You're not going to fall. Think about the eggs,* she told herself.

Leaning against the flat stone, she felt her body relax and closed her eyes. She remembered how it had been when she was young. She could almost hear her mother's encouraging words as she'd guided her daughter onto the cliffs. Mary had been afraid then, too, but with reassurance and urging from her mother and her mother's friend, Polly, she'd found the boldness of the young. She'd hunted eggs, feeling honored to be included with the other gatherers. Brisk wind whipped Mary's hair about her face and carried the pungent odor of seaweed and sand.

She smiled, feeling exhilarated rather than frightened. Now, as it had when she was a child, it had taken time to adjust to the uncompromising environment of the cliffs, but once gaining confidence, she relished egg gathering. It was an adventure—one that held the reward of a luscious egg feast.

Ignoring the birds, she moved on. While considering how odd it was that Murres laid and hatched their eggs on unprotected ledges, she grabbed a pear-shaped egg lying on flat stones. Stuffing it into her bag, she crawled forward, her eye already on another.

Mary collected several dozen before deciding to return to the cabin. Taking more would be greedy, and she left the rest to their parents. Maybe in a few days, she'd return with Sean to gather more. It would be fun to share this with him.

The weight of her bag gave Mary confidence and a sense of satisfaction as she cautiously climbed down the craggy rocks. Although she'd stuffed dried grass into the bag to cushion the eggs, she had to move carefully to make certain none were damaged. When her feet settled on soil again, she looked up at where she'd been. *It will be good to come back,* she thought with a bit of melancholy. If she needed to return for more eggs, it would mean no one had rescued them. Hoping to sight a boat, her eyes searched the ocean to the horizon. She saw nothing but shimmering waves and seabirds.

Mary turned and headed toward home. As always, she scanned the landscape searching for Trent. She didn't see him. He'd kept his distance since the horrifying day when he and

Sean had fought, and Mary had relaxed a little. If he were going to hurt anyone again, he'd have done it by now.

Keeping a casual pace, she looked at newly sprouting grasses, stopping more than once to stoop and study a sprout, hoping to find budding flowers. But it was still too early. *Soon,* she thought. *Soon.*

As she moved further inland, the winds became soft breezes and the sun warmed her. Mary wanted to run but dared not for fear of breaking her precious cargo. She imagined Sean's pleasure when he saw the eggs and his delight in eating them. She didn't stop to consider why she felt such satisfaction at the idea of pleasing him. Her attachment to Sean had grown so gradually and casually that she was almost unaware of it. All Mary knew was that she looked forward to Sean's company and that his happiness gave her satisfaction. Of course, that's what she would expect between friends.

Hidden beneath her reserved exterior lay the reality of what she felt for her husband. It waited to be ignited and she could ignore it only so long. One day she would be forced to face the truth. Then she would have to decide if Paul's betrayal would keep her from loving Sean. Would she be able to grab hold of the joy awaiting her?

Mary stepped inside the cabin and hefted the duffel bag. "Guess what I've got?"

Sean looked up from where he sat at the table, his rifle parts scattered about and waiting to be cleaned. He smiled. "I s'pose I've got to play the game or never know?"

"That's right," Mary said, setting the bag on the counter and facing him.

"Hmm. As I recall, ye were goin' to the cliffs. There wouldn't be any eggs in that bag, now would there?"

"There would be," Mary said proudly and untied the band on the satchel and reached inside. Pulling out two eggs, she held them up. "They're going to taste wonderful." She transferred all the eggs into a large bowl. Wearing a smug smile, she set it on the table.

"Ye were busy this mornin'," Sean said. "There's enough here for several days."

"I hope there are enough to last until we're rescued."

"I worried about ye bein' out there on yer own. I almost came lookin' for ye. It could be dangerous."

"Yes, but I know how to climb the rocks."

"Well, ye should have let me go with ye."

"Next time. I would like to show you. But this time I needed to go on my own. It felt good. Almost like when I was a girl." A sad smile settled on Mary's lips. "I miss home."

"I know. Someone will soon come for us. The weather is getting better every day."

"Yes, but it's still unsettled. One day it's nice and the next there's another storm. And spring storms can be wild. It isn't safe for anyone to come yet."

"Try not to get discouraged. It will happen."

"I know you're right, but I've never been very patient." She smiled and folded her arms over her chest. "I'm hungry. Would you like to sample these?"

"The sooner the better."

Taking a pan from the shelf, she placed it on the stove and spooned out a scant amount of grease. Dropping it into the skillet, she said, "The lard is nearly gone." She watched as it melted and slid across the pan. "Have you seen Trent?"

"When I went out to the shed a while ago, he was

whittling and scowling as usual. He's bidin' his time. He'll be gone first chance he gets."

"Good riddance. I wish he'd already left. Why do you think he's stayed this long?"

"Maybe common sense has gotten a hold of him. He'd be foolish to take off in that small boat with the weather so skittish and with help comin' soon."

"I hope that's all it is," Mary said, the familiar apprehension setting in. What if he were waiting for a chance to hurt either Sean or herself? *That's enough, Mary. That kind of thinking will get you nowhere,* she told herself as she washed six eggs and cracked them into the pan. Scrambling them with a fork, she said, "I suppose we'll have to share these with him."

Sean smiled. "I s'pose." He eyed the eggs. "They smell good. I'm starvin' and I can hardly wait to taste them." He reassembled his rifle and scooted away from the table. "I'll call Trent."

Knowing Trent would be sharing in her harvest displaced some of Mary's pleasure at cooking the eggs. She'd rather never see Trent again. He did nothing for her except stir up fear.

Sean stepped outside and hollered for Trent, then returned to the kitchen. Standing very close to Mary, he watched her cook. "I sure wish we had some flour so we could make bread. Toast would taste good with these."

With a half smile, Mary said, "Eggs will have to do for now. I'll make bread our first day back in Unalaska." She looked into Sean's gentle eyes, and a longing to do something special for him welled up. Without thinking, she reached out and caressed his cheek. "When we get home, I'll make your favorite meal. What is it?"

Sean covered her hand with his. For a long moment he said nothing. Then, with his voice quaking slightly, he said, "Me mother used to make an Irish stew. I'd be proud if ye were to make me some." Taking her hand, he pressed his lips to her fingers.

Mary could feel her face flush, and a fluttering sensation unsettled her stomach. *What am I doing?* She stepped back. She hadn't meant to become so familiar. Her voice purposely calm, she said, "I'll need my hand if I'm going to cook." She gently removed her fingers and turned back to her work.

Sean walked to the window and stared out. "I'll be glad to get home. This has been a long winter." He sighed.

The door flew open and Mary jumped. Slamming the door, Trent walked in.

"Do ye have to come into a room that way?"

Ignoring the comment, Trent said, "You called me. What do you want?"

Mary held out the pan. "We thought you might like some eggs."

Trent gazed at the food and a smile appeared, which he quickly hid. "So, you've decided to share with me?" He pushed his hands into his pockets and leaned against the wall.

"We've never withheld anything from you. You've always eaten what we have." Mary turned back to the stove. "Even if you don't deserve it," she added under her breath.

"What?" Trent demanded. When Mary didn't answer, he said, "Tell me what you said."

"I said, they're ready." Mary spooned the delicacy onto three plates. She set one in front of Sean and another at the end of the table and took the last for herself, then sat across from

Sean. She watched as he took a bite. Just as she had imagined, he smiled and nodded, then took another bite. Mary scooped up a spoonful and put it in her mouth. It was hot and rich. She chewed slowly, relishing the hearty flavor.

Sulking, Trent sat down, and without a word shoveled eggs into his mouth. A few moments later, his dish was empty. Without a word of thanks, he left the house.

Mary stared at the door. "Why does he have to be like that?"

"Don't let him bother ye. He's not right in the head. He's angry, and anger shuts out everythin' else."

"I don't understand him. What makes him so angry and rude?"

"He hasn't forgiven his parents or the people who turned their backs on him, for one. As to the rest, I don't know. But anger will rob him of joy. It's sad. God wants so much more for him."

"You think so? Someone like him?"

"Yes. Even someone like Trent. God loves everyone. He wants us to know he loves us and that we can have peace and joy."

The idea that someone like Trent was loved by God unsettled Mary. She wasn't at all sure she believed Sean. She speared another bite. "These are good. They don't taste like chicken eggs, but they're good. I think I might like them better."

"Oh, I don't know about that. I'm a bit partial to chicken eggs."

———————————

After eating, Mary and Sean sat on the driftwood log out-side the cabin door. "I need to put the eggs in the shed," Mary said. "They'll keep better in the cool air."

"Not just yet. Just sit a while," Sean said.

Mary leaned her back against the cabin. "All right."

A breeze blew, and fragments of beach sand lifted into the air. Mary watched as the tiny granules settled on the new grasses. "I love spring. It always smells of growing things. When I walked back from the cliffs today, I looked for flowers, but there aren't any—not yet, anyway. I can hardly wait for them." She looked around. "In another few weeks the grass will be shoulder deep."

"We'll be gone before then," Sean said. "And I'll be glad to go. Although when I think on it a bit, I've got to admit to being a little attached to this island."

Mary sighed. "Me too." She leaned her elbows on her thighs and rested her face in her hands. "I like it here, but the island is so small; there's not much exploring to be done."

Something crackled in the brush and the grass trembled. Sean pressed a finger to his lips and leaned forward as he watched the spot at the edge of the clearing. A twitching black nose appeared, then a snout, and finally the face of a fox parted the grass. Its small pointed ears turned forward.

"This week, she's visited a couple of times already," Sean whispered.

Her ears sharp and turned forward, the small fox crept forward, her belly low to the ground. She took a few steps, then stopped and sniffed, her tail twitching. Then she turned and disappeared into the grass.

"Why do you think she's coming here?" Mary asked.

"Can't say exactly, but I did set out a fish head after her first visit, and it disappeared."

Over the next several days, the fox returned again and again. Each time Sean set out a fish head or an occasional egg, she would sneak into the clearing, snatch the morsel, and disappear. Her visits became the highlight of each day. As the days passed, she became a little less nervous and a bit braver, until one day she actually approached Sean. She came within a few feet, and although he extended a treat to her, she wouldn't accept it from his hand until he set it on the ground. This occurrence became a daily routine.

On one such visit, Sean said quietly, "Ye know, I think she's got a litter about. She has milk." He grabbed an egg. "Maybe she'll take it out of me hand today."

"She'll never do that."

"Oh, I don't know. I think she trusts me." Sean stepped cautiously toward the fox and knelt in the wet dirt. At first she darted away, then with her tail between her legs, she stepped toward Sean. Sniffing the air, she edged forward.

"Come on, girl. I've got an egg for ye," Sean said softly, extending his arm further and keeping his palm completely flat, the egg in the center of his hand.

Transfixed, Mary held her breath. She was as much mesmerized by Sean's tenderness and gentleness as she was captivated by the fox and waited to see if the animal would take the food from Sean's hand.

Her eyes fixed on the egg, the animal stepped closer. When she was less than a foot away, she jumped back but didn't run, then inched toward Sean again.

"I won't hurt ye none," Sean said, his voice quiet and kind. The fox sniffed Sean's hand. "Come on," he encouraged.

She nudged the egg with her nose, then swiftly grabbed it between her teeth and darted away. She stopped several paces from Sean, broke the egg, and licked up the slimy insides.

"Amazing!" Sean said. Beaming, he looked at Mary. "I told ye."

"I can't believe it."

A couple days later the fox returned, and this time she brought her kits.

"Will ye look at that," Sean said. "She's brought her family along." He shook his head. "I would never believe this if I weren't seein' it for meself."

The kits stayed at the edge of the grass and watched as their mother grabbed an egg and quickly devoured it.

Sean held out another. The fox approached cautiously, one pup following close behind. *He is so cute,* Mary thought, wishing she could scoop up the tiny fox and cuddle it against her. The mother grabbed the egg, carried it back to her litter, and broke it open. She stood back while the kits pounced upon the meal, whimpering their delight and beating the air with their tails. Sean offered another, saying, "Good thing there are a lot more of these." This time, the mother fox ate some of the egg before the pups got their share.

A sudden blast shattered the air and a kit squealed, then bounced into the air, its body destroyed. The mother and other kits scrambled for the protection of the grasses. Before they disappeared, another shot reverberated and, with a yelp, another pup died.

Stunned, Mary looked in the direction the blast had come. Trent stood at the edge of the clearing, rifle still resting on his shoulder. "You animal!" she screamed and ran at him.

Sean grabbed Mary and held her against him. He whispered, "Hush. Don't give him a reason to shoot ye too."

Mary stopped struggling, but her insides churned, and she couldn't keep her words to herself. "How could you? How could you? What kind of monster are you?" Mary said crying. "They were innocent little animals who never did a thing to you. They trusted us. Why?"

"What do you care? Your husband kills them for a living."

Mary felt as if she'd been slapped. She didn't know what to say. Finally, she answered lamely, "Sean only does what he has to do. He doesn't kill for pleasure. There's a reason he does what he does."

"They're only dumb animals. I don't have to have a reason," Trent said. His gun slung over his shoulder, he turned and walked away.

Chapter 21

*W*hat is wrong with him? What kind of man is he?" Her hands balled into tight fists, Mary paced. "I hate him! I hate him!" Against her will, her eyes wandered to the two dead kits. Only moments before they'd been curious, lively babies. Their bodies, lifeless and splayed, looked like bloodied smudges of fur. Unable to hold back her tears, she looked at Sean. "Why did he have to kill them?"

Sean shrugged. "Ye can't tell about some men." He placed a hand on Mary's shoulder. "I'll take care of them."

Mary grabbed Sean's hand. "We have to get off this island. Trent is crazy. He's getting worse. Next time it might be you or me."

"The only way to leave is to use his boat." Rubbing his chin, Sean glanced toward the bay. "The weather is still unpredictable. It's too dangerous." His eyes followed the path Trent had taken. "Although I despise what he's done, it doesn't mean he's crazy. There are a lot of people who don't think anything of killin' an animal."

Shocked, Mary stared at Sean. "How can you defend him?" Mary knew her next statement was ridiculous, but she couldn't hold back the words. "Do you think it's all right to kill a baby fox just for the fun of it?"

"I thought ye knew me better than that," Sean said quietly.

Immediately, Mary was sorry for her accusation. "I do. I'm sorry." She paced again. "I don't know what I'm saying."

"Just because Trent killed those pups doesn't necessarily make him dangerous, even if he's been unpredictable as the weather and has a sour disposition." He looked at the dead kits. "I don't know what to think."

"I think he could do almost anything." Mary glanced at the trampled grasses left by Trent when he'd walked away.

"Mary, even if I thought it were safe to leave, Trent's not just going to let us take his boat."

"We can sneak away after dark."

"And what happens to Trent?" Sean shook his head. "I don't like him, but it's not right to leave him."

"Sean, he's dangerous."

Sean walked across the open ground to one of the kits and knelt beside it. "I kill fox for a livin'. Does that make me bad or dangerous?"

"It's not the same and you know it. You do it only to make a living. He enjoys it. You saw the way he looked. You've seen how he is. When you got into that fight, he would have let you drown, and that day in the boat, you saw him point his rifle at us. And what about the night he aimed his gun at me and threatened to shoot me? He probably would have if you had not been holding your rifle."

Sean straightened. "I think he's a lot of bluff. Trent hasn't done anythin' to us in all these months. We'll wait. It will be safer. Someone will come for us soon."

Mary didn't know what more she could say to convince Sean. In anger and frustration, she blurted, "No, Sean, you're wrong—very wrong." If not for the fear of running into Trent, Mary would have walked to the beach. It always calmed her. This time she stomped into the cabin, slammed the door, then paced the small room. Her mind replayed the shooting. Trent's expression had been cold and empty when he'd walked away. *He has no feelings. He's dead inside,* Mary decided. *We've got to take his boat and get off this island.*

She made a decision. With or without Sean's approval, she would prepare to leave. *I'll set the fish out to dry and gather extra mussels and dry them. We have plenty of eggs. When the food runs out, we can fish. I'll convince him to borrow the boat. We can send someone back for Trent.*

Several days passed and Mary worked on her plan. She set up a rack on the far side of the island and used it to dry the extra fish she'd been catching and the mussels she'd found. While she worked, she watched for Trent, but he seemed not to care about her or Sean and spent most of his time whittling. On several occasions she caught sight of the fox and her two remaining kits, but they never returned to the house. Mary wished the trust that had built between Sean and the fox hadn't been destroyed, but she was glad they were staying away. There would be no way to protect them if Trent decided to kill more of them.

When Mary thought she had enough supplies to see them through several days of travel, she approached Sean. He was bundling up the last furs of the season when she approached the shed.

Setting the furs on the ground outside the door, he said, "This is the last of them. I'm glad to be done with it."

"Me too. And I'm glad you won't be doing this again." Mary scanned the clearing and nearby hillsides. She wondered where Trent had gone to.

Sean walked back inside the shed, and Mary followed him. She closed the door. Silently, she watched Sean clean the tanning tools, then drop them into a burlap bag. She practiced what she would say in her mind.

"Is somethin' wrong?" Sean asked. "Ye look a little tight."

"No. I just wanted to . . . I just want . . ."

Sean stopped what he was doing and studied Mary.

Mary gathered her courage and took a deep breath. "Sean, there's something I have to tell you. I've been gathering food for the last several days. The weather has been good, and I think we need to leave."

"You mean take Trent's boat?"

Mary nodded. "The food is packed. There's enough for several days. We can leave right away. We'll wait until Trent is napping. He won't know we've gone until we're well on our way."

"I told ye how I feel about that."

Mary folded her arms over her chest. "Sean, I think a lot of you, and it's good you care about Trent, but we've got to think about ourselves this time." Afraid Trent might be listening, Mary stopped and peeked out the door. She saw no sign of him and closed the door softly. "We can send someone back for him."

"And what if we don't make it?"

Mary hadn't thought of that and didn't know how to respond. Finally, she said, "We don't have any other choice. We must leave."

"Mary, I'm for it if ye want to make a try, but I'm not leavin' anyone behind, not even Trent. We'll all go together, or we don't go at all."

Mary felt sick at the idea. How could she spend several days in close quarters with Trent? "He could kill us and take the furs," she said.

"He could have done that already if he'd wanted to."

"I know, but I think he enjoys scaring people. He might just be biding his time, relishing the thrill of watching his prey squirm."

Sean smiled. "Ye're bein' a bit melodramatic, don't ye think?"

Jutting out her chin, she said, "No, I don't think so. That's how I feel."

With a sigh, Sean said, "I'll go down with ye and take a look at the boat to make sure it's seaworthy. Then we'll decide what to do."

When Mary and Sean approached the boat, Trent was already there. Hurriedly, he stuffed a bundle under the bow and straightened, then faced them. "What are you doing here?"

"We could ask ye the same."

"I don't answer to you."

Sean said nothing for a moment. Mary could see the muscle in his jaw working and knew he was struggling to keep his temper in check. "We were thinkin' that maybe the three of us could use yer boat and make our way back to Unalaska. The weather's been holdin'."

"The three of us?" Trent asked incredulously. "I won't be needing company." He turned his back and set a fishing pole on the bottom of the boat.

"You're going?" Mary asked.

"Yep. I'm heading out. I'll send someone back for you."

As the words left his lips, outrage and understanding surged through Mary. She felt betrayed but understood what Sean had been saying. She'd been prepared to abandon Trent without a thought to anyone but herself. Sick at heart over her own selfishness, she took a step toward Trent. "I know how you're feeling, wanting to get off the island, but you can't leave us."

"I said, I'd send someone back."

Mary hardened her resolve. "How can we trust you to do that?"

"You can't." Trent grinned cruelly.

"We're not staying here. We're going with you," Mary persisted.

"Three is better than one," Sean offered amiably. "With three the rowin' can be shared. We'll be able to rest and still keep movin'."

"I'm taking no passengers," Trent said flatly and started up the hill.

"Ye'll wait and hear me out." Sean stepped in front of the man.

Trent's face turned red, then purple. "Get out of my way. I have some things I need to get."

"Ye'll not leave us here."

In an instant, Trent's hand shot out, grabbed Sean around the throat and squeezed, as if wanting to crush the life out of Sean. With his face only inches from Sean's and his teeth clenched, Trent yelled, "No one tells me what to do. I'm going alone. No passengers." He pulled out his revolver and pressed it hard against Sean's cheek. "I've dreamed of this moment. For months you've been giving me lip, and it's time I shut you up." Keeping his grip tight, Trent pushed Sean against a rock outcropping.

When Trent had grabbed Sean, the Irishman's rifle had fallen to the ground. Mary glanced at it. *He's going to kill Sean. I need that gun.* Keeping her eyes on Trent, she took a step toward the weapon. Trent didn't seem to notice she'd moved.

"Trent, I understand that this has been a tough winter for ye," Sean said, his voice strangled but calm. "I meant ye no harm." Sean's voice was steady.

Mary took another step. *Just a little ways and I'll have it.* She visualized how she'd grab it up and . . . *And what? Shoot him?* She realized if she managed to get the rifle, she'd be forced to shoot Trent. Her stomach knotted, and she felt dizzy. *I have no choice,* she told herself. *He's going to kill Sean.* She took another small step.

"You're always *so* calm. You make me sick." He smiled wickedly. "You're not going to talk your way out of this. I'm going to kill you. It's simple. I don't need you. With you gone, the furs are mine, and so is Mary." He pressed the gun harder against Sean's face and pulled back the hammer. "You feel calm now?" he taunted.

Mary froze.

Trent glanced at her.

"It's not as bad as ye think," Sean choked out. "Ye can take the boat and the furs. We won't stop ye."

"You're right, you won't."

Mary's heart slammed against her chest. She had no time to spare. She had to do it now. She rehearsed the proper use of the rifle in her mind. It had been a long time since Sean had taught it to her. As she realized what she was about to do, she could feel her stomach knot and bile began to rise up in her throat. *Only two more steps and I can grab it.* She kept moving slowly. *Now!* she thought and lunged. Landing flat out, she grabbed the gun and snapped up the bolt. Trusting that a cartridge had been placed into the chamber, she pointed the rifle at Trent. "Stop! Now!"

Disbelief painted Trent's face red as he looked at Mary.

Her finger resting on the trigger, Mary said, "I'll shoot you."

"Mary, you don't want to shoot anyone," Trent said, his voice sweet as honey. A smile played on his lips. With his fingers still squeezing Sean's throat, he leveled the pistol at her.

Without thinking, Mary pulled the trigger. A shot reverberated over the hillsides and across the water, and the butt of the rifle slammed into Mary's shoulder.

Almost simultaneously, Trent fired. Mary jumped but quickly realized he'd missed her.

Trent's sick smile turned into a grim line. He let his arm fall and looked down at his shirt, horror and disbelief on his face. Blood seeped through the blue material and spread into the fabric. Still gripping his gun, he pressed his free hand against his chest and fell to his knees.

Mary watched, stunned and horrified. "I didn't mean to . . . I didn't want . . ." Trent fell forward, the impact of his body making a sickening thud as it hit the ground. Silence settled over the island. Even the birds were still.

"Mary, ye all right?" Sean asked. When she nodded, he leaned over Trent. He pressed his fingers against the man's neck, then held a hand in front of his nose and mouth. Dropping back on his haunches, Sean said in disbelief, "He's dead."

"I . . . I didn't mean to do it. I only wanted to help you. I didn't want to kill him."

Sean hurried to Mary and pulled her into his arms. "Ye did what ye had to, only what ye had to. He would have killed ye, Mary. He would have killed us both. Ye were right about him. I should have listened to ye."

Mary's legs felt wobbly, and she thought she might faint. She leaned heavily against Sean. "I didn't mean to kill him. I didn't mean to."

"I know. I know," Sean said, stroking her hair gently as he would a child's.

"I . . . I think I'm going to be sick," she said and turned away just as she emptied her stomach.

She felt Sean's touch on her back.

"Are ye all right?"

"No. I'm not all right." She looked up at Sean. "I killed him."

"Come on, let's get ye back to the house," he said gently. "I'll make some coffee. And then ye can go on to bed. I think a little rest will do ye some good."

Mary glanced at Trent's body. He stared without seeing, and blood oozed onto the ground around him. "What about him? We can't just leave him there."

"I'll take care of it. But first let's get ye to bed." Sean bundled Mary within an arm, and like a mother hen, escorted her to the house.

"I didn't mean to kill him. I didn't mean to," Mary repeated.

"I know. I know."

Sean had gone to take care of the body, and Mary lay in bed. She felt anxious and sick. Closing her eyes, she longed for the comfort of sleep, but Trent's horrified face and the blood that spread across the front of his shirt and onto the ground filled her mind.

She rolled onto her side, tucked her hands under her cheek, and drew her knees up to her chest. "I killed him. Oh, God, I killed him. What am I going to do?" She remembered Sean's Bible. Maybe it would help. It had always seemed to bring comfort to her parents and to Sean.

Throwing the blankets back, she stood and walked to the cupboard where Sean kept the black book. Taking it down, she held it away from her, as if she were afraid of it, and walked to the table. She sat and placed the book in front of her. For a long while she stared at it, her hands resting on the cover. Tentatively, she opened it. *Where do I begin?* she wondered. Turning a page, she looked at it but didn't see. The words were a blur. Feeling lost, she turned another page. Where should she read to find comfort? She wished she'd paid attention when her mother and father had quoted Scriptures and taught her about the Lord.

She scanned the pages, hoping something would speak to her, but the words were a jumble. She closed her eyes. "God, if you are real, I need help. I need quiet inside," she said, agitation churning. "I think I'm going crazy." Her eyes fell upon Psalm 4:8. *"I will both lay me down in peace, and sleep: for thou, Lord, only makest me dwell in safety."*

Mary let out a groan. *Yes, I need peace. Please, God, give me peace.* She closed the book and laid her head on the table. With her hand still resting on the Bible, she closed her eyes.

Wind whistled around the house as a storm descended upon the island, but Mary slept.

Chapter 22

*T*he cabin's interior consumed the muted light of morning. The storm raged, and Mary slept a weighty sleep. Like a shroud, it suffocated. She fought her way toward consciousness, battling against the heavy emptiness blanketing her. *Why the grief?* she asked, then Trent's horrified and stunned face burst into her thoughts. *I killed him.* Her eyes opened and she stared at the driftwood ceiling, unaware of anything except the young man's face.

Gradually her surroundings penetrated—the storm's screams, her skin's coolness, the wool blanket's scratchiness became real. *How did I get here?* she wondered. The last she remembered, she'd been at the table. *Sean. Sean must have carried me here,* she decided.

Weak and spiritless, she closed her eyes, rolled onto her side, and pulled the blanket tightly under her chin. She listened

to the wind punish the cabin. Like a relentless executioner laying the lash across a prisoner's back, it whipped the fragile
cabin. Mary didn't care.

She felt as if she needed punishing. If not her, then the
cabin. As the magnitude of what had happened laid itself over
her, she moaned. *"What have I done?" What have I done? I
didn't have to kill him. I could have shot him without killing
him.* She stared at the curtain shutting her away from the house,
but she saw only Trent's bloodied body and vacant eyes. She
squeezed her eyes closed and pressed the blanket against her
mouth, smothering a cry. As much as she'd detested and feared
Trent, she hadn't wanted him dead, had she? "I didn't mean to
kill him. I didn't mean to," she whispered.

"Mary, ye all right?" Sean asked from the other side of the
curtain.

Mary struggled to shove aside the painful emotions and
answered hoarsely, "Yes." She heard Sean yawn and throw back
blankets. *He must have slept alone,* she thought.

"I'll make coffee," he said.

Although the draping separated them, Mary knew Sean
would be stretching his arms over his head, then leaning from
side to side as he did every morning. Glancing at the empty
place beside her, she rested her hand on the place he usually
slept and realized she'd missed his presence during the night.
Since arriving on Unalga, she'd become accustomed to having
him beside her. Now with Trent gone, they had no reason to
share a bed. A sadness separate from the sorrow she felt over
shooting Trent settled over her.

"Ye goin' to be long?" Sean asked.

"No. I'm coming." Reluctantly, Mary sat up. She didn't

want to do anything. "I'll cook some eggs," she offered. Wind screeched and the cabin shuddered.

"I was hopin' the storm would pass quickly."

Mary climbed out from under the blankets and pulled on her boots. Stepping into the room, she found Sean gazing out the frosted window. It looked like winter had descended. Unreasonable panic rose in her. "Sean, winter has returned. I have to get off this island. I can't stay." She stared at the window. "What are we going to do?" Then tears came, and she covered her face with her hands and sobbed. "I can't stay. I can't stay."

Sean took Mary's hands, pressed them against his chest, and enfolded her in his arms. "It will be all right, Mary. Winter will pass and we'll return to Unalaska. And our lives will be the way they used to be. And all this will only be a memory."

Mary looked up at Sean. "But when? How long do we have to wait?" Her eyes moved to a new totem Trent had carved and left in the cabin. "All I can think of is . . . is him. He's here. He's everywhere. I can't stay."

"Mary, ye must stop tormentin' yerself. Ye did nothin' wrong. Trent did this to himself. He would have killed me. I saw it in his eyes. He would have done it. His hate was strong." He gently caressed Mary's upper arms. "Do ye hear me, now? It wasn't yer fault."

"I hear you, but I still feel like a murderer." Mary's body trembled. "If I hadn't shot that gun, he'd be alive."

"And I'd be dead."

Mary searched Sean's eyes and realized how empty her life would be without him. "I thought he was going to kill you."

"He was," Sean said soberly. He kneaded her shoulders. "Yer muscles are tight. Take a couple of slow, deep breaths and calm yerself." His steady hazel eyes stared into hers. "Take nothin' on that doesn't belong to ye. Give this burden to the Lord. He'll carry it for ye."

Mary looked away. Although she'd heard the expression many times, she didn't understand what it meant to give burdens to Jesus. "I tried, but I still feel awful inside."

"I know how ye feel. Once, a long time ago, I killed a man. It was an accident," he quickly added. "Still, afterwards, guilt tormented me, and I wished there were some way to bring him back, but there was no changin' it." He caressed her hair. "Trent's gone, and we've got to go on." He smiled gently. "Maybe some coffee will lift yer spirits. I'll get us some." He walked to the stove and filled two cups. Handing one to Mary, he said, "Sorry. It's only lukewarm and weak as me mother's tea."

Mary sipped the drink, but she didn't taste it. She stared at the door. For a moment, she expected Trent to step in and demand breakfast. She shuddered. His life was over. He'd never demand anything again. "Maybe Trent's dead because I wanted him dead," she almost whispered. "I hated him. Maybe I shot him because . . ."

"Mary. Stop it. Ye've got to quit this. It's not goin' to help. Have ye forgotten what Trent was like? Since our first day here, he was trouble. And those types almost always end up like he did. He brought it all on himself."

Mary nodded. "I know what you're saying is true, but I still feel as if it was my fault."

"Our feelin's often lie to us." Sean's stomach rumbled and he grinned as he patted his stomach. "It's time to think of somethin' else, like breakfast. I'll make it."

Mary managed a smile. "No. I'll do it." She walked to the stove, took a sip of her coffee, then set it on the counter. Moving the frying pan onto a burner, she spooned a tiny bit of lard into it. When it had melted, she broke four eggs and, one at a time, dropped them in. "There may still be a few good eggs left to be gathered. We'll have to get them soon."

"Maybe the weather will clear this afternoon, and we can have an adventure searching for more."

"I don't want any more adventures," Mary said woodenly. She stared out the window. Snow still fell at a slant. "Sometimes it feels as if we'll never leave this place." She turned back to the eggs and, using a fork, scrambled them. "Sean," she began hesitantly, "do you think God forgives a person who kills someone? I mean, will they go to hell?"

"I thought ye didn't believe in any of that stuff."

"I don't know what I believe. I was just wondering."

Sean thought a moment. "I think God forgives them. From what me mother used to tell me, he forgives all of our sins if we ask him to. But I think ye have to know Jesus Christ as yer savior to be forgiven."

He took his Bible from the shelf and opened it. Turning the pages, he stopped occasionally and studied the words. Finally he pressed the book open and read, *"But if we walk in the light, as he is in the light, we have fellowship one with another, and the blood of Jesus Christ his Son cleanseth us from all sin. If we say that we have no sin, we deceive ourselves, and the truth is not in us. If we confess our sins, he is faithful and just to forgive us our sins, and to cleanse us from all unright-eousness."* Tender eyes settled on Mary. "If ye believe in the Ten Commandments, ye know killin' is a sin. But if this word is right, if ye're one of God's children, all ye need to do is tell him ye're sorry for what ye did and he'll forgive ye. It says here he cleanses us from *all* unrighteousness."

"He must hate me. I've ignored him all my life and now, this. It seems selfish to expect him to help me now."

"Ignoring him was your decision, not his. He's been waitin' on ye. Accordin' to the Bible he wants to spend time with us."

"I don't even know if I believe in him. I don't feel his presence. When I used to go to church, I'd watch the people. They would have their eyes closed and be praying and seem so happy and content, but I never felt it."

Sean placed his arms on the table and leaned forward. "Ye know from the readin' I've been doin' I don't think we're supposed to depend on feelin's, but on what God says. And he says right here if ye love him and ask for his forgiveness, he'll forgive ye."

"But I don't love him. I don't even know him." Mary scooped eggs onto two plates. "So, how can he forgive me?"

Sean thought. "Don't ye believe at all?"

"I don't know."

"I think ye just have to believe in him, nothin' more." He thumbed through several pages then stopped. "Here it is. *For God so loved the world, that he gave his only begotten Son, that whosoever believeth in him should not perish, but have everlasting life. For God sent not his Son into the world to condemn the world; but that the world through him might be saved. He that believeth on him is not condemned: but he that believeth not is condemned already, because he hath not believed in the name of the only begotten Son of God.'"* He let his hands rest on the open book. "See, ye just have to believe. When Jesus died on the cross, he took all our sins onto himself. That way *we* don't have to carry them."

A mixture of trepidation and hope filled Mary. She set a plate in front of Sean. If she believed, she would be saved from her sin, but the trouble was that she didn't believe. She sat across from her husband. "I don't know what to think," she said and took a bite of egg.

The storm pounded the island the rest of the morning, but as the day passed into afternoon, it began to ease. Mary cleaned the cabin, laundered clothes, and mended tattered socks, but she felt restless. She couldn't push Trent from her mind.

Sean sat at the table repairing torn crab nets. Occasionally he'd make a comment, but for the most part, they worked quietly.

As Mary considered Trent, she wondered where he was. If there were a hell, he'd certainly be there. Is that what awaited her? Fear clawed at her as she considered her own inevitable death. One day she would face it and its frightening secrets. Was there any way to know what happens when you died?

I wonder if Sean's Bible will tell me, Mary thought. But if the answers were there, how could she find them? As long as she could remember, her parents had told her it held the secrets of life and death. *Maybe I should read it,* she thought.

Late in the day, the clouds thinned, the snow stopped falling, and sunshine looked down through white pillows and brightened the landscape. The air warmed, and the new snow immediately began to melt.

"It's time to do some fishin'," Sean said.

Mary set her mending aside. It would feel good to get outside. "We have two poles. I'll go with you."

"I'm gettin' a bit tired of freshwater fish. Do ye think we could land a salmon from the cove?"

"Maybe, but the lake is more dependable." Mary smiled. "We need the food. Let's go to the lake first, then we can go to the bay."

"Sounds good," Sean said, tying off a knot. "I'm finished here." Throwing the nets over his shoulder, he crossed the room and grabbed his coat.

Mary took her coat from its hook and pulled it on, then followed Sean out the door. When she stepped into sunlight, she stopped and turned her face into it. It warmed her skin. "It feels good," she said, breathing deeply. She'd hoped to smell new grasses, but there was no fragrance. Cold and snow had buried the aroma. "I hate snow."

"It will melt fast," Sean said. "The grass will be back in no time."

After exchanging nets for fishing poles, they headed for the lake. Wet snow created a slippery surface forcing Sean and Mary to walk slowly and cautiously. Mary stepped on the occasional tufts of grass poking up through the freshly laid white carpet.

As they approached the lake, the mournful call of a loon echoed from below. Sean held a finger to his lips and whispered, "She's been nestin' in the grass at the lake's edge." He and Mary crouched as they approached the water.

The heavy-bodied loon glided across the lake while a lone chick swam along the water's edge. Although feeding, the mother remained alert. Like a sentry she watched her baby and the grasses along the bank for possible predators. Oblivious to danger, the chick pecked at grass shoots and twigs and paddled aimlessly.

"It is so cute," Mary whispered.

Unexpectedly a fox shot out of the grass and plunged into the shallows, lunging at the chick. He came away with a mouthful of feathers, and the chick chirped hysterically and darted for deeper water.

Beating the air with black and white wings, the mother loon sprinted across the water's surface, placing herself between chick and fox. Flapping wildly, she attacked the intruder, using her long, sharp beak as a weapon. With a sharp yelp, the fox retreated. The loon chased after him, climbing onto the bank in her determination. Tail between his legs, the fox disappeared, and the mother extended her feathered arms in triumph, then returned to the lake and her offspring. The chick flitted its tiny wings and clambered onto its mother's back. Calmly the two headed into deeper water.

As Mary watched, something Sean had said nudged her. She searched for the memory. He'd said something about sacrifice. *That Jesus loved so much he'd sacrificed his life for mankind. Just as the loon was willing to die for her chick, or any parent would give their life for their child, he died.* As clarity came, Mary felt excitement pierce her. She knew it was important to understand. Aloud she said, "The mother loon is very brave. That fox could have killed her."

Sean smiled. "She wasn't about to let anything get her baby." He sat on a log as he set up his pole. Giving Mary a sidelong glance, he said, "It's a perfect picture of how someone chooses to die for another."

Although Mary had had that very thought, she wasn't about to give in so easily and said in a caustic tone, "They're birds, Sean. It's natural for them to do that."

"Yes. And it's natural for God to sacrifice for his children."

"They're birds," Mary repeated dryly, uncertain why she couldn't yield.

Sean allowed his eyes to wander over the hillsides. "It's not by accident God shows us truth in creation. I think he does it so we can know him even if we don't have anyone to help us, or if we don't have his book. He wants us to understand. He wants us to know him. We only miss it if we choose to," he added pointedly.

Mary flushed with irritation. Sean seemed to have an answer for everything. "So, you read your Bible for a few weeks and now you know everything."

"No. I only know a little, but I'm learnin'. Every time I read the Bible I learn more and, as I watch how the world works, I keep learnin'. Through God's Holy Spirit, he helps us understand. He shows himself to us, but we have to be willin' to see." He paused, then added, "Open yer eyes, Mary."

Mary stared at the lake. What if what Sean said were true? She'd be a fool to ignore him. Then again, if it were all just a fantasy, she'd be a fool to believe it. And Mary hated to look foolish.

Chapter 23

*L*uba refilled Michael's cup with coffee. "When are you going to talk to Nick? The weather has been good for several days now. It should be safe to get Mary and Sean, and I don't want to wait any longer."

Michael took a drink of his coffee. "I plan to talk to him today. I decided last night. I'll go over this morning."

Luba set the coffeepot on the stove and returned to washing dishes. "I pray they're all right. It's been such a hard winter."

Michael sipped his coffee. "It has been, but they haven't been alone." He stood and walked to the sink. Taking two more drinks, he set the cup in the wash water. "I think I've had enough coffee for one day." He circled his arms around his wife's waist and rested his cheek against her hair. "Praying is the best thing we can do. God listens to our petitions." He kissed Luba's cheek and straightened. "I believe they're alive. In fact, I'm certain of it; and it is time to bring them home. I'm not waiting any longer. Although the weather's been changeable, it's held for the last four days, a good sign."

Luba turned and wrapped her arms about her husband's waist. She pressed her forehead against his chest. "I pray and pray, but I'm still afraid. I keep seeing them starved or sick, or even worse. Plus, I think about how they must feel about us and their friends. When Nick left them, they expected him to return soon, but he didn't. They must have waited and waited. How do they feel about no one coming for them?"

"Winter hit there just like it did here. They know how dangerous it is. They'd understand."

Luba nodded, rested her cheek on Michael's wool shirt, and closed her eyes. Tears she'd kept in check for too long began to flow. They traced a wet path down her cheeks. She looked up at Michael. "It has been so long. What if they're dead? I couldn't bear it."

Michael caressed Luba's hair. "They're not dead. God is faithful, and Mary knows how to survive. Plus, Sean is strong and won't give up."

"What if Nick won't go after them? What will we do?"

Michael remained silent for a moment, then said with determination, "He'll go. He's a good man, and he'll do the right thing." He kissed the top of his Luba's head, then turned her face up and met her eyes. "He'll do the right thing."

"I wish I felt as certain as you. I don't trust him. Leaving them through the winter was cruel. I've tried not to hate him, but . . . he should have gone back. He was their only way home."

Michael took Luba's hands in his. "Luba, you're being too hard on him. I have to admit to getting angry myself, but Nick has a right to protect his own life. And as much as I believe a boat isn't as important as two people's lives, that boat is his only way of making a living. We need to try to see this from his perspective, and it serves no purpose to brood over what should have been. Now we need to focus on bringing them home."

Luba nodded. "I just pray they're safe and waiting for us."

"Me too. I better get going. If Nick is willing, I want to start for Unalga today." He walked to the door and grabbed his coat and hat off the hook. "Keep praying," he said, planting his hat on his head and pulling on his coat. He opened the door and stepped outside.

Green hills blushed, and splashes of wildflowers swaggered in the sun's light. Still, the wind cut like a cold knife. *We won't have any real warmth until late summer this year,* Michael thought, pushing his hands into his coat pockets. He glanced out at Unalaska Bay. Small whitecaps skipped across dark waves. Was another storm moving in? He scanned the horizon. The skies were clear. *No. No storm. Not today anyway,* he thought. *Father, please hold up the good weather until we can get Mary and Sean home safely.* He hurried his steps. The sooner he talked to Nick, the earlier they could set out.

As he approached the German man's house, Michael prayed, "Father, please speak to this man's heart. Show him we can't wait longer. Help him see that going after Sean and Mary is the right thing to do, and then help him to do it." He stepped onto the wooden porch, took a deep breath and knocked.

Heavy steps came from inside, then the door creaked open and the rotund man stepped into the doorway. "I've been expecting you. This seems to be a day for travelers." With a nod, he said, "Come in."

Michael took off his hat and stepped inside. Paul Matroona sat in the front room. Immediately, Michael's anger flared. He gave Paul a curt nod.

The young man stood. "Mr. Calhoun, good to see you."

"Paul, I heard you'd been wounded and were recovering here in Unalaska. How is your leg?"

Paul patted his thigh. "It gives me some trouble, but it's healing. I'll be ready to get back into the battle again soon."

"I wouldn't be so anxious. Too many men have died already."

Nick sat in a large, cushioned chair and rested his broad arms on the ample wooden armrests. He motioned for Michael to sit on the divan across from him.

"No thank you. I'd rather stand," Michael said.

"Suit yourself. I know why you're here—Unalga. Seems the weather has you both thinking about Unalga."

Michael glanced at Paul.

"Yep," Nick said. "He wants to go, too, and bring back that daughter of yours and your son-in-law."

Michael felt his ire rise again. Why would Paul feel responsible for Mary? She was Sean's wife.

"I understand how you two feel," Nick said. "But I'm sorry to have to say . . ."

"Nick, please hear me out," Michael cut in. "The weather has been good for days now. Clearly, spring is here. It's time to go and get them."

Nick leaned forward slightly. "Michael, it's still cold. A storm could roll in any time. You know this has been a bad spring, and we had a wicked winter. There will be more storms, you can count on it, and the ones coming in are more like winter gales." Running a hand over his balding head, he continued,

"I'm gonna' go after them, but I'd like to wait a little longer, until the weather settles down." He shook his head. "I can't go now. It's still too dangerous. I barely made it back after I dropped them off, and I don't want to chance it—not yet."

"We can't wait. It's been months. There's no telling what they're facing now—hunger, illness . . . death."

"If they were going to die, they would have already done it," Nick said matter-of-factly.

Shock hit Michael. Nick's words had been callous. He hadn't expected that from his neighbor.

Immediately Nick added, "I'm sorry. I didn't mean that the way it sounded. They're probably fine. I was just saying if they weren't fine, it would probably be too late now. They faced their toughest days back in January and February. Now they should have a little more to eat if they know how to use what's around them."

"Mary knows," Michael said solemnly.

Paul pushed himself out of his chair and paced the floor, stopping directly in front of Nick. "We have to go after them now. Mary might . . . " He glanced at Michael. "I mean, she needs to be home where she's safe. We can't leave her and Sean there any longer. Anything can happen."

"Paul's right. Sean and Mary could be in trouble. We need to get out there. No more waiting for perfect weather." He shoved his hands into his pant's pockets. "This winter has been horrible for Luba and me. We can't wait any longer. We need to know. When I left Luba this morning, she was in tears."

"I know how you feel," Nick said kindly. "But I don't think a few days is going to make any difference." He rested his huge arms on his thighs and leaned forward. His tone somber, he said, "I wasn't honest with you before. It's time we faced the truth." He paused. "I don't think they're all right. I don't think they could have made it through the winter. I'm sorry to say it, but it has to be said."

Michael's heart constricted as he heard his fears spoken out loud. Still, he wasn't ready to give up. "Nick, you can't know that, and we won't know until we get out there."

"Nick, you don't know anything," Paul said, his voice angry. "She's all right. She's strong. I'll take a dory and go on my own if I have to."

Nick didn't respond.

"All right," Michael said. "I understand you're not wanting to go out, but would you let me take your boat? You know I'm a good seaman. I'll take good care of it. I'll bring Sean and Mary home myself. You won't have to be involved."

Nick pushed his large bulk out of the chair and plodded into the kitchen. He poured a cup of coffee. Looking at Michael and Paul, he hefted the pot. "You want any?" Both men shook their heads no.

Nick stared out the kitchen window. "I want you to know I feel bad about all this. I like Sean and Mary. When I couldn't return, it was torture. Every day my mind has been with them, every day. I wait and wonder—and I pray. I'm not a heartless man."

"Then show me your heart. Let me take the boat," Michael prodded.

Nick continued to stare out the window. Finally, he turned and faced Michael. "All right. You can have it, but I still think you should wait. If a storm comes in . . . Well, we don't need to have you lost out there too."

Taking long strides, Michael crossed to Nick. He gripped the big man's hand and shook it hard. "Thank you. Thank you." He placed his hat on his head. "You'll see, they'll be fine. And I'll bring your boat back good as new." He walked to the door, then turned. "I want to leave today. Is the boat ready to go?"

"Yes, I've had her ready for a couple weeks, just in case."

Michael opened the door and stepped onto the porch. "Thanks, Nick," he said and started to pull the door closed.

Paul grabbed it. "Wait. I'm going with you."

"You? Why?"

"I need to know Mary's all right."

"Mary's none of your concern."

"I know I have no claim on her. I don't mean to cause trouble, but I have to know. I can't wait any longer."

"No. It's not a good idea."

"You'll need another man on board, and I don't think you want to take your sons. They're still awful young."

"I don't want you coming along. I'm not crazy about spending days crammed onto a small boat with you. What you did to Mary is unforgivable. And I can't help but think about how Sean will react when he sees you're one of the men who's come to rescue them. Mary belongs to Sean, and you have no business being involved in their lives."

As Michael stepped off the porch, Paul jumped down and blocked his path. "I have to go. You can't keep me here. I'll swim out to the boat if you try to leave without me." Defiantly, he met Michael's eyes. "I still love Mary. I need to know she's all right. But I promise I won't cause any trouble."

Michael thought for a long moment. He did need another man to help him, and it seemed that Paul would go no matter how hard he tried to stop him. Knowing he was probably making a mistake, he finally said, "All right. You can come. But I'll hold you to your promise. I'll see you at the dock in an hour." With a nod to Nick, Michael turned and hurried home.

Michael burst into the house. "Luba, can you help me get packed? We're leaving in an hour."

Luba set her sewing aside and stood up. "Nick is taking you?"

"No. He's letting me use the boat."

"You can't go alone. It's too dangerous. If Nick's not going, I'll go with you."

"I won't be alone. Paul Matroona is going along."

"Paul?"

"He insisted. No matter what I said, he wouldn't accept no for an answer. And I don't want to fight him over it. Besides, I do need another man along."

"I'm still going," Luba said stubbornly.

Michael took Luba's hands. "I understand how you feel, but I want you safe here with the boys. If the weather turns bad, I don't want . . ."

"I'm going. You can't make me stay. I've sailed in rough weather before. I'm not afraid. I need to see that Mary's all right. And if she isn't," she hesitated, "then I still need to see her."

"What about the boys? Where will they stay?"

"They are always welcome at the Jesse Lee Home. They have friends there. It would be a treat for Eric and Alex and for the orphan boys living there, and we know they will get good care."

"And what if something happens . . . to us? They'd be left alone."

Luba's face remained resolute. "Then they will be in the very best place they can be, and we'll see them in heaven one day."

Less than an hour later, Luba and Michael joined Paul at the docks. After stowing bedding and supplies, the boat was released, and they headed out into the bay. Michael steered for the open sea, and the tiny town of Unalaska quickly disappeared.

Chapter 24

---

*H*ands on the wheel of the boat, Michael squinted into the sun. The deck rolled under his feet. *The sea's running a little heavy,* he thought as he peered at the waves. The trenches were deeper and closer together than they'd been just thirty minutes before. An alarm sounded inside of him, and he scanned the horizon. Gray clouds spread across the sky, but they didn't look threatening. *It's not a storm. Relax. It's just a heavy tide.*

Michael turned his gaze on Luba. Sitting on a wooden crate alongside the railing, she rested her arms on the sun-blistered rail and stared out over the ocean. Michael studied his wife. Although her waist had thickened a little over the years and her black hair was now tinged with gray, she was still beautiful. She looked up at her husband and flashed him a smile, her brown eyes warm. Feeling the same rush of admiration he'd had when he'd first met her at the general store in Sitka, Michael waved back.

The cabin door opened, and Paul stepped in. His irritation immediate, Michael barely glanced at the young man. Every moment he spent with Paul challenged him. All Michael could think of each time he looked at him was how this man had hurt Mary. The wounded expression on Mary's face when she'd learned about Paul's betrayal was etched into Michael's mind. He hated Paul. Keeping his eyes on the sea, he ignored the young native.

"I'd heard you were a better man," Paul said. "I didn't expect you to be a friend, but your hard heart is a surprise."

Michael said nothing. His anger was billowing inside like thunderheads.

"Say something. I've tried to talk to you for days, and I'm tired of hitting a stone wall every time."

Michael's anger surged, and through clenched teeth, he said, "What do you want me to say? That it's all right you broke my daughter's heart? That it's fine for you to commit adultery whenever you feel like it?" He turned angry eyes on Paul. "What is it you expect from me? I didn't ask you to come on this trip. In fact, I told you I didn't want you to come. You're here only because you insisted."

"First of all, I tried to explain about the other woman."

"I don't want your explanations. And it doesn't' matter any more anyway. It's in the past."

"If it's in the past, then why do you still hate me?"

Michael didn't answer. He couldn't. He knew his anger was out of line, and he had no excuse.

For several moments neither man said anything. Finally Paul said, "It looks like we might be heading into a storm. I thought you could use a break." He approached Michael. "You look tired. I'd be happy to take over for a while."

Michael didn't respond, but gazed ahead, his jaw set.

"I can take over . . ."

"I heard you. I'm fine. I don't need your help. I'll let you know when I do." Michael bit off his words at the end of each sentence, unwilling to spare even one extra breath on the man.

Paul shrugged and walked out of the cabin.

The young man strolled to the bow and stood, legs apart and slightly bent to absorb the rise and fall of the boat. He clenched his hands behind him and watched the horizon. *He's as arrogant as ever,* Michael thought. Then he noticed the droop of Paul's shoulders. Paul glanced over at Michael once, then returned to staring at the building waves.

Michael told himself that he had every right to be angry. Any father would have trouble forgiving a man who'd treated his daughter so badly. *He had an affair with a married woman while being promised to Mary.* Michael fumed as he thought about it.

Luba opened the door and peeked inside. "May I come in?"

Michael smiled. "Please. I could use some company."

"You had some. Did you chase him off?"

"Yes," Michael admitted. "I tried to control my anger, but . . . I can't."

"Can't, or won't?"

"I tried . . ." He looked at Luba. "All right. I didn't try very hard. I know it's wrong." He sighed. "I'll do better next time."

"Michael, I can't know what you're feeling." Luba approached him. "I was angry in the beginning, but what happened is part of the past. It can't be changed."

"I know, but every time I see him I remember Mary's face when we told her about . . . about him and that woman." He tightened his grip on the wheel. "I feel guilty about being so angry. I know God says we're supposed to forgive and to love, but I just can't seem to keep from hating him."

Luba rubbed his arm. "I understand, but what good will your anger do?"

Michael had no answer.

"God doesn't want you to hate because he loves you." Luba paused. "And he loves Paul. He knows what hating will do to you." Luba continued gently, "Your hate doesn't hurt Paul as much as it hurts you. Bitterness will change you."

Michael grimaced. "You're right. You always are," he added with a grin. "But it's one thing to forgive and another to live in such close quarters with him. It's too much. I didn't want him to come with us. But he is so bullheaded, he gave me no choice."

Luba patted her husband's hand.

Michael wrapped his free arm around her shoulders and pulled her close to him. "I'll try harder."

Luba kissed his cheek. "God will help you."

"I know. Actually, I didn't think much about Paul until we got on this boat. Now he's in front of me every time I turn around. His presence is a constant reminder of what he did to Mary, and what really makes me mad is his insistence on going with us to get Mary. What is it he wants? I don't trust him."

Luba leaned against her husband. "Maybe he's telling the truth and just needs to know she's all right."

"If he'd waited in Unalaska, he'd know as soon as we got back. No. It's more than that. He's going to try to get her back. I know it."

"No. You don't know that," Luba said firmly. "Maybe you should ask him why he's here instead of making a rash judgment."

Michael pulled his coat collar up around his neck. "Maybe. I don't know if I can talk to him."

The boat rose sharply, and Luba grabbed hold of the wheel to steady herself. "It's getting rough. The wind is picking up, and the clouds are turning black. Are we heading into a storm?" She drew her shawl closer.

The placid gray had changed. In their place stood dark mountains of clouds above the horizon which were moving toward them. "I wish I could say no, but it doesn't look good."

"I had hoped we'd make it without facing a storm. Do you think this is a bad one?"

Michael studied the ocean and the swelling clouds. "You never know for sure, but it looks like we're in for a challenge."

"How far are we from Unalga?"

"Three days, maybe. It's hard to say. With this, it could take longer."

Luba stepped back. She smiled at her husband. "It won't be the first storm we've faced together." She kissed him. "I better get you men fed. I'll brew some coffee and warm up the stew."

"Sounds good. I have a feeling we're going to need a good hot meal."

The gale boiled across open water and hurled itself at the small craft. Luba had barely finished serving the meal when it hit. Waves became small mountains, and the boat rode up one side and down the other, wallowing in the deep valleys that lay between. Each set of waves seemed to come closer than the ones before.

Luba secured anything that wasn't already tied down in the living quarters, while Paul battened down loose equipment up top. Michael stood at the helm, battling to keep the ship heading nose first into the waves.

With everything fastened down in the kitchen, Luba pushed open the hatch and peered at the deck. She couldn't see Paul anywhere but assumed he was in the bow finishing his duties. She knew Michael held the wheel. The boat dipped into a wave, and frigid water spilled over Luba. She stumbled backwards but managed to grab hold of the railing and held her ground. Gripping the balustrade, she pulled herself up onto the deck. The boat plowed into another wave and Luba braced for the onslaught of seawater. It cascaded down the steps and into the cabin.

This is serious, she thought, fighting panic. She wiped burning salt water from her eyes. *Stay calm. We're going to be fine. All storms seem bad when you're in them.* She looked at the pilot's cabin but couldn't see Michael. *Where is he?* "Michael! Michael!" she yelled, but her words were drowned out by shrieking wind. Hanging onto the balustrade, she pushed the hatch closed with her foot. Another wave flung the small boat and it bobbed like a toy. The boat nosed to the top of a wave, and Luba scrambled across the small deck and clung to the railing. She huddled there a moment, trying to get her breath, then pressing close to the inside wall of the boat, she made her way to the pilothouse. Yanking open the door, she stepped inside and pulled it closed behind her.

The storm's roar quieted slightly. Michael stood at the wheel. Relief swept through Luba. "Michael, you're here."

"Where else would I be?"

"I didn't know. When I looked up here, I couldn't see you."

"What are you doing out of the cabin? It's dangerous. You could get washed over and no one would know."

Luba brushed wet hair off her face. "I had to see you." The boat tipped, then plunged, and Luba was tossed against Michael. She grabbed hold of his arm. "How bad is it?" Michael's grim face told Luba before he even spoke. "It's bad. Real bad. We need to start praying," he said.

Luba's stomach turned at Michael's tone. She knew him well enough to know their future was precarious. Taking a deep breath, she said, "I am praying already. What else can I do to help?"

"There's nothing for you to do up here. Go below where you'll be safer."

Luba chewed her lip and nodded. "All right."

"Please stay below." He pointed at a rope coiled on a hook on the wall. "Cinch that around your waist, then tie the other end to the outside door handle. That way, you won't get washed over."

"All right." Luba grabbed the rope, and with shaking hands, she tied it about her waist, then opened the door and secured it to the knob. Wind shrieked and wrenched the door out of her hands. Luba stumbled back toward Michael. He caught her in his arms. Pressing his cheek against hers, he said, "Be careful. I love you."

Luba kissed her husband. "I love you too."

Another wave lifted the boat. "You better go."

Luba lunged toward the door. When she reached it, she called "Michael."

"What?"

"If we don't make it, neither will Mary and Sean. We have to get to Unalga."

"We'll make it. Pray."

As Luba stumbled out of the cabin, she bumped into Paul. She stopped and looked at the young man's face. She could see worry but not fear. "I'll be praying," she said.

Paul gave her an encouraging smile. "We're going to be all right," he said. "Pull on the rope when you get below so we know you made it."

Luba nodded and stepped into the tempest.

Paul lurched into the cabin. "Everything is secure. What can I do now?"

"Nothing. I have it." Michael's voice sounded sharp. A mountain of water roiled toward the boat, slamming into it and lifting them. Michael fought to hold the wheel steady, keeping the nose into the wave, but the ocean's strength was too much and spun the wheel out of his hands. The boat pitched sideways.

Paul grabbed the wheel, clamping his hands down beside Michael's. For the moment, Michael forgot his hatred for Paul. Together the two men pulled the wheel back around.

"Thank you," Michael said when they had stabilized.

Keeping his hands beside Michael's, Paul shouted over the roar of wind and water, "I've never seen a storm come up so quickly."

"The weather's unpredictable here. The cold waters of the Bering Sea meet the warmer currents of the Pacific, and the sea can get churned up." Michael kept his eyes on the rebel waves. "I've got it now. See if Luba is secure," he added, nodding toward the door and the rope securing his wife.

Paul let loose and staggered to the door. When the rope was jerked tight several times, he returned to Michael. "She's down safely." For several minutes, both men stared at black waters. A wave rolled them sharply left, and a chair tumbled across the room. Paul righted it, then wedged it beneath a heavy metal desk.

"You know how to ride out the waves?" Michael asked.

"Yes. I did a lot of sailing when I was a boy."

"Can you take the wheel? I've got to check our heading."

Paul gripped the wheel and took Michael's place. Keeping his eyes on the cresting waters, he said, "I never meant to hurt Mary. I loved her. I still do."

Michael looked at Paul. He didn't want to hear excuses.

"What I did was wrong. I'm not proud of it. I was young and foolish, but not any more."

"What do you want, Paul? My blessing to steal Mary away from Sean?"

"No. I know it's too late for me. When they were first married, I had trouble accepting it, and I went a little crazy. But I'm over that now. I wouldn't do anything to hurt Mary."

"Then why are you here?"

"I told you. I just need to know she's all right."

"And after that?"

Paul was silent for a long moment. "If I'm sent back to Europe, I'll finish out my time, then move back to Barrow. That's where I grew up, and it's where I belong."

A wave rammed the window, making the glass shudder and creak. Both men braced for shattered glass and salt water, but the pane held.

"You still haven't explained why you insisted on coming with us. You would have known about Mary as soon as we got back to Unalaska."

"I have to talk to her. When she gets back, it'll be too late. She'll be overwhelmed by friends and family. There won't be time for me. I need to talk to her now—to explain what happened and why."

"You can't make excuses for your behavior."

"I'm not. I know I was wrong. I just want to apologize. And if . . ." A volley of waves buffeted the boat, and Paul tightened his grip on the wheel. Nothing more was said until the boat was, once more, heading straight into the waves. "And if Mary's . . ." Paul stopped. He swallowed and tightened his jaw.

Michael watched the young man grapple with anguish, and his heart softened. "She'll be all right." He laid a hand on Paul's arm. "I'm sorry for the way I've been treating you. I was wrong. My anger got the best of me. But not anymore."

"I don't blame you. I deserved it."

Dark water lifted the boat, then dropped it into a deep trough. Before they had time to recover, another came, twisting the boat sideways and burying it in a green tide.

"Pull it around! Nose into it! It's going to swamp us!" Michael yelled, grabbing hold of the wheel and pulling hard.

"It won't turn. It's going to sink us!" Paul shouted.

Michael thought of Luba waiting below and of Mary and Sean on Unalga. He had to survive. They needed him. "Father, help us!" he yelled.

Chapter 25

$\mathcal{M}$ary removed a pair of socks from the wire clothesline Sean had strung. The sun felt warm through her shirt and gave her a sense of well-being. *If only the sun would stay,* she thought as she stretched from side to side. *Our clothes will smell like outdoors. Even if the sun appears only occasionally, it's better than not at all.*

She smiled as she recalled how eager Sean had been to get his fishing line into the bay. "The salmon are beginnin' to run," he'd said. "I've seen some big ones." She'd watched him walk down the path, pole resting on his shoulder and his step light. Although thinner than when they'd arrived, Sean looked much as he had when she'd first met him. His hazel eyes remained bright, a smile prevailed, and his disposition remained steady.

The wind gusted and nearly snatched the socks out of her hand. She quickly grabbed its mate and folded them together, then placed the pair in a box. Next, she removed Sean's work shirt from the line. She started to fold it, but instead, pressed the cloth to her face. It smelled of him, and along with his scent came comfort and serenity. She didn't understand why, but being close to him made her feel secure.

Closing her eyes, she pictured her husband. Dark brown hair curled onto his forehead, and a crooked smile matched his easy stance. And when he looked at her, his eyes warmed with tenderness. Peace emanated from him.

Despite the distance Mary had placed between herself and Sean, he'd never complained. Instead, Sean had worked hard and sacrificed for her. She remembered how on their wedding night he'd not claimed his husbandly rights. He'd told her he would wait until she was truly ready to become his wife. Then he'd made his bed on the floor in the front room. The memory of that night stirred something in Mary. *I don't know any other man who would give so much for his wife,* she thought. *But then, Sean's not like other men.* Tenderness and pride for her husband swept through Mary. *Maybe I do love him. He's a good man.* She smiled softly. *It's silly being afraid to love my own husband. Why am I afraid?*

Paul's image intruded on Sean's. He wore his usual pretentious smile. A pang of hurt stabbed Mary as she considered how he must have had to pretend he'd loved her. *If he were pretending, he must have hated it. I was a fool to trust him. I thought he was a good man.* The realization that she'd been fooled before hit her like a slap. How could she trust her feelings for Sean?

"No," she said aloud, flattening the shirt against her chest and folding it. "I thought I knew Paul and didn't. Men can't be trusted. Not even Sean." She folded her husband's shirt, and as she smoothed the material, his genuine, kind face returned to her thoughts. *Sean isn't Paul. It's wrong to judge him by Paul's actions. Not all men are like Paul. My father never betrayed my mother,* she thought, but as soon as the idea entered her mind, she remembered that Michael wasn't her real father. Nicholas was, and he'd been a philanderer and a drunkard. Hurt swept over her, and she wished he'd been different. She'd always wanted to know him. *If he'd been a better man, he would still be alive. I would have grown up with him.*

She finished folding the shirt and set it on top of the socks. *I can't let myself be fooled again,* she decided. *Loving someone is too complicated and risky. Men can't be trusted. How do I know if Sean is different? I can't trust my feelings. I'm too gullible.*

"Take a look at these," Sean called as he stepped into the clearing and hefted two large salmon.

Mary could feel heat rush to her cheeks. How long had he been there? What if he'd seen her dreamily pressing his shirt to her face and smelling it? Embarrassed, she forced a smile and faced him.

"It was a great day for fishin'," he said. "I did better than I'd hoped. But the fish were in a fightin' mood. I'll tell ye,' neither of these was easy to land." He hefted the larger of the two. "I thought he was goin' to break me pole."

"They're huge. This one alone is big enough for several meals," Mary said as she took the biggest fish from Sean. "I'm starved. I'll cook some right away."

"I was hopin' ye'd say that. I already gutted him."

Carrying the larger fish, Mary headed toward the cabin.

"I'll hang this one in the shed," Sean called after her.

As Mary set the salmon on the counter, she replayed the scene in the yard. *I hope he didn't see me mooning over his shirt,* she thought. She could feel the heat in her face as she considered the possibility. She then went about her work, adding wood to the stove; then, using a large knife, she cut off the fish's head and set it aside. *This will make a good stew, especially when I add the beach peas and crowfoot plants I found.*

Mary sliced into the fish, and the flesh fell open, exposing red meat. After cutting two steaks, she scraped out the last remnant of lard from the bucket, dropped it in a pan, and placed it on the stove. While it melted, she cut up the remaining fish and placed it on the counter. Sean would hang it. When the lard had completely liquefied, she dropped the steaks in the pan. They sizzled and spit.

After they'd fried for a few minutes, she turned them. "While these cook, I might as well take down the rest of the laundry," Mary said and walked to the door. Opening it, she started out but stopped when she spotted the mother fox and two kits in the yard. Sean crouched at the edge of the clearing with a piece of salmon in his hand. Amazed, Mary watched silently as the fox approached, her nose extended. After what Trent had done, Mary had never expected to see her again. *How can she trust any man?*

As this thought unfolded, Mary considered how she'd been unable completely to believe in Sean. The fox struggled too. She shrank back, stopped, then continued forward as she tried to decide if she could trust the Irishman. *You're acting like me,* Mary mused.

Sean held very still but kept the food extended. "It's good to see ye girl," he said gently. "Come on, now. I have a piece of fish for ye. Would ye like that?" He tipped his head to the right a little, the way he did when listening, as if waiting to hear what the fox might have to say.

Mary held her breath and waited as the fox whined and took a tentative step forward. The kits held back.

"That's all right. I know ye're scared," Sean continued. "I can't blame ye."

Mary let out her breath slowly, afraid any sound or movement would frighten the fox. Keeping perfectly still, she waited, her muscles tight as if her own decision depended upon what the fox decided.

Sean continued his sweet talk while offering the fish. The fox moved closer.

What is it about Sean? Mary wondered. *I've never heard of a wild fox trusting anyone enough to take food from his hand. And after what Trent did, how can she trust anyone?* Mary nearly gasped as the two youngsters also approached the young Irishman. At that moment, Mary was overwhelmed with devotion for Sean. He was special. She'd known it but had fought accepting it, refusing to let it touch her. Now, as she watched the animal move closer and finally take the offering from Sean's hand, trusting him with her life, Mary knew she could too. Sean quickly held out another piece, and a kit snatched it. The other young fox tried to steal it from the first, and in the end, the two pounced on the tidbit.

Sean glanced at Mary and whispered, "Incredible, isn't it?"

Mary nodded. "It's you, not them. You're amazing." Sean didn't act as if he'd heard. He was already cutting off another hunk of meat. Mary didn't understand what it was that was special about Sean; she only knew she could trust him and that she believed in him. *The fox must feel the same peacefulness in Sean that I do,* she thought, wishing she possessed the same serenity.

"Can I try?" she asked. Sean nodded and she took a step into the yard. The fox immediately flinched and darted into the grass. The two kits scrambled after her.

Sean straightened. "I guess she's not used to ye. If she comes back, ye can try again."

Deflated, Mary sat on the log beside the house. "No. I'm not like you. She won't come to me." She plucked a blade of grass. "I never thought we'd see them again."

"Me neither." Sean sat beside Mary.

Mary stripped away the outer leaves from the stalk. "Sean, why do you think the fox trusts you and is afraid of me?" She looked at him. "What's different about you?"

"I don't think I'm any different. I just think she's used to me. I'm the one who fed her the eggs and fish heads before and coaxed her."

"No. It's more than that. Why would she trust any man after Trent shot at her and killed her babies? It happened right here. I can't believe she'd even come back." Mary tossed the last remnant of grass to the ground. "And when you were feeding her before, I was here. She knows me almost as much as you."

"I'm sorry if yer feelin's are hurt . . ."

"No. That's not it. My feelings aren't hurt. I just want to know what it is that she trusts in you. You're not like most people, Sean. As long as I've known you, you've been steady and good-natured, but since you almost died in the snowstorm, you've been more than that. There's something inside you—gentleness and contentment, and you're never afraid, and your faith is strong."

Sean grinned. "Don't be thinkin' better of me than I am. I've got plenty of faults, includin' bein' afraid. I'm not different from anyone else."

"But you are. Remember when you said that with God living in you, you were a new creation? I didn't believe you then."

Sean nodded thoughtfully. "I remember. I did say that. And that's what the Bible says, so it's true. I'm not the same as I was before I met Jesus."

Afraid of what Sean might say after her next statement, Mary hesitated. She took a deep breath. "I want to be like you. You're steady, and as you've said, I'm tight. You have peace, and I'm afraid. You're happy, and I'm troubled."

"Mary, it's not me ye want to be like. You want what God has done in me. He's the one who gives peace and happiness." He smiled. "Ye can have those things. He wants to give them to ye." He took her hands. "All ye need to do is believe in Jesus and give yerself to him."

"Are you sure? There must be more to it than that. At our church we always had a lot of tradition and ritual, and people had to take religious classes. There seemed to be so much to do."

"I'm no Bible scholar. I'm sure classes aren't bad, but from what I've been readin' in the Bible, it seems God made it simple. When I read about Adam and Eve, it said that God planned for humans to have a straightforward and pure relationship with him, but evil got in the way. When ye trust in Jesus, he takes the sin away so ye can have the bond with him he intended all of us to have. And that changes ye."

He caressed the top of Mary's hand. "I never told anyone this before, but I used to be a fake. I'd appear calm on the outside, but inside I'd be torn up. The only reason people believed I was unruffled is because I could manage to keep control. Now I don't have to keep control because I'm filled with God's peace. I know he loves me and watches over me. Everythin' is in *his* control." His eyes met Mary's. "Do ye believe Jesus died for ye?"

Mary nodded.

"Then, ye only need to tell him that. Do ye want to pray with me?"

"I'm afraid."

"Of what, Mary?"

"I don't know exactly. What will I be like? Will he love me even though I'm ugly inside? Even though I killed Trent?"

"He loves ye just as ye are."

Mary thought a moment, then said softly, "I'll pray with you."

Still holding Mary's hands, Sean closed his eyes and bowed his head. Mary did the same. He took a breath. "God, Mary knows that she needs ye. She understands that without ye she's truly alone. Help her to know ye better and to understand how much ye love her." He glanced at Mary. "Now repeat what I say." He closed his eyes. "Dear Lord in heaven, I know that without ye I'm lost, and I need a savior."

Mary could feel tears behind her eyes as she repeated the prayer.

"I know Jesus died for me, and I can be free from me sin by believin' in him."

Mary said the prayer after Sean, and the tears came, washing away her hurts.

"Thank ye, Jesus, for lovin' me and givin' me a new life."

Quiet gratitude enfolded Mary like a warm blanket. She could barely speak as she recited the words.

"Help me to follow ye," Sean said. "Amen."

Squeezing her eyes tightly, Mary said, "Help me to follow you. Amen."

Sean and Mary looked at each other for a long moment. Then Sean, after pressing his lips to Mary's hands and hugging her, held Mary away from him and said, "Ye belong to him now. Ye're his—a new creation."

Rivers of tears made paths down Mary's cheeks. Exhilaration and a new sense of freedom filled her. She laughed and cried at the same time. "Thank you. Thank you, Sean."

"Don't thank me. Thank God." He pulled her back into his arms. "After I met the Lord durin' the storm and began readin' me Bible, I've been wantin' this for ye, but ye wouldn't let me speak of it. And as God continued to show me more and more about himself, it was so hard not to say anythin' about him. I saw him in everything around me, and as I read his Bible, I understood more about who he is and who I am. I don't think the learnin' ever stops." He caressed Mary's cheek. "Now we can discover him together. He will withhold nothin' of himself from us if we love and obey him. Mary, ye don't have to be afraid any more. He's here inside us."

Mary had never felt this way before. It was as if her birthday, Christmas, and every other wonderful thing she'd ever experienced were all happening at once. "I think I know true joy now," Mary said breathlessly. "And I'm not afraid." She glanced at the hills all around as the reality of God's presence struck her. "He's been trying to show himself to me all my life, but I refused to see." Using the back of her hand, she wiped at her tears. "If he'd given up . . ." She let the sentence hang, unable to voice the possibilities.

Sean turned serious and asked, "Should I give up on ye?"

Mary looked down at their entwined fingers. Softly, she said, "No. Never. Please don't give up." She gazed into Sean's ardent eyes. "I'm glad I'm your wife. I've been afraid to believe in you, but not any more. I love you. I love you."

Joy blazed in Sean. He gently cradled Mary's face in his hands. "It's been my constant prayer that ye would love me, but I was afraid to believe ye ever would." He pressed his lips to hers and wrapped her in his arms.

Shivers spread through Mary as she returned Sean's kiss. When they parted, she cuddled against her husband's chest and whispered, "I love you, Sean." She stepped back, keeping her hands on his arms. "I'm sorry for the way I've treated you. I was afraid. After Paul . . ."

"I know. It's all right. I understand. Ye don't have to be afraid anymore."

Mary stepped back into his arms. "It feels good to love you."

Sean took a deep breath. "Yes, it feels good. I thank God for ye. God has been good to me." Swinging one arm away from her, he said, "He gave us each other and all this." His eyes traveled over emerald fields and beyond to the steady billows in the bay. "He's given us so much, Mary. All the beauty around us is a reminder that he exists. Have ye ever asked yerself why the sea steadily washes ashore, day upon day, or the sun rises and sets without fail, or how plants know when to push through to the sunlight?" Sean grinned. "Only God could do such things." He closed his eyes and lifted his face toward the sun, then looked at Mary. "Each day we live is a gift, and each one spent together is priceless and rare."

Taking her hand, he walked toward the beach. As they strolled side by side, they said nothing. When they reached the sand, Sean sat on a driftwood log and pulled Mary down next to him. "Today, we will just enjoy what is around us."

As Mary watched the waves, a dark cloud intruded upon her joy. Trent was dead. She'd killed him. Could God really forgive murder? "Sean, do you think God truly forgives me for killing Trent? Every time I think of it, it seems unforgivable."

"He understands. Ye did what ye had to."

"But does he forgive murder?" Mary felt panic rise as she waited for Sean's answer. What if God couldn't forgive her? What would happen? She searched her husband's eyes. "Sean?"

"God's not like us. He can forgive anythin'. Me mother used to tell me God forgives all sins. And she knew the Bible better than anyone I know. There was only one sin she said he didn't forgive."

"What is it?"

"She called it blasphemy of the Holy Spirit."

"What does that mean?"

"From what I understand, it's when a person doesn't listen to the Holy Spirit when he draws them to Christ, and they don't believe Jesus is the Son of God and our Savior."

"I do believe Jesus is my savior. So even though I killed Trent . . ." Mary couldn't finish.

"Ye're forgiven, Mary. God loves ye and understands that ye killed Trent to save me, and he knows ye wish it didn't happen."

Mary wiped her eyes. "Do you think it's murder when you kill somebody to save someone else?"

"No."

"What is it then?"

"I think I would call it defendin' yerself."

Mary looked at the bay. "When I shot him, I hated him. He was trying to hurt you, and I hated him."

Sean pulled her close. "Do ye hate him now?"

"No."

"Then it's over and best put behind ye."

"Sean, do you think we could read the Bible when we get back to the house?"

"Yes. Are ye ready to go back now?" Mary nodded, and Sean stood and took her hand, helping her to her feet.

When they stepped inside the house, smoke greeted them. "Oh! No! The fish!" Mary cried and ran to the stove. Grabbing a towel, she removed the overheated pan and the charred meal. "Our dinner. It's ruined."

Sean took the skillet and tossed out the fish, then filled the pan with water. "It's all right, just a little smoke."

"But what about dinner?"

"I'm not really hungry any more," Sean said. "There's somethin' I've been waitin' on for a long time." He circled Mary's waist with his arms and pulled her to him. "There was a time I thought ye'd never truly be mine." He ran his hand through her hair. "I still have a lot to learn about trustin' God." He smiled. "I love ye, Mary Calhoun. I'll love ye forever."

"I love you." Mary kissed Sean, then whispered against his cheek. "I'm thankful to be your wife."

Sean lifted her and cradled her against his chest. "Ah, me wife. How good to meet ye Mrs. Calhoun," he said with a grin and carried her to their bed.

Chapter 26

*M*ary opened her eyes. She studied Sean's back. Lean muscles flowed smoothly, one into the next. There were no blemishes. His back rose and fell with each breath. She gently ran her hand over his skin. It felt smooth. Content and happy, Mary snuggled close to her husband, resting her forehead against his skin. Remembering Sean's tenderness and passion, she smiled softly. Love had finally found her.

I wish I had opened my eyes to you sooner, she thought. *I was such a fool. Why did it take me so long to see who you really are?* Still asleep, Sean rolled onto his back. Mary laid her hand on his forehead, gently pushed a black curl back, then ran a finger down his cheek. His mouth turned up in a smile. *Even when I was indifferent, you loved me.* "You're a fine man, Sean Calhoun," she whispered.

His smile widened, and Sean opened his eyes. "I am, am I?"

"Sean, you've been awake all this time?"

"I don't know how long ye've been admirin' me, but I've been awake a while." He kissed Mary. "Good mornin' to ye, Mrs. Calhoun."

"Good morning."

He cupped her face in his hand. "Ye look beautiful even first thing in the mornin'. I always thought so; I just didn't think ye'd want to hear it."

"What I think is that your vision must be blurred from sleep."

Sean shook his head. "Nope. I've got perfect eyesight. And me eyes are tellin' me ye're beautiful."

"I was hoping you'd wake up so I could tell you how much I love you." Mary kissed him again, then snuggled close. "And I wanted to tell you I love being your wife."

Sean draped his arm over Mary and pulled her tight. Pressing his lips against her hair, he said, "I've hoped and prayed ye'd say that to me one day." Closing his eyes, he breathed deeply. "I'm afraid I'm dreamin' and I'll wake up."

"It's no dream. I only wish I hadn't been so afraid. We could have had this sooner."

"Ah, I'm just glad ye woke up to it." He pressed his lips against her neck. "We'll have a wonderful life together."

"Mmm, wonderful. My family will be ecstatic. I know this is what my mother was praying would happen." Mary pushed herself up on one elbow. "Are you hungry? I can make us something to eat."

Sean chuckled. "No. My stomach can wait. I want to stay right here with ye. I don't want to waste another moment."

For a long while, Sean and Mary silently lay in each others arms. Soft breezes caressed the house, whispering beneath the eaves while the two dreamed of their future.

Finally Mary ended the silence. "Do you think there will be any more big storms?"

"Hard to say. We've had a couple of clear days; we can hope and pray it will hold."

"Do you think someone will come for us soon?"

"That last storm was pretty bad, and it's only been a couple of days since it came through." He rolled onto his back and stretched his arms over his head. "And I don't know if I want to be rescued right away." He gave Mary a mischievous look and winked.

"We can be this close at home in Unalaska, and I'd like that better." She rested her hand on Sean's chest. "It seems someone should have come for us by now. What if no one ever comes to get us?"

"They will. The weather is still unpredictable. They're probably waiting for it to settle down. It's a big risk. I mean, the storm we just had was the worst I've seen this year. I wouldn't have wanted to be out in it."

"What if something happened and they can't get here? Could we take Trent's boat?"

Sean thought a few moments. "We could. But it's small. It would be a long trip and dangerous." He put his arm under Mary and pulled her to him. "And why would I climb into a tiny boat and row for days and days when I've got ye to meself right here? With the summer months comin', there'll be plenty to eat, the weather will be warm, and we'll have each other. It's our own little paradise."

"Sean, I'm serious. What if no one comes for us? Summer only lasts so long, then winter begins again. We have to get back to Unalaska."

"We will, even if we have to take Trent's boat. But I think if we just sit tight, someone will rescue us. Try not to worry. God is here." Pushing himself up on one elbow, he looked down at Mary. "Now, I don't want any more glum talk this mornin'. It's a special day. And I just want to look at me beautiful wife and spend the day kissin' her, not talkin' about what-ifs."

He moved to kiss her, but Mary rolled to her side, giggled, and sat up. Planting a quick kiss on the tip of his nose, she said, "I'm starving. I want breakfast." She climbed out of bed. "I just wish there were some coffee left. When we get back to Unalaska, I'll be ready for some."

"I really don't miss it. We've been reusing the grounds so often, it wasn't much more than dirty-lookin' water." Sean pulled the blankets back and stood. "I'll get us wood for a fire. Seems we used the last of it last night." He pulled on pants and a shirt, then his boots. "I'll be right back."

Sean stepped outside and pulled the door closed. Sunshine brushed lush hillsides with warm light. The grasses were knee-high and dappled with blue, pink, and purple flowers. Some gathered into crowds while others remained detached, standing alone. Sean strolled to a single lavender flower and picked it. "Ye remind me of the way Mary used to be. Beautiful and standoffish." He sniffed the blossom. It had a faint sweet smell. "But no more. I'll pick a bouquet and make ye a part of it."

Sean closed his eyes and took a deep breath, relishing the fragrance of the flowers and grasses that mingled with the pungent aroma of the sea. "Before I start pickin' flowers, I'd better get that wood." Tucking the blossom into a buttonhole of his shirt, he walked to the shed.

It was dark and moist inside. Sean waited for his eyes to adjust, then crossed to the dwindling pile of driftwood. "I'm goin' to have to start searchin' the beaches for more wood," he said as he piled several pieces in his arms.

When he could carry no more, he walked to the door. Balancing the firewood in one arm, he grabbed the door handle and pushed it aside, then elbowed it open. Stepping outside, he immediately heard a man's voice. He stopped and listened, barely breathing. Another voice carried up from the beach, only this time, it was a woman's voice.

Someone's here! They've come for us! Dropping the wood, he raced to the top of the knoll. Scanning the bay, he spotted Nick's boat resting in the cove. He searched the shore but saw nothing. Then his eyes moved up to the trail. First he saw Michael, then Luba, and finally Paul. Sean studied Paul, his heart sinking. All these months and miles, and the man was still tormenting them. *He's come for Mary.* Fear and jealousy filled Sean. Then he remembered Mary. She loved him. Paul was no longer a threat. Taking a deep breath, Sean smiled. He had nothing to fear.

With a shout of, "Hello," he waved. "Up here!"

The visitors looked up, smiled, and waved.

"We're saved!" Sean shouted and ran to the cabin. "Mary! Mary, they're here!" He pushed open the door. "Your father and mother are here!"

"Mama and Daddy?"

Sean nodded. "Come on! They're coming up from the beach!" He grabbed her hand and dashed out the door, Mary in tow. Excited and out of breath, they stood at the top of the hill and watched Michael, Luba, and Paul climb the trail.

Michael stopped, then with a broad smile, waved. "Sean! Mary! It's good to see you!" he shouted.

Gazing at the top of the hill, Luba pushed past her husband. "Mary? Mary!" Her face radiated joy as she hurried up the track.

"Mama!" Mary ran down the path, easily skirting holes and jumping over clumps of grass. When she reached her mother, she threw herself into her arms. The two clung to each other. Both women cried. Finally loosening her hold a little, Mary looked at her mother. "I can't believe you're here. It's like a dream."

Luba brushed Mary's hair back and gazed at her daughter's face. "My sweet little girl. I was afraid I'd never see you again."

Paul hung back several paces, saying nothing.

"What about me?" Michael said, holding out open arms.

Mary stepped into her father's embrace.

"Thank God you're all right."

"I was beginning to be afraid no one would come for us," Mary said.

Michael stepped back and held his daughter at arm's length. "Not come for you? We'd never leave you here." His eyes took in Mary's thin condition. "But it looks like we've made it just in time. You've gotten awfully thin."

"I'm fine, really. We managed to find enough to eat."

Sean joined them, and shaking Michael's hand, he said, "It's good to see ye. We'd been hopin' ye'd get here sooner, but now is good." He hugged Luba. "I'm surprised to see ye here."

"I wasn't about to sit at home and wonder a minute longer. I had to know Mary was all right." She gazed lovingly at her daughter and rested her hand on Mary's back.

Sean glanced at Paul. His presence tempered his joy. He nodded at him and held out his hand. "Good to see ye."

With a surprised expression Paul gripped Sean's hand and shook it. "I'm glad to see you're all right."

"Daddy, there was a bad storm. Did it catch you?" Mary asked.

"Oh, yes. It felt as if the ocean dropped out from under us, then came up to beat us. It was a bad one. For a while there, we had a time of it."

"I thought we were going to end up at the bottom of the ocean," Luba said. "I prayed and prayed."

"And we're thankful for those prayers," Michael said with a grin. "We definitely needed God's help." He nodded at Paul. "We were real lucky to have Paul with us. We needed another man."

Paul smiled modestly.

Mary hadn't acknowledged Paul yet. Now she looked at him and said, "It's good to see you, Paul."

Paul nodded. "I know I should have waited in Unalaska, but I had to see that you were all right. There's something I've been needing to say to you. I couldn't wait any longer so I forced your father to bring me along." He paused, looked at Sean, then back to Mary. "I don't think I can wait any longer." He looked back at Sean. "I don't mean any harm to you, but I need to speak to Mary."

Sean draped an arm around his wife's shoulders and pulled her close to him. "It's up to Mary."

"Can we talk?" Paul asked Mary.

"Mary, ye do whatever ye have to."

Mary placed her hand over Sean's. Smiling reassuringly at him, she said, "It's all right. We'll be right back." She looked at Paul. "We can talk privately up here." She turned and walked toward the cabin, then stopped and looked back at her parents. "I was about to make breakfast. There's not much, but what we have is yours."

"We brought supplies. They're on the boat," Luba said. "We'll bring them up." She looked at Michael and Sean. "If you men will haul it, I'll cook it."

"I'm ready," Sean said eagerly. "What do ye have?"

"There's some cold storage fruit, oranges and apples, and I've got bread and butter and eggs, plus smoked ham."

"Me mouth is waterin'."

"I've been dreaming of fruit. And butter and ham?" Mary gave Sean a smile. "We won't be long," she promised and headed up the hill.

Mary stopped at the shed. Stepping around to the side of the building, she sat on a log. "It's private here." She clasped her hands in her lap, working hard to maintain a calm exterior while her heart hammered and her hands shook. *What could he possibly want to talk with me about? I'm married, and there can be nothing between us. I can't believe that even Paul would have the nerve to ask me to leave Sean.*

Hands shoved in his pockets, Paul paced in front of Mary, his eyes on the ground. When he stopped, he still said nothing.

"Paul, what is it?" Mary prodded. "If it's about the fight we had . . ."

"No. It's not that. Well, it is, but it isn't." He paused and took a shaky breath. "I want you to know I meant it when I said I loved you. I do."

"Paul, I . . ."

"Please, hear me out." He looked directly at Mary now. "I do love you; I can't help that. I always will, and I will forever regret my stupid behavior. Because of it, I lost the best thing I've ever had." He looked back toward the sea for a long moment.

"Paul, why are you here?"

"I needed to see with my own eyes that you're all right. I couldn't wait weeks for Michael and Luba to return. I had to know."

"I thought you were off fighting a war. Is it over?"

"No. I was sent home because I was wounded."

"Wounded?"

"I'm all right. Just a single bullet in my thigh. It's healing." He stared at the rough, weather-beaten wood of the shed wall. "I need to say something to you."

"Paul, you need to know I'm in love with Sean," Mary said gently.

"I know. I can see that. And I'm happy for you. I really am. You deserve a good man." He met Mary's eyes. "I wish I'd been a better man. I'm sorry for everything I did. I was wrong. That woman meant nothing. I want you to know that in spite of my dishonorable behavior I loved you and didn't want to hurt you." He blinked hard and wiped his eyes with the back of his hand. "I don't expect a thing from you, but I needed you to know the truth of how I feel. I wish I could go back and do it right."

Mary studied the handsome man. Sorrow shadowed his dark eyes. Although Paul's tenderness stabbed at her heart, Mary felt exultation, for she knew she didn't love him anymore. She was free. She loved Sean.

Mary stood and rested her hand on Paul's arm. "Thank you for telling me. I have wondered if you never really did love me. Hearing you say that you did means a lot."

"Mary?" Luba called.

"We're here," Mary said, removing her hand.

"Well, that's all I had to say." He looked at the ground, then back at Mary. "I'm glad you're all right." Paul walked away.

Luba appeared a moment later. She hugged her daughter. "It feels so good to hold you." She stepped back. "It's been a horrible winter. Every day I wondered if you were alive or if you were suffering." Her eyes filled with tears. "I was afraid that when we got here we'd find your bodies. But you're all right." She sat on the log and patted it. Mary sat beside her mother.

"Mama, God watched over us all these months, and Sean and I make a good team. I remembered a lot of the skills you taught me when we lived in the village. We ate mostly fish and mussels, plus some seaweed, berries, and eggs. Sean and I both gathered food." She stopped, and her eyes filled with tears. "When Nick didn't come back for us, I was really scared, but God used this time to help me find him."

Luba's eyes brimmed. "You know God?"

Mary nodded. "I know that he is good and never leaves us and always loves us." She smiled. "I found him here. He showed himself to me in so many ways. As usual, I was stubborn and wouldn't look, but finally . . ."

Luba pulled Mary into her arms. "I've been praying and praying, hoping we'd find you and Sean alive, but God has given so much more." She held Mary away from her. "I've always known this would be yours one day." Luba untied the leather necklace with a walrus tooth hanging from it. "It is right that you have it now."

"No, Mama. It belonged to Nana. It's the one Grandpa Engstrom gave her, the one he found on the beach after the tidal wave. You've always cherished it."

"I have, but it was given to me so I could pass it down to my daughter. It is a reminder of who we are, where we come from. You have shown that you are a true native. And it is time for you to have it." She draped it around Mary's neck and tied it.

Mary ran her finger over the rough leather and smooth ornament and remembered her grandmother's story of love and survival. She looked at her mother. "What happened to Nana is like what has happened to me and Sean. When Nana would tell me the story of how she and Grandpa struggled to survive and fell in love, I always thought it sounded exciting and romantic. I used to wish I could have such an adventure." She smiled. "Living it is different than dreaming about it."

Mary looked at the necklace. "Grandpa gave this to Nana. I'm honored to wear it." Mary realized she belonged not only to her ancestors, but also to God and his family. And no matter where she lived or died, she would never be abandoned or alone. "One day, I'll give this to my daughter," she said softly.

Sean stepped around the corner of the shed. "What are ye two women doin' out here? It's time to eat." His expression turned to concern. "Is somethin' wrong?"

"No. Everything is right." Mary took her husband's hand and rested her cheek against it. "God has been talking to me all my life, but I didn't listen. He loved me enough to place me on this tiny island so I would finally see." Mary scanned the deep grasses and the small cabin. "I never thought it could happen, but I'm going to miss Unalga. This has been a sanctuary, a place for me to find the truth. I thank God for it." She smiled at her husband. "But I'm ready to go home now."

Author's Note

*A*lthough this story is fiction, my grandfather, Thomas Francis Roberts, and my grandmother, Vera Nadzda Anderson, inspired it. They left a heritage their children and grandchildren cherish.

Just as Mary did in this story, my grandmother loved a native man, but a Welshman named Thomas Roberts wanted to marry her. He went to her parents, seeking their permission, and in spite of the fact that she loved another, they gave him their blessing. I can only guess at my grandmother's reaction, but I do know she did as she was asked and married my grandfather in 1920.

In 1921, Thomas accepted a job caretaking a fox island for the winter on Unalga, and he and my grandmother were left there with the promise of supplies. The supplies never arrived. There was no poacher on the island of Unalga, but survival was challenging enough. Using all the skills they possessed, my grandparents endured and lived. In the spring, rescuers arrived and were astonished to find that Thomas and Vera were still alive.

My grandparents' marriage lasted until my grandfather's death in 1947. They had eight children and passed down the richness of their heritage to each of them. I am one of the grandchildren who has gladly inherited their legacy of love and endurance. It is so similar to God's plan, and I am forever grateful.

ALSO BY BONNIE LEON:
THE SOWERS TRILOGY

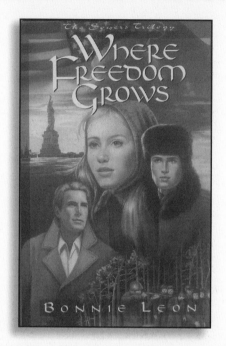

WHERE FREEDOM GROWS
ISBN: 0-8054-1272-7 • $12.99

After two young Russian siblings lose their parents to the Soviet State under the control of Joseph Stalin, they must endure this dark and perilous time—alone. Yuri Letinov, a brave young man, decides to stay in Russia and stand against the terrible oppression of the communists, yet he forces his sister, the beautiful and spirited Tatyana, to sail to America alone to avoid the gathering danger. With no family and no home—they rely on their faith in the Lord's gracious providence. And with that assurance, they valiantly pursue their separate destinies. Yet they realize through their hardships and triumphs that freedom grows in the heart of every Christian.

AVAILABLE WHEREVER FINE BOOKS
ARE SOLD OR CALL 1-800-233-1123

BROADMAN
&HOLMAN
PUBLISHERS

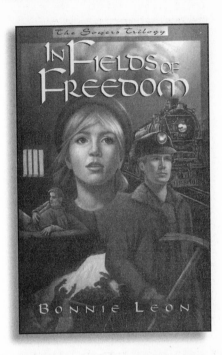

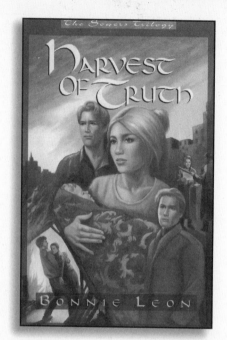